solstice

Kate Christie

Bella
BOOKS

2010

About the Author

Kate Christie was born and raised in Kalamazoo, Michigan. After high school, she left Michigan to attend Smith College in Massachusetts, where she studied women in a major way—the motto of Smith's Women's Studies department. More recently, she earned a Master's in Creative Writing from Western Washington University. A marketing and development writer by day, Kate spends most evenings writing fiction. Currently she lives in Western Washington with her partner of nine years and their two wonderful dogs. *Solstice* is her first published novel.

To Kris for, well, you know.

Acknowledgments

Thanks to my parents for supporting my writing aspirations from a young age, and for giving me my first word processor more than two decades ago. Thanks also to my partner for supporting me during the variety of occasions when I "took time off to write"—as the movie says, put it on my tab.

Chapter One

~SAM~

Just before the summer solstice, my still-new life in Seattle began to shift until it was as unpredictable as the fault lines buried beneath the city. Trees and plants were in full bloom that week and clouds rushed overhead on trade winds, casting shadows over Puget Sound and the buildings dotting the city's hills. Outside the window of my office on the fourth floor of a Belltown walk-up, winos and executives shared the sidewalk peacefully, moods augmented by massive doses of sunlight on these, the longest days of the year. Gazing out my window toward the ferry terminal where mammoth white and green ferries drifted in to rest against the wooden pilings before reversing again into the Sound, I sensed something brilliant not too far off, portended by clear skies and the scent of seaweed.

Friday morning a week before the solstice, my manager paused in my office doorway. "Do you have a minute?" Jim, a forty-something who dressed in Gap khakis and dyed his hair to hide the gray, was among the older people in our tech start-up, one of the many proliferating throughout Seattle.

I minimized the window where I was hard at work comparing mountain bike models at REI.com over my daily decaf mocha latté. "What's up?"

"There's a Web technology conference in Chicago next month I thought we might send you to. What do you think?"

For anyone else, attending a conference in Chicago would have been a treat. For me, though, Chicago was awfully close to home. I faked a smile. "Sounds good."

He gave me a thumbs-up and disappeared down the sunlit hallway, his trail runners squeaking softly against the laminate wood flooring.

Last time I'd been home, Christmas lights had glowed bright from the other houses on our street. Now, in mid-June, the Michigan countryside would be a blend of green and gold, winter wheat nearly ready for harvest, row upon row of young corn reaching for the summer sun. I knew those fields intimately from frequent train rides between Chicago, where I used to live, and Logan, where I grew up. When I moved to Seattle, I was sure I was leaving those treks behind for good.

By the end of the day, Jim had e-mailed me an itinerary to review along with a link to the conference Web site. Knowing I had family in the area, he added, he'd given me some extra time in the Midwest. Rubbing my temples where a headache had suddenly begun to threaten, I examined the itinerary. The conference ended on a Friday, but my return ticket wasn't until Sunday. Which meant I would have two whole days with my parents—assuming I told them I was coming.

I closed Foxfire and replied to Jim that the trip plans passed muster. At least I had a month to get used to the idea. And anyway, I didn't have a choice. I had to go home. Even my brother went home again.

* * *

The next morning, I dozed in the sunlight pouring in through my half-open blinds, until my cat Chloe managed to convince me that her hunger had reached a true crisis point. After feeding her, I donned workout gear and rode my bike to Green Lake, a nearby city park, where I stretched out on the boat stadium steps, watching geese and ducks cruise past under a wide blue sky. No doubt about it, Seattle was fabulous in the summer. Too bad I would have to spend a week away from the city in July, arguably the best month of the year.

Before I moved to Seattle, my friends and family in Chicago and Michigan warned me that I would find the Pacific Northwest a dismal, rain-drenched place to live. Their dire predictions didn't sway me, though. I packed my Ford Ranger, crossed the Mississippi, and headed west. I reached my new home in summer, which in western Washington, I discovered, consisted of five or six months of cloudless, low-humidity days and nights. I e-mailed my relatives and friends regular updates on the gorgeous weather, but I knew it would take more than anecdotal evidence to alter their image of my new home.

When the winter rains finally did arrive, I learned that Seattleites possessed nearly as many words for rain as Michiganders had for snow. But despite all the talk, the winter precipitation ended up being pretty close to what we got back in the Midwest. The difference was that while snow retained and reflected light, the dead vegetation, steel-blue water, and low sky common to Northwest winters didn't. Seattle felt grayer, even if it wasn't. Fortunately, spring and summer came sooner to Seattle than in other parts of the country.

My first year on the West Coast had passed quickly, and I hadn't even once regretted leaving Chicago and the level Midwest for Seattle and its San Francisco-grade slopes; windy Lake Michigan and sailboats for choppy Puget Sound and car ferries; Lincoln Park for Phinney Ridge; the Cubs for the Mariners.

By now I was nearly used to waking to melancholy animal calls from the Woodland Park Zoo, just across the street from my apartment building. I was still learning Seattle's urban landscape, though, so different from Chicago's glass and steel skyscrapers and old-school stadiums—colorful murals of orcas and fir trees decorating the whitewashed sides of brick buildings downtown; Safeco Field, with its giant retractable roof designed to let in the sun and keep out the rain; the Pink Elephant Car Wash sign guarding Denny Way; the many bridges in and around the city, floating, draw and stationary; and, of course, the Space Needle, a fixture at the northwest edge of downtown. On sunny mornings on my way to work on the number 5 bus, I would watch the gleaming skyline of Seattle approach, the glaciated dome of Mt. Rainier looming over Capitol Hill, and I would realize yet again how lucky I was to live here.

Suitably stretched, I started around Green Lake on the gravel trail near shore, dodging the hordes of weekend walkers, stride lengthening as my muscles warmed and loosened. I loved running, loved the sensation of my body moving freely, deliberately through space. Soon I was lost in my own world of wind and sun and water, so when I passed a familiar face, I barely paused. She was younger than me, with short brown hair and an athlete's body in tank top and shorts. I knew her immediately. But I didn't stop until she called, "Hey, Sam! Wait!" and jogged after me.

"I thought that was you," she said when she reached me, slightly breathless. Her companion, a tall, muscular woman, had stopped a little farther down the path and was checking her watch. "Sam Delaney, right?"

"Right."

"You don't remember me, do you?"

With her dimples and smooth, unlined skin, she looked just the same. "Emily, right?" Emily Mackenzie had been a freshman when I was a senior in high school back in Michigan. We'd played soccer together.

"You do remember," she said, smiling. "My mom told me you moved out here."

"My mom told me you lived here, too." Which wasn't a lie, exactly. I'd just known she lived in Seattle before my mother mentioned it.

"I heard about your brother. I'm really sorry."

"Oh. Thanks." I ran a hand over my ponytail. The last time I'd talked to Emily, I'd recently finished my junior year of college and was in Logan for a short visit before heading back to Chicago for the summer. Chris, my brother, was home, too, visiting from New York. We'd gone to see a Logan High soccer game and afterward had headed down to the field to say hi to some of the players and Tony, my old coach. Emily had hugged me and told us about the Division I soccer scholarships she'd been offered. She'd decided on the University of Washington.

"I'll be a Husky next year," I remembered her saying, a big grin on her face. And Chris and I had both grinned back. It was hard not to smile around Emily.

"I have to go," I said now, abruptly. "Nice seeing you."

"Oh." Her friendly look faded. "I guess I'll see you around, then."

"Right." I turned and started to run again, concentrating on the sound of my shoes crunching over gravel and trying to blot out the disappointment I'd seen in her eyes just before I turned away. At some point, I was bound to bump into someone who knew Chris. After all, he'd been gone for a year now. I just hadn't been expecting it this morning.

I picked up my pace and ran faster than before, pushing my legs and lungs harder than either wanted. By the time I reached the stadium again, I was slightly dizzy and soaked with sweat. As I unlocked my bike, I looked up to see Emily and her friend run past the boathouse. If she turned her head, she would see me. But she didn't.

Which was better, I assured myself, pedaling out to the main road and heading for Café Lulu, my favorite neighborhood coffee shop and usual Saturday morning destination. Normally I would have taken the path around the lake, but this time I stuck to the street, my mother's voice haranguing me as I rode along at the edge of the road: "Samantha, where's your helmet? Do you want to become a vegetable, young lady?"

And I should have worn a helmet, especially in traffic. But it wasn't like you lived forever.

At the café, I ordered my usual bagel and juice. Paper bag in hand, I rode my bike over to the lawn next to the Green Lake community center. There, I kicked off my shoes, dug my toes into the grass, and started in on breakfast. In high school, Tony, our coach, had informed us that we had thirty minutes after a workout to fill our glycogen window, and I'd never forgotten. Around me weekend warriors congregated on the community center playing fields, volleyball and softball players sharing the lawn with a women's soccer team. I watched the women play while I ate. They kept shanking the ball, which told me they hadn't played much soccer. Unlike Emily Mackenzie. Or me.

When we were five, my best friend Natalie Sipsma and I joined a youth soccer league in Logan. For a few years, we were the only girls on our neighborhood team. Then more and more girls in the area took up soccer, until eventually there were separate, gender-specific leagues. My mother tried to convince me to play in the girls' league in junior high, but I refused. So did Nat. No way were we going to miss out on our last few years of playing with the boys.

Nat and I were among the first generation of Logan kids who'd played soccer for ten years already when we started high school. But by the time we were senior co-captains, girls like Emily Mackenzie were trying out for the team. Emily grew up playing club soccer, traveling to tournaments in all corners of the United States and Europe. While Nat and I played a couple of years on the state team as alternates, Emily led her age group's state team in scoring.

I crumpled the bagel wrapper and lay back on the grass,

watching a lone cloud meander across the sky. Sometimes I thought I could remember every moment of every soccer game from the time I was eight or nine on. Which was strange, given that so much of the rest of my life off the soccer field was a haze. Trips I went on with my family, classes I took in school, even the night Chris ran away from home and the day he returned years later were pretty much a blur. The main thing I remembered about the day Chris came back was thinking that he'd grown up to look like Jude Law.

But I could call up important soccer moments easily. Like the first time I put a penalty kick over the goal at the age of eight and everyone, including me, was impressed I could kick the ball that high. Or the goal I scored on a banana kick from the corner of the field when I was twelve. Or the penalty kick I made in District Finals senior year to win the game.

Emily, the future star, lurked in the background of most of my soccer memories. Her older sister Beth was my age. But while Beth was the semi-hippie, future environmental activist offspring of intellectuals, I was the jock daughter of the lead counsel at Helix, the pharmaceutical giant based in Logan. Emily was nothing like her sister. The first time I saw her play she was only ten, and she was already the best female soccer player I knew. She was still just a kid when we played together in high school, her feet almost too big for her body. Now she was about my height with a medium build—a good size for a soccer player I'd thought when I watched her play the previous fall, her senior season at U-Dub. She was the same scoring machine I remembered, only more confident, more mature. After each game, I thought about walking down to the field to say hi, but something had stopped me.

I hadn't played soccer since leaving Chicago, a fact that now struck me as nearly inconceivable. Lying on the grass thinking about my soccer past made me realize how much I missed it. Maybe I should think about playing again.

I'd been lying there for a while when a shadow passed over

me and stayed. I squinted up at the culprit, trying to pick a face out of the halo of short brown hair. Emily.

I sat up and knocked over my juice. "Shit." I righted it again quickly.

She lowered her mountain bike and herself to the ground next to me. "Lulu's, hmm," she said, eyes on my crumpled bag. "Good coffee there. I'm a fan of Revolutions myself."

That didn't surprise me—Revolutions was a hipster coffee shop right off the lake, its ultra-modern interior as different from Café Lulu's family atmosphere as another coffee shop could get.

My silence didn't seem to bother her. "Filling your glycogen window?" she asked, her voice teasing.

I couldn't help smiling at that. "Yeah."

"Tony has no idea the lasting impact he's had on us. I'm glad I ran into you again, Sam. It's really good to see you."

"It's good to see you too." I wasn't convinced, though, not really. I couldn't forget the look on her face when she had mentioned my brother earlier. I wasn't sure how I wanted her to look at me, but pity definitely wasn't it.

Emily and her smile, though, were just as hard to resist as they had ever been, and for a little while, as we discussed soccer (naturally) and our Seattle lives, I even started to relax. But before either of us had revealed much of ourselves, she asked, "Do you miss your brother?"

I pictured Chris the last time I'd seen him, lying in a hospital bed in our childhood home the previous spring too weak to even lift his head. Something inside me shut off. A minute later, I was lacing up my shoes.

"I have to go," I announced, and there it was again in her eyes, just for a moment, that disappointment I didn't get. Her life was clean, untrammeled. Mine was not.

"You should come play soccer with my rec team," she said, standing up beside me. "E-mail me if you're interested—my address is my name, all one word, at Gmail."

"Maybe," I said, inwardly cringing at my own coldness but

unable somehow to stay still around her. And then with an awkward half-wave I was off, pedaling away from the community center, ignoring the urge to look back. I guided my bike around Green Lake toward home, dodging the people crowding the gravel path. I couldn't shake the sense that the life I'd built for myself in Seattle was on the verge of losing its careful order. Running into Emily now, having my past and present collide only a month before I was due to return home, was too much for my brain to wrap itself around.

I crossed Green Lake Way and followed a dirt path in among the trees of Woodland Park. From my building, it was all downhill to Green Lake. You could pedal a couple of times and coast the rest of the way, practically. But on the way home you had to work.

I preferred the ride home.

Chapter Two

~EMILY~

Summertime, summertime, sum-sum-summertime. My favorite season of the year. Or second favorite, after soccer season. This summer was different, though. I had a couple of months to wait until soccer started, like always. But this time, when the season began, I would be an assistant coach at U-Dub. The previous year I'd been an All-American striker trying to break the school's single-season scoring record, but now I was an alum relegated to the sidelines. I wasn't sure I was ready for that particular change of life. Where did it say you hit twenty-two and stopped playing soccer? In the men's game the world over, you were a rookie at twenty-two. But I wasn't a man, and this was America. WUSA, the fledgling pro-league for women soccer players, had folded after only a few seasons, though rumor had it that a spin-off league was in the works. There was no guarantee that I would make the cut, though. I could head to Europe or Japan to play pro, but I wasn't the traveling type. Fortunately

Michelle, my coach, had offered me the opportunity to stay on as an assistant. For at least the next six months I wouldn't have to make a decision on where to go or what to do next.

This summer I planned to hang out and watch women's pro basketball games and get sunburned, and for once I wouldn't have to worry about blowing my knee along with my scholarship during rec league. I could rock climb as much as I wanted, roller blade without pads if I felt like it. I could even go to FOB—Festival of the Babes, a lesbian soccer tournament in San Francisco I'd heard mucho about but had never actually attended. Or, at least, I could have gone had the tournament not been over Labor Day weekend, when I would be busy with my coaching duties.

I woke up the second sunny Saturday of June to Liz pounding on my bedroom door, demanding I go for a run with her. In December, I'd moved from the University District to Wallingford, near Green Lake, with my friends Liz and Jessie. They were a couple and could be nauseatingly cute together at times. Up until school had ended a few weeks back, I'd sort of been part of a couple too. Then Alex, the woman I was dating, went home to Portland for the summer, and that was that. We weren't serious or anything. I didn't believe in being serious. Too many fish in the sea. Or to paraphrase a quote I once heard, women are like buses—miss one and another will come along shortly.

Despite the fact that I'd been out the previous night till two and it was just now seven-thirty, the sun was pouring through my open window and I knew I'd never get back to sleep. I threw a shoe at the door and said, "I'll go, just give me a minute," my throat scratchy from smoking the night before. I smoked socially when I was out with the girls, which in the off-season was kind of a lot. Not enough to get lung cancer, though. Or addicted.

I fell off my futon and turned on my iPod in its dock already cued to Queen Latifah. I stripped off the boxer shorts and T-shirt I'd slept in, admired my body in the mirror over the dresser, and pulled on running gear. Life was good, my arms looked good, and I had new running shoes. Sometimes all it took was sunlight to make the world seem perfect.

Liz and I stretched on the front steps, watching our neighbors walk their dogs and sip coffee on their front porches. Our rental house was located on a quiet, residential street a few blocks north of the heart of Wallingford, just south of Green Lake. Jessie had gotten it—she was an Eastsider in real life, originally from the suburb of Bellevue. Her father was an investment banker and had no idea that Liz and I were dykes. And even less of a clue about his daughter. Jessie had studied business in college and now worked downtown for a financial consulting firm. She could afford the rent all on her own if she ever wanted to kick Liz and me out. Liz, meanwhile, would be a senior at U-Dub in the fall. She was great, except when she pulled her rower attitude: "Athletes row; others just play games." To which I always responded, "Which sport is it that anyone can pick up and do well? (Yours.) And which sport takes decades to perfect? (Mine.)" Uh-huh.

Green Lake was only ten blocks away. We took off down the street at a jog, warming up for our usual sprint around the lake. We always started out easy, but then Liz had to be so competitive with that tired "Rowers vs. Everyone Else" attitude, and then I had to make sure she realized I was a soccer player, see, and we didn't let anyone outrun us. Except, maybe, runners.

While we jogged, I regaled Liz with tales of my previous night's escapades, going to a WNBA game—I always seemed to know someone with an extra Seattle Storm ticket—and hanging out afterward with a bunch of U-Dub soccer and softball girls. After a few drinks at Pasha's, a bar near Key Arena owned by Storm season ticket holders (code for lesbians), we'd gone to Rebound, a club downtown, to dance.

"We heard you come in, Mac," Liz said, giving me one of her looks. Liz was always looking at people like they better say what she wanted to hear or she'd mess them up. We'd been friends for two years, though, so I knew that underneath that butch exterior she was even more softhearted than me.

"I was pretty sure I heard you and Miss Thang myself," I said.

"No way. Jessie was trying to be quiet."

"Please. As if that girl has ever been quiet in her life. I'm surprised the neighbors haven't called the cops on you two."

"Tell me about it," Liz said, and giggled. "Just think what they'd find, all of Jessie's little toys."

At Green Lake, we pushed each other until we were going too fast to talk and breathe comfortably. We ran hard, Liz grunting occasionally, me focusing on the gravel path and dodging traffic. And scoping like I always did.

We were halfway around the lake when I caught sight of this woman running toward us along the water, and it was like we were in slow motion as her eyes locked with mine. Sam Delaney.

Afterward, I knew I acted like a fool. Sam barely paused in running and didn't seem remotely interested in seeing me after all these years. At first I thought she didn't recognize me, but she came up with my name easily. I wouldn't ever forget hers. My first year of high school, Sam had taught me what I needed to know to go from good soccer player to excellent. She'd schooled me in the principles of defense, which as a striker I'd never given much thought to before, and she taught me how to slide tackle. That alone was enough to earn my eternal worship.

But the worship clearly hadn't been mutual. Before I could find out anything about her life in Seattle, she took off again, running on at the edge of the lake.

I watched her disappear around a curve in the shoreline. A few feet away, Liz cleared her throat. She hated having her workout interrupted.

"Don't even start," I said. "That's Sam Delaney. Remember— the girl from home whose brother died last year?"

"That's her? Damn, I don't think I went to high school with anyone that hot."

This seemed likely—Liz had grown up in Walla Walla, Washington, a small college town out in the boonies at the edge of the desert.

"I told you she was."

"Yeah, but your definition of hot is pretty broad," she said, and accelerated to avoid the punch I sent her way.

We didn't pass Sam again. I kept an eye out for her, but no dice. Near the playing fields at the eastern edge of the lake, we veered off toward home. By the time we got back to the house, my stomach was growling so loudly Liz could hear it too.

"I'm going to Revolutions," I said as we walked up the front steps. "Want anything?"

"Nah, Jessie's making waffles. We're going to the beach later. Want to come?" she asked, holding the door open.

"No, thanks." I wasn't in the mood for our usual summer hangout. Nicknamed Daikiki for its popularity among Seattle's lesbian community, Denny-Blaine was a public beach on Lake Washington between Madrona and Madison Park. On a summer day like today, it would likely be packed with queer beachgoers there to see and be seen.

Liz paused. "You okay?"

"I'm fine," I said, and headed upstairs. "Later."

Liz and Jessie shared the master bedroom-bathroom suite downstairs, while I got the upstairs bedroom and bathroom all to myself. I loved my room, with its wood floors and wide, tall windows. Liz had a bunch of her stuff in the spare bedroom across the hall, but we hadn't used that room much since we moved in. Mostly it was for show in case Jessie's family dropped by. I didn't think I could ever get serious about someone as far in the closet as Jessie was, but Liz was my buddy, so I tried to keep my judgments to myself.

I tossed my wallet into a backpack along with a beach towel and sunscreen. On my bike, I was at the lake in five minutes, in line at Revolutions in ten. Zucchini bread stowed in my pack and vanilla latté in hand, I pedaled carefully over to the lawn near the Green Lake playing fields. I liked to watch sports while I ate. On TV or live, didn't make much difference. And that's where I saw Sam again, lying on the ground, eyes closed. I paused a few steps away and watched her for a moment. Then she opened her eyes and squinted up at me.

I copped a squat next to her on the ground. "Dude, I don't see you for years and now I run into you twice in one day." Not that I was complaining.

She sat up, knocked over her juice, and righted it again all in one motion. Did I make her nervous? Maybe she'd heard through the hometown grapevine that I was gay.

I spotted the pastry bag near her foot. "Cafe Lulu's, hmm," I said, looking for something innocuous to talk about. "I'm a Revolutions fan myself."

She watched me sip my latté, but didn't say anything. This new, grown-up Sam wasn't as open as the girl I remembered. She'd always been a little standoffish, but once you got to know her she warmed up. Apparently enough time had passed that I once again qualified as a stranger, judging from the guarded look she was casting my way.

"I see you're filling your glycogen window too," I tried again. This time, I drew a reluctant smile from her. Apparently our soccer past was safe territory. But I didn't want to talk about our past. I wanted to know about the current Sam Delaney. A couple of years back, I'd heard she landed her dream job, writing for a newspaper in Chicago. How had she ended up in Seattle? I Googled her a couple of times after my mom mentioned she'd relocated, even looked her up on Facebook, but no luck—turned out there were a lot of Samantha Delaneys in the world, and this one had dropped off the grid when she left Chicago.

"What have you been up to?" I asked, munching my breakfast.

"Not much. What about you?"

"I just graduated from U-Dub a couple of weeks ago."

"You played soccer there, didn't you?" she asked.

"Totally." She shouldn't have asked me that, though, because I could talk about soccer for hours at a time. I managed to restrain myself and keep it to a few minutes recounting my recent past as a player and my future coaching plans at my alma mater. "But what about you?" I asked eventually. "What are you doing in Seattle? Still writing?"

"Not exactly." She described her job, managing the corporate Intranet for a start-up software company downtown. "We make Xynotes, electronic Post-it notes. 3M sold off their rights to the idea to the partners in my company, who used to work for—"

"Let me guess," I said. "Microsoft." Seattle was awash with former Microsofties who'd made millions in stock options and moved on to new careers.

"Sun, actually."

"My bad." I couldn't picture Sam in a software company. I'd known guys at U-Dub in computer science, and they were all total hard-core geeks. Sam was no geek. "So you design Web pages?"

"Among other things."

"You still play soccer?"

She shrugged and looked away. "Not really. I haven't found a team here yet."

"My rec team needs players." I tried to sound casual. "Why don't you play with us? It's mostly U-Dub players, but you're better than half of them."

"You're kidding."

"No way. You were awesome, even in high school. You were like Beckenbauer, so smooth. You never let the pressure get to you. I loved that about you." The last part slipped out. I hoped she wouldn't notice—no need to let her know I'd had a towering crush on her back in the day.

"But you were better than I was," she said.

"I could score, but I couldn't do half the things you could."

"You were only a freshman. Three years makes a big difference in high school."

I wanted to ask if she thought it made a big difference now, but I refrained. Barely.

"Anyway," she added, "your sister went to Brown, didn't she? What's she up to now?"

"She just got back from two years in Benin with the Peace Corps." Beth, my older sister, and Sam had taken the same advanced placement classes throughout high school. Beth had never seemed to like Sam—she referred to her as "future yuppie Republican wife material." I'd wondered if my sister would return from the Peace Corps as judgmental as when she signed up. She hadn't struck me as particularly altered at my graduation a few weeks before, despite the colorful West African clothing and jewelry. Though, admittedly, I might have been a bit distracted during her visit.

"Africa? Sounds about right," Sam said, smiling sideways at me.

"I know. Beth says I must be adopted, since I'm the lone jock in a family of brainiacs."

"You look just like your dad, though."

"So I'm told." I paused. "You and your brother looked alike too." She had yet to respond well to me mentioning her brother, but I wanted to know what she thought about Chris being gay. Even more, I wanted to know what she thought about me being gay, assuming she knew. If she had fulfilled Beth's expectations, she'd freak out because someone who once saw her naked in the locker room had turned out to be a lesbian. "Do you miss him?"

She nodded, silent again.

"Of course you miss him," I said, plucking a few blades of grass from the ground and letting them fall. "Sorry, that was a stupid question."

"No, it wasn't. I do miss him, but I'm used to it. He ran away when I was in junior high. I grew up missing him."

I reached out and covered her hand with mine. "I'm sorry you had to go through that."

"Thanks," she said, looking down at our hands.

What was it about her that impaired my thinking? I moved my hand away quickly, hoping she wouldn't think I was hitting on her. "My team really does need subs," I said to fill the space between us. "We always lose players in the summer."

"Maybe." Without warning she pulled her shoes on and stood up. "I have to go."

And what was it about me that made her want to flee? I stood too. "Where are you living, anyway?"

"On Fiftieth, across from the zoo."

Score one for Beth—Phinney Ridge was unmistakably the realm of Yuppies. "I live on Forty-ninth in Wallingford. We're practically neighbors."

This fact didn't seem to thrill her. "I guess so." She picked up her bike. "Nice to see you."

"You too." I made one last effort to convince her to play soccer, told her to e-mail me if she was interested. But she just said "Maybe" again and pedaled away.

I stood where I was and looked after her until she disappeared around a curve in the path. She seemed so different. But then, it had been a while since we'd hung out. Besides, losing a brother would change most people. Chris Delaney was the first person I'd known to die from AIDS. Officially, my mother had told me, Chris had died of liver complications, but he'd been fairly open with Logan friends and neighbors about his HIV positive status. Thanks to advancements in antiretroviral therapy, being HIV positive didn't mean an immediate death sentence anymore, not like it used to when we were kids. But Sam's brother's death was a reminder that people were still losing the battle with AIDS, even when they had access to seemingly miraculous medications.

I dropped back to the ground and stretched out, head cradled on my arms. On a Saturday morning in Seattle, high school seemed impossibly far away. The one person from Logan I'd always wished I'd kept in touch with was Sam. She'd been the kind of girl who breezed through adolescence. Editor of the school newspaper and an all-conference soccer player, not to mention pretty and well-liked by most people I knew, she seemed to skate along, acing tests and winning awards. When I made the varsity soccer team my first year of high school, she never called me a "shmen" or otherwise hazed me. I even got the feeling she liked me. I was a starter right from the beginning, which meant that in practice when starting offense scrimmaged against starting defense, Sam and I matched up against each other.

Through most of the season, I couldn't seem to get past her. I would try my best moves, but Sam didn't bite. In fact, she had this fake that I always fell for, even when I knew it was coming: She would appear to shift her weight forward, as if she were committing herself to a tackle. Assuming I'd caught her off balance, I would try to accelerate past only to find that her balance was in fact on her back foot. She'd neatly knock the ball away from me, clear to the defensive midfielder, and I would groan or curse my way back to a restart, where Tony would pull me aside and tell me that while he loved my aggressiveness, a back pass and run off the ball might be the safer option.

After one practice during which Sam schooled me so often that I finally switched sides to play against Cindy Holtmeier, a much less talented defender on the opposite side of the field, Sam called me over as practice broke up. I could still see her in grass-stained sweats and a long-sleeved shirt (it was only March—the snow had barely melted from the practice field, and Jenna and I hadn't become glued to each other's side yet), one foot on a ball, a water bottle in hand. Even then she'd had this quiet self-containment you couldn't help but admire. I'd approached shyly. She was a captain and hadn't talked to me one-on-one much before.

"Who's your ride?" she asked.

I shifted from one foot to the other. "Um, my sister," I said, and pointed at Beth, who sat a little ways away reading in our mom's red hand-me-down Corolla.

"Go tell her I'll take you home, okay?"

I raced over to tell Beth, who rolled her eyes and jammed the Corolla into gear, grinding the transmission noisily as she pulled away. Beth had orchestra after school and usually waited for me to finish practice. While she never let me ride with her and her friends on the way to school, she didn't mind being seen with me after everyone else had already gone home.

Back at Sam's side, I waited as she threw her water bottle at her Adidas soccer bag and picked up the ball, tossing it from hand to hand. A few other players remained, stripping out of their cleats and shin guards and chatting about non-soccer things. Natalie Sipsma, the other captain, was watching us curiously, and a strange sort of pride welled up in me. Sam wanted to talk to me.

"Come out here for a second," she said, dropping the ball and dribbling it onto the field.

I followed (like a puppy, it seemed to me later when I replayed the encounter alone in my bedroom) and waited to see what she would do next.

"What do you think it is that makes Mia Hamm such a good player?" she asked suddenly, facing me with the ball at her feet.

I blinked. "Um, her ability to score?" I offered. "Or, no, her ball control?"

"Those are your strengths, too," she said, "so maybe it shouldn't be a surprise that I think her greatest asset is her ability to play good defense."

That was the first time we stayed after practice until it got too dark to see, which in Michigan in March wasn't all that late. For whatever reason, Sam had decided to teach me the basics of defense: how to push someone in the direction you wanted them to go; how to close a gap gradually without overcommitting; how to figure out what a player was going to do before she did it.

"Don't watch her upper body," she told me. "Just keep your eyes on her hips. Hips never lie."

I wasn't sure why Sam chose me as her senior year soccer project, but I wasn't about to ask. At the end of the season I thought she might even come to blows for me. At District Finals we drew a high school known for rolling over opponents, literally. Midway through the second half I went on a breakaway, and the other team's sweeper took me down hard from behind. I ended up sprawled inside the penalty box, wind knocked out of me.

All of a sudden Sam was there, lifting my skinny fifteen-year-old body off the ground and brushing the dirt from my uniform. She walked past the girl who'd tripped me and said, low so the ref wouldn't hear, "Try that again and you'll regret it." Then she took the penalty kick, smacking the ball a thousand miles an hour into the right corner of the goal where it hit the side netting and spun around the back post. That goal won the game for us.

We made it all the way to State semifinals that year before losing in a sudden death shoot-out. I sat on the ground at the end of the game, tears spilling over as I ripped off my shoes. Sam came over and sat down next to me, her arm around my shoulders.

"Don't take it so hard," she said. "You still have three more years."

I just hid my face on her shoulder because I knew that without her we would never win States. I was right—we never did win States. And Sam never did cry, that I saw. She was the only one who didn't.

The day she won Districts for us, maybe she was just being a good captain and would have done the same for anybody on the team. But today, with her flat gaze and unsmiling mouth, it was hard to believe that Sam had ever cared that much about anything. Had Beth been right, after all?

I would have to see Sam again, I decided. I had to know for sure how she'd turned out. I closed my eyes and listened to the sounds of Saturday morning sports enthusiasts, daydreaming about the past Sam Delaney and I had once shared.

Chapter Three

~SAM~

The night after I ran into Emily Mackenzie, I sat bolt upright in bed at two a.m., sheets tangled around my ankles. Chloe meowed from her corner of the bed, watching me in the dim light from my clock radio as if I were possessed. In a way I was—I could feel sickness swirling through my blood, disease carried along with oxygen and genetic code from one end of my body to the other, infiltrating every cell, every organ. I couldn't stop it. I could only turn on the light and go to the bathroom to check myself for outward signs of infection.

It was silly, of course, and by the time I finished looking myself over in the mirror above the sink, wakefulness finally managed to chase away the delusion of disease. Reason asserted itself, forcing fear back to my subconscious.

This was not the first time a panic attack had struck me in the middle of the night. Usually, though, it hit just as I was falling asleep, and I would lie motionless in the dark, heart pounding so hard it felt as if my bed were shaking. Sometimes I was convinced I was dying of Ebola, or E. coli, or some flesh-eating bacteria. Other times I was certain an earthquake had jarred me from sleep. There had been two since I'd moved west, both around five on the Richter scale. Supposedly we were getting ready for the big one. And to think I'd picked Seattle over San Francisco partly because of the San Andreas fault, ignorant of the plates rubbing shoulders beneath Puget Sound.

I leaned over the sink and splashed cool water on my face. With one last look in the mirror, I turned off the bathroom light. I wasn't sick. I'd been tested for HIV more than once since my last sexual encounter and had been negative each time.

In bed again I tried to keep my mind blank, but I couldn't quell a recurrent nightmare image—Chris's back covered in painful, oozing lesions. He had to lie on his stomach at the end, IV feeding him life-sustaining fluids as his liver function and T cells dwindled. Our mother sat in the chair next to the rented hospital bed in the downstairs den reading to him and wiping his back occasionally with a medicated washcloth, her hands protected by latex gloves. She had to leave the room periodically to cry.

It was no use. I turned on the bedside lamp and reached for the book I'd been using recently to read myself to sleep. I went through a book a week, sometimes more. Lately I'd been on a Jane Austen kick; something about escaping into the gently ironic, non-mechanized world of Austen's England appealed to me. Without books and exercise, my sleep would probably have been more disordered than it already was. On this particular night, though, even reading failed. Five in the morning found me staring at the ceiling, wisps of dreams lingering like cobwebs in my mind. In one I was in my childhood bedroom with its half-circle paint swirls on the ceiling and wallpaper covered in stars and planets. I picked that pattern when we redecorated the upstairs of our house in Logan. I was twelve. Chris selected wallpaper dotted with musical scores for his room because, he'd said, his life was a melody he was in the process of composing.

I could still picture his room—light-colored wallpaper and solid wood furniture, guitar propped against his desk, flute lying unassembled on his twin bed. He left everything behind when he ran away, even the old top hat our paternal grandfather had left him. Before he died, he told me he had some doubts about our grandfather's "proclivities." He made me swear never to tell anyone he'd said that, not even after he was gone. The top hat currently occupied a shelf in my hall closet.

Images of Chris and our house in Logan wound through my mind, preventing sleep. At times, like now, it felt like he'd died only a few weeks ago, not an entire year. Fortunately, those times were fewer and farther between now. In general, it was getting easier to think about him. Though, apparently, not to talk about him.

Around seven, I gave up, made a pot of coffee, and read the Sunday paper from cover to cover, Chloe asleep on my lap. An article previewing the upcoming Husky football season reminded me of Emily, and I wondered what would happen if I accepted her offer to join her soccer team. But even as I considered it, I knew I wasn't going to e-mail her. I missed soccer, but I'd come to Seattle to forget. If my late-night panic attack were any indication, Emily Mackenzie represented the opposite of forgetting.

* * *

On Monday morning, I rode my usual bus downtown to Xytech's Belltown headquarters. I'd started temping at the newly formed company when I first arrived in Seattle and was still crashing at my friend Tina's apartment. They'd offered me a full-time, permanent job after six months, and at this point, I thought I would probably stay for a while. I liked the pace of the software industry. A month in Internet time was like a year in the outside world. If you only stayed busy enough, you wouldn't have time to think about where you used to be.

This particular Monday found me exhausted from my semi-sleepless weekend. But as the days passed in a blur of work, meals, bus-rides and exercise, my routine settled me down. By the time another weekend rolled around, I'd practically forgotten about Emily Mackenzie. Really.

When the phone rang mid-morning Saturday, I paused in the middle of dusting the lower level of my coffee table, books in untidy piles on the carpet around me. None of my friends in Seattle got up before noon on the weekends, which meant it was probably my mother calling to check in on my impending trip home. Again. She'd already called twice to make plans for my visit.

But when I checked caller ID, I saw a local Seattle number, no name. A thought occurred to me, and I almost didn't answer. Almost.

"Is this Sam?" the voice at the other end asked.

I sat down on the couch. My premonition had been spot-on. Was I developing latent psychic abilities? Didn't those sorts of things usually show themselves in childhood?

"Hello? Are you there?" she asked.

"Yes, I'm here."

"This is Emily Mackenzie, from Logan. You know, we ran into each other last weekend at Green Lake?"

"I remember." It was cute, in a way, that she kept thinking I wouldn't be able to place her. Endearing somehow.

"I was wondering if you wanted to play soccer tomorrow," she said. "We were a player short last week."

I leaned back on the couch and focused on the DVR player in the entertainment center on the opposite side of the living room. It was Saturday—maybe there would be an MLS game on later.

"Sam? Are you there?"

"I'm here."

"You don't have to decide now. You can call me tomorrow if you want. I can give you my cell number. The game's at

Marymoor, off 520 on the East Side. Do you know where that is?"

"Yes."

"Good. The field isn't grass, it's dirt, so wear turf shoes," she said as if I had agreed to play.

Maybe I would. When I was a kid, if someone had told me there would be a time in my life I would go twelve consecutive months without playing soccer, I would never have believed it. "What time is the game?"

"Five. Do you want to play?"

"Maybe. What color do you guys wear?"

She gave me the details quickly, sounding excited that I might show up. Why did she even care? And why had she seemed happy to run into me? She had a whole other life away from Logan, and so did I. Our lives couldn't really intersect again.

"I hope you come," she said. "You're one of the only people from high school I wished I'd kept in touch with."

She didn't seem to be afraid of anything. "It's been a while since I played. I'm probably going to be rusty."

"Don't worry. I'll tell everyone you're not very good, okay? That way you'll be better than they're expecting."

"That might work."

"I'll say you're this chick I know from high school and you practically begged me to play, and now we're stuck with you."

"You don't have to go quite that far." I tried to remember the last time I'd heard someone use the word chick.

"Just kidding," she said. "What are you doing now, anyway? I didn't wake you, did I?"

"No, just cleaning my apartment."

"Do you have your own place?"

"Yeah." I looked around at the furniture, wall decorations and hanging plants. The "office" in one corner of the living room held my computer and the framed painting I loved, horses etched in red against a gray wall, a modern cave painting.

"I have roommates myself," Emily said. "I couldn't afford a

26

house on my own."

"Me, either."

We were both quiet. Then she said, "Guess I should let you get back to cleaning."

"Guess so." But I was liking talking to her. I pictured her in an older Wallingford house with the morning sun coming in the window, her hair tousled from sleep, her eyes lit by her smile. Whenever I thought of Emily, she was smiling.

"See you tomorrow?" she asked.

"Okay." And just like that, I had a soccer date.

I hung up and sat on my couch. The need to cleanse my surroundings of dust and germs, a compulsion that struck at least once a week, had faded prematurely. I tossed the dustrag on the floor among the books, got up and walked away from the mess I'd created.

* * *

A little before five on Sunday afternoon, I stopped my truck in the parking lot at Marymoor. Around me, twenty-something women spilled from their cars and swaggered toward the field, athletic bags slung over toned shoulders, shin guards hanging unstrapped from muscular legs. I was out of my league, I could tell already. What had I been thinking? I hadn't even played Division III in college.

A knock on the passenger window startled me. Emily, a soccer ball under one arm, athletic bag on the other, grinned at me through the glass. I reached for my own bag and stepped out of the truck.

"You made it," she said.

"I did." I pressed a hand against my stomach, willing the butterflies to calm their spastic flight. I used to throw up in high school before big games. This hardly counted.

"Nice wheels," Emily said, nodding at my Ford Ranger.

"Thanks." I'd bought it barely used the previous summer

with money saved from my job at the *Tribune*. This truck had brought me to Seattle.

We joined the trickle of players heading toward the bleachers on the opposite side of the dirt field. Emily told me she'd thought it was bizarre when she discovered that most rec soccer in Seattle took place on dirt fields. City officials claimed it rained too much in the Pacific Northwest to maintain grass fields.

"Which is ridiculous. It's mismanagement, pure and simple," she said as we crossed the field, kicking up dust along the way. "All they'd have to do is keep off the fields in the winter and they'd be fine. Idiots."

"Yo, Mac," a girl in a tank top said as we reached the bleachers.

"What's up, Mel?" Emily dropped her bag on the ground and slapped hands with the other girl. With their short dark hair and slim soccer player hips, they looked like sisters. Cousins, at least.

"What happened to you last night?" Mel asked. "I looked around and you were gone. Didn't you get my text?"

I sat down on the bleachers away from everyone else, eavesdropping on the conversation as I pulled on my cleats.

"I was tired." Emily took a pair of turf shoes from her bag. "I wasn't in the mood to dance, that's all."

"I heard a rumor you're still single," another player put in. "Damn, girl, it's been all of, what, six weeks? Is that a record?"

I looked at Emily and she looked at me quickly and then away. I could have sworn she was blushing. I knew she was gay, both from hometown gossip and from looking at her. Didn't take a genius. But it dawned on me at that moment that she probably didn't know I knew.

"Yeah, yeah," she said. "What's the deal with Frenzia? They get new uniforms this summer?"

The conversation turned from her private life to our competition, rivals apparently who had yet to beat Emily's team in several years of trying. I double-knotted my laces and resolved to tell her at some point that I knew she was gay, that it was cool with me. My brother was gay. I was fine with the whole thing,

28

really.

This chain of thought conveniently distracted me from pre-game jitters, and I dressed and stretched and warmed up in my own little world. When I jogged back from a circuit of the field, Emily introduced me around. I nodded at the other women and they nodded at me. I felt them looking me over, checking my clothes, my shoes, the way I wore my hair, how many times I juggled the ball with my feet as I waited for the game to begin. Did they see a real soccer player in me? What had Emily told them? And would I be any good, or had I lost it all in a single year?

We trotted onto the field and took our positions. We had just enough players, no subs, while the other team had five subs and a coach. And matching uniforms. Despite the dirt field, I got the feeling they took their rec leagues seriously in Seattle.

The referee blew the whistle, and the game was on. The first realization hit me five minutes in: I was in nowhere as good of shape as I'd believed. Not that I was in bad condition. I just hadn't done any speed work recently and, as a result, was slower than I was used to. My reflexes were off. I couldn't seem to anticipate passes either from my team or the other, couldn't read the bounce of the ball, couldn't convince my body to react the way I wanted it to. In other words, I had lost it all in a single year.

I played poorly at outside defender the entire first half. We got scored on midway through, but fortunately it was the other outside defender's mark who got the goal, not mine. One of the central backs, Anna, who looked about my age, covered for me when I screwed up and gave me orders the rest of the time: "Sam, you need to be goal side of your player," and, "Look for your midfielders when you get the ball," and, "Try to get rid of the ball sooner."

The rules of defense that I'd known and practiced most of my life, the principles of play that I'd taught to other players. I just gritted my teeth and nodded. After all, it was her team.

At halftime, I stood apart from my teammates, staring out to where the referee was juggling the ball in the center circle, dust rising about him. I didn't belong. What had I been thinking? Maybe I'd been away too long for a good tackle or a perfect pass to lift me out of myself even briefly. Maybe it was time for me to accept that soccer no longer had a place in my life.

Just then, Emily walked over. "Don't worry, takes a little while to get back into it. You'll settle down. Just give it a chance." She smiled at me, and I could see the certainty in her eyes, the confidence in me that I couldn't seem to muster.

I'd counseled her often enough back in high school almost a decade before. Now she was giving my words back to me. I nodded. Apparently satisfied, she punched me in the arm and turned away.

Maybe she was right, I thought, gulping water. Maybe it would just take time. But at some level, even as I tried to psych myself up for the second half, I knew I would probably never be the soccer player I used to be, back when I loved the game purely and simply. All these years later I couldn't even imagine how to resurrect that kind of passion.

Most of the second half for me was a blur of hard work and missed passes, my judgment poor and reflexes still slow. But on several separate occasions, I actually felt in the flow of the game. The first moment occurred early in the half. Anna got caught on the opposite side of the field, and the other central defender got beat. The opposing team's forward headed straight for the box, only the goalkeeper between her and a certain goal. But I was already streaking back on an angle, chasing her down. She didn't notice at first. Then she saw me flying full speed at her and wound up, trying to get off a quick shot at the top of the box. She was too late. I extended my body, timing my slide-tackle, and nailed the ball from in front of her, knocking it out over the sideline and sending her to the turf.

No whistle sounded—my tackle was legal. I got up and extended a hand to the player I'd taken down, but she just glared at me and picked herself up. She was not pleased that I'd wrecked her easy goal. My teammates were happy, though, and as Anna dusted me off and patted me on the back, I saw new respect in her eyes.

The rest of the game was considerably more enjoyable. We scored twice and held them scoreless, stealing the game away at the end of the second half. Emily scored both goals. That was her job, after all, and she executed beautifully. At the final whistle, the other team stalked off the field without shaking hands. We won, even without subs and with only a core of people who had ever played together before.

As I stripped off my heavy socks and shin guards, listening to the other players chatter, I learned that I wasn't the only non-U-Dub player recruited at the last minute. And I wasn't the worst out there, even if I'd played terribly for me.

When I finished changing, I caught Emily's eye, waved and started to walk away. Something about this group of women made me nervous. Maybe it was that I knew they were still sizing me up. I was the new kid, the one who hadn't made it in college soccer for whatever reason. I didn't like that role. Especially when I knew I could play better than I just had.

"Hey, Sam, wait up," Emily said, stepping into soccer sandals.

"Nice playing," Anna, the back, said to me as I waited.

I made a face. "Thanks. I'm a little rusty, though."

"You were fine. You two coming to dinner?"

"Maybe," Emily said.

We were exactly the same height, I noted, as Emily and I walked toward the parking lot. I remembered her as this skinny teenager, but she wasn't skinny or a teenager anymore. She was strong and had beautiful muscles in her arms. I wished I had arms like hers. But I'd inherited my mother's body type. No matter how many weights I lifted, my arms refused to take on Emily's sculpted look. Her legs too.

"Anyway, you seemed to relax in the second half," she said.

I'd been checking her out fairly blatantly, and she was smiling this little smile that let me know she'd noticed. What was I doing?

I didn't want to give her the wrong impression.

"I did feel better," I said. "I had no idea it would be so hard to pick it up again."

"That slide you had when their striker went on the breakaway was awesome."

"Thanks." One of those plays I would file away for future reference in my mental collection of soccer memories. "You weren't so bad yourself."

When we reached the parking lot Emily watched me unlock my truck and toss my bag in.

"Thanks for inviting me," I said, belatedly remembering my manners. "Your team is great."

"I'm just glad you made it. We usually stop by Pagliacci's on Capitol Hill after our games. You interested?"

I hesitated. Pizza did sound good. But then I pictured trying to make conversation with the women on the team. "I can't. I already have plans." I wasn't sure why I made it sound like I had a date or something, except that I really didn't want Emily to get the wrong idea. She was great, but I was straight.

"Fine." She started to turn away, but stopped. "By the way, think you might want to play with us regularly? We could use you."

"I don't know. Maybe."

"Just think about it. I'll call you later in the week and you can let me know, okay?"

"Okay." I slipped into my truck, rolled the window down and turned the key in the ignition. For some reason, I was glad Emily was going to call me. I looked up, and she was still standing on the sidewalk in front of my truck. She smiled at me, sweetly almost. It was the first time in Seattle that I'd seen her do anything slowly.

"Bye," I said.

"See you, Sam."

I backed my truck up and left Marymoor behind, drove west toward Seattle with the evening sun still high above the Olympic Mountains. I felt good. I felt relaxed and tired, and I knew some of the warmth spreading through my body came not only from losing myself to soccer but also from the way Emily had looked at me. Which didn't make sense, but I hadn't felt touched by another human being in any way in such a long time that I didn't question it.

I drove home knowing I'd probably end up playing the following week mostly for the chance to feel this way again. Both on and off the field.

Chapter Four

~EMILY~

At Pagliacci's after the game on Sunday, I tried not to glow too much. I still couldn't believe Sam had actually showed up. I'd hoped she would the previous weekend, of course, but it wasn't like I'd been holding my breath. But this weekend, after I'd gotten up my nerve Saturday morning to call her and thought for certain that she still didn't remember me, I couldn't stop smiling. Sam had played soccer with us, and we'd won. Double bonus.

Kristin McConnell and Mel Brady, my two best friends other than Liz, picked up on my mood right away. As soon as we'd ordered, pushed several tables together in the back of the restaurant and tossed our keys and cell phones into the middle, Mel elbowed Kristin and leaned across the table toward me. "So who's the straight chick, Mac?"

"Yeah, who is she?" Kristin echoed, a straight girl herself and the upcoming season's captain at U-Dub.

"Just a friend," I said, attempting to dim my lightbulb smile as I sprinkled crushed peppers on a slice of cheese pizza.

"Then why are you so amped?" Mel pressed.

"I don't know what you're talking about."

"Whatever," Kristin said.

"Exactly," Mel added.

They let it drop for the time being as we all swigged soda and rehashed the game. It was always good to beat Frenzia, one of our biggest rivals in the Seattle league. Anna Patterson, who'd been a senior captain at U-Dub when I was a frosh (though personally, I didn't think she'd ever relinquished her authority), said at one point, "Mac, your friend is better than I thought she would be."

I bit my lip against the smile I could feel threatening. "She's pretty good, huh?"

There was consensus around the table—Sam was worthy. Which, coming from these women, was a huge compliment. I released a slow breath I hadn't realized I'd been holding.

"Try to get her to play with us if you can," Anna directed. "That slide tackle in the second half was solid."

The conversation moved on from there, but I stayed stuck on Sam, different moments from the game flickering through my mind disjointed, out of sequence. On the breakaway, with the Frenzia striker on a beeline for the goal, Sam had executed one of her trademark slide tackles that sent the ball flying off the edge of the field and the striker to the ground. When she stood up and let Anna brush dirt from her back, I could see a flicker of the old Sam, the tough Sam I used to watch when I was just a kid and she didn't even know I existed.

Before that play, though, she'd seemed miserable. Her timing in the first half stunk, and she was noticeably unfocused. Had little to do with ability, though I could tell that her body was also trying to readjust to the game. She was not having fun. At halftime, I pretended she was one of my future players in a mental rut, frustrated, and I'd smiled at her and squeezed her shoulder and told her to relax. After a moment, she'd nodded. Our eyes had held for too long, and I was certain that she would see the emotion in mine. Damn, the girl was hot, even sweaty, dirty and frustrated. I'd walked away hoping I wouldn't have the same feeling for any of my future players.

Then, after the game, when we were walking across the field and I caught her checking me out. What was that, anyway? Sam had to be straight. Even I knew there was no use thinking otherwise. But for a moment as we'd crossed the soccer field, I could have sworn she was looking me over in an un-straight way. She must know I was gay. My sister had told me that everyone from high school knew.

Kristin kicked me under the table, interrupting my train of thought. "Yo."

"Earth to Mac," Mel said.

"What was the question?" I hedged.

"No question," Anna said. "Pass the red peppers."

"Yes, ma'am." I passed the jar and resumed pondering. I had a date to talk to Sam again later in the week. I wondered how long I'd be able to wait.

* * *

That night I went out with Mel and our usual crowd of friends, soccer and softball players, and we hung out on Capitol Hill and at Rebound for the hundred thousandth time. But like the night before, when I'd ignored Mel's text and headed home early, somehow I wasn't in the mood for the same old scene. I walked out of the club before it even got going and caught a bus to the U District. The route wound past the U-Dub athletic fields, and I felt again the usual pang. Out there under the night clouds were the fields where I'd trained and played and made my best friends and done what I'd always wanted to do. But now, what was I supposed to do?

For sixteen years I'd had something to do—school—but suddenly college was over and my liberal arts degree, while making me a better-rounded human being in touch with societal and cultural influences, wasn't exactly opening any employment doors. Jobs were neither plentiful nor stable, which made it hard to commit fully to any one path knowing it might be temporary. All at once the known road was behind me, and I had to figure out what to do with the next eighty years, assuming I was lucky enough to live that long.

For now I only had to make enough money to cover the basics until September, when my coaching stipend from U-Dub was due to kick in. Jessie had offered to get me a job at one of her father's friend's businesses downtown, but I was pretty sure that a stint in corporate America would make me want to slit my throat. I'd seen a "Help Wanted" sign in the window of Peloton, a Wallingford bike shop, just before graduation. I was hardly a bike expert, but Lori, a hip thirty-something dyke who co-owned the shop with a guy named Josh (Lori called him an "honorary lesbian"), had recognized me when I stopped in to fill out an application. Seemed she'd played some soccer herself back in the day, so I got the job.

Most of my friends from U-Dub had launched major job searches well before graduation and still ended up at Seattle's Best Coffee or one of the many local temp agencies. They'd done research and set their sights on high-paying jobs with good benefits and room for growth, while I'd aimed for the neighborhood bike shop. I was pretty sure I'd lucked out.

When the bus stopped at Forty-fifth Street to take on passengers, I let myself off and walked west through the heart of the University District. Here, away from Logan, I'd come out and played Division I ball and loved every minute of it. But my NCAA eligibility was up, and I would have to start over again and whittle a new me out of the world. The thing was, even though I'd always known it was rented time, I still liked my old life. I wanted to keep playing college ball, to keep playing college dyke. What else would I ever be as good at?

It was one in the morning before I unlocked my front door and crept quietly upstairs. Tonight I had walked away from my

U-Dub friends. Some day soon I would get up the nerve to call Sam Delaney again. Life was good, I told myself, and maybe, just maybe, about to get even better. I peeled off my clothes and lay back on my futon, nearly naked as I hummed along with Annie Lennox.

* * *

The following day, Monday, my alarm went off at seven, which felt way too early. Even after two weeks of working mornings at the bike shop every day except Sunday, my body still wasn't used to the regular schedule. Yawning all the while, I showered and dressed in khaki shorts and a clean T-shirt. Then I tugged on a waterproof jacket (one of my first ever REI purchases freshman year of college) and walked through the cool rainy morning to Peloton on Forty-fifth. I stepped through the door at the back of the building right on time. Lori was already there, standing behind the main counter not far from the door, leafing through a sheaf of papers. She was attractive, with short black hair, a muscular frame and funky wire-rimmed glasses. Not my type, though. More like what I'd look like in a dozen years. Or what I would look like if I were Asian.

My interview with her a few weeks earlier had had its less-than-impressive moments. I'd known she was gay right off, of course, which had somehow caused me to state at one point, "I'm a fast learner and I'm good with my hands." And then my face had turned red as I'd realized how that might sound coming from one lesbo to another. Nice.

Despite such moments, and in spite of the fact I hadn't held very many jobs (I'd spent summers in Seattle conducting "research" for the Exercise and Sports Studies Department, which meant I was a jock getting paid to work out), Lori and Josh had seen fit to hire me.

"Good morning," she said when she saw me.

"Good morning," I said, and went to open the register.

"How was your weekend?"

I was struck by the urge to tell her about running into Sam, but instead I made small talk with her and the other morning shift guy, Brett (whose skater's duds and goatee smacked of Bellevue to me), until it was time to unlock the front door and welcome in the purchasing public.

As I worked that morning, stray thoughts kept finding their way into my brain. One notion in particular repeated: Wonder what Sam's doing. She was probably at work. I pictured her in a glass-walled office with slick, sharp furniture and computers equipped with video-conferencing and speech-recognition software. My only exposure to Seattle software companies came from articles about Microsoft and the Michael Crichton movie, *Disclosure*, which, incidentally, was totally unrealistic because how often in the history of Western society has sexual harassment been directed at a man? Get real—only men possessed the actual power to rape other men. But I had to admit, Demi Moore was hot in that movie, which was why I'd seen it three times. No wonder Ashton was into her.

I pushed the thought away—of Sam, not of Demi. I didn't need to be thinking about Sam Delaney. She had nothing to do with the world I'd built for myself in Seattle. I'd left Logan behind because I couldn't be myself there. Logan High was not exactly a comfortable place to be gay. The one kid I knew who was out back then, Isaac Washington, got knocked around at least once a week by some meatheads who gave the rest of us jocks a bad name.

Isaac was beautiful. Not in a physical sense. He just didn't care what anyone else thought. He was flamboyantly gay in an unapologetically homophobic environment; he even wore make-up sometimes to school. A few people accepted him for who he was but most didn't. Among the majority were the ones who wrote "faggot" on his locker and shoved him in the hallway and even outright beat on him, sometimes in front of hall monitors. What did the hall monitors do? Looked the other way because

Isaac was a self-proclaimed fag, and everyone in Logan knew fags were fair game.

I kept my silence and so had the other GLBT students, and we'd let Isaac hang out there all alone. Looking back, it wasn't something I was proud of. But I probably wouldn't have changed it either, even if I could have. Hard enough to come out in a moderately supportive atmosphere like U-Dub.

When my shift ended at one, I walked home from Peloton thinking about my new job and identity, bike store employee, and the thought that popped into my head, galling me, was whether or not Sam would think it was cool. But I didn't care what Sam Delaney thought and I'd done awesomely without her the last five or six years and she was straight anyway so I shouldn't even be thinking about her, I reminded myself.

But the worry that she might think I was a slacker for not landing a "real" job like hers persisted as I tried to sleep alone that night on my queen-sized futon. If I thought about it, I knew why Sam's opinion seemed to matter. However, reviving an ancient crush on an unattainable woman was hardly prudent, so I chose not to think about it. Which didn't, of course, mean I could avoid thinking about her.

* * *

I only made it to Wednesday afternoon before giving up and planning my phone call. The previous Saturday I'd caught Sam at home and behaved on the phone more like the nervous teenager I used to be than the smooth player I liked to think I'd become. Before I made that first call, I was in bed staring at the digits of her phone number scrawled on the back corner of an *Advocate* magazine until they blurred and ran together. Should I call her or shouldn't I? Did she know I was gay or didn't she? Would she pick up on my crush on her or wouldn't she?

But after a nearly aborted start, the conversation had seemed to go well. We'd even joked around a little, and talked about what she was doing (cleaning) and where she lived. She had her own place, and I imagined it would be neat and well ordered. Everything in her apartment probably matched, unlike my furnishings, a jumble of stray pieces I'd inherited mostly from older friends. As we'd talked, morning sun had poured in the open window along with a slight breeze and the sound of birds singing. Three sunny Saturdays in a row, and it wasn't even July yet.

Wednesday afternoon was sunny, too, and warm. If I called now, I would fulfill my promise to call without actually having to talk to her, thereby avoiding possibly acting like the doofus she seemed to bring out in me. I lay in bed thinking about what I was going to say, then took the plunge and located her number on my cell. Her voice mail picked up after four rings. Score! All too soon the beep sounded, and I cleared my throat and said, like the dork I wanted to avoid being, "Um, hi, Sam. It's Mac–um, Emily, that is. Emily Mackenzie. From soccer? Hope your week is going well. Just wanted to check in, see what you thought about playing this weekend. Everyone thought you were great. So, um, if you want, you can give me a call, or I'll try you back another time. Okay, talk to you soon."

Only after I hung up did I realize that I'd failed to leave my phone number, which might not be such a problem in the era of caller ID. I flopped into the middle of the bed and rolled my eyes at the ceiling. What an idiot. Now I'd have to call her back. But it was nice, too, talking to Sam, even if it was only her voice mail. She would hear my voice when she came home from work, and maybe she'd save the message and replay it.

Then again, why would she do that? It wasn't like she had any hidden feelings. Those were strictly on my side. Aargh.

Liz rapped on my open door. "What's up?" she asked, coming in and dropping onto the bed next to me.

"I was just leaving a message for Sam Delaney about soccer this weekend," I said, trying to play it cool.

"Go, tiger." She punched me in the arm.

41

I hid a wince. Liz really didn't know her own weightlifting-pumped strength sometimes.

"Speaking of," she added, "Jessie's hanging out with her family on Sunday and I need my car for a crew meeting. Can you find a ride to your game?"

"Sure." Now I had a genuine excuse to call Sam back.

"You can thank me later," Liz said, rolling her eyes. "Wanna go to the beach?"

"Why not?"

"Cool." She hopped off my bed. "Come downstairs when you're ready."

I turned on Queen Latifah and danced around while I got ready for Daikiki.

Chapter Five

~SAM~

Apparently I was too old to play ninety minutes of soccer without stretching afterward. On Monday, my calves and quad muscles felt like rubber bands stretched to their limit, my body tired from the unaccustomed strain of a full soccer game. But mentally, I felt lighter as I started my weekly routine, the memory of playing soccer with Emily's team fixed in my mind.

After a day or two back in the same old same old, though, rising early and feeding Chloe and showering and dressing and running for the bus and working at my PC as developers and tech supporters and marketers flashed past my office door, I settled back into my old self, my dull self. God, I bored me. Or maybe my job was the culprit. I missed the energy of the newsroom at the *Tribune* where everyone had coexisted in a large, open room, sans cubicles, trading lines and copyedits, working toward the same deadline. That same energy had proven too much when I went back after Chris's funeral. I couldn't take the pace, couldn't focus on the details that made a story. Worse, I kept lapsing into passive language. When Tina, my best friend from college, suggested I take a break from the Windy City and come visit her in Seattle, I surprised everyone, including myself, by making the move permanent. When I left Chicago, I gave up both writing and soccer. Now I was starting to wonder why I'd thought I had to.

When my work phone rang on Wednesday afternoon, I answered the way I always did, "This is Sam," my voice low and soft. Business boring.

"Hey, Sam," a cheery voice blared.

I turned down the volume on my phone. "Hi, Tina."

"What are you doing tonight?"

"You know, a couple of parties, maybe an orgy."

"I have a better proposition," she said. "Want to go to the zoo with me?"

"The zoo? Why?"

"What do you mean, why? To see the animals, dummy."

"Huh." I frowned at my computer as the screen saver kicked in and the graphics dissolved into a mass of bleeding colors and mutated text.

"Do you want to go or not?" she asked. "I just thought it's a beautiful day, and I have a free pass from work. And you and I haven't hung out in a while. We could do dinner at your place afterward, if you wanted."

I hadn't been to the zoo since I'd moved to Seattle. "All right, I'm in."

After we hung up, I looked at the Sierra Club calendar on my desk. My parents' anniversary was approaching. Maybe I would take them a box of their favorite smoked salmon next month. Assuming they were still together by then—after my last visit, when they'd only spoken to each other when absolutely necessary and even then in clipped tones that hinted at unspoken hostilities, I wasn't making any bets.

* * *

After work that afternoon, I discovered a message on my voice mail from Emily. I listened to it twice, smiling at the way she'd given her full name—as if I might know another soccer-playing Emily in Seattle. I hung up without deleting the message and got ready to meet Tina.

The sun was out again today, after a drizzly Monday and Tuesday. I waited for Tina on the front stoop of my apartment building. She was easy to pick out of the crowd of zoo-goers—red-orange hair and a turquoise shirt, both luminescent in sunlight. Tina's color clashes were usually intentional. This, according to Seattle fashion, qualified her as a hipster, or so she claimed.

"Hey, stranger," she said, stopping before me. She was wearing the silver and turquoise snake nose ring her mother had given her. Frieda Hoffman was a famous second-wave feminist who traveled the country giving lectures and "activizing," as her daughter called it. Sometimes I wondered what it would have been like to grow up with a mother like her. Chaotic, according to Tina.

She narrowed her eyes at me. "How are you?"

"Fine."

"Really?"

I rolled my eyes. "Yes, really."

Tina and I had been friends since our freshman year at Northwestern when we lived next door to each other. Since my brother's death, she'd been treating me like a sickly child. Sometimes I wanted to shake her and tell her I was the same me. But that wasn't quite true, as she would undoubtedly have pointed out.

At the zoo, Tina flashed her corporate pass. Families were everywhere, harried-looking adults with children by the hand, in strollers, running free. When I was little, my mother had taken Chris and me to Binder Park Zoo in Battle Creek practically every week in the summer. Chris and I had both waited eagerly each year for school to let out so that we could watch tigers pace in and out of dusty caves, elephants communicate in their alien tongue, monkeys fly across a massive jungle gym. But one summer, when he was eleven and I was eight, Chris stopped short beside the lion enclosure and refused to go any farther. As we drove home, he said he'd never noticed the cages before. Now that he had, he didn't think he could ever go back. I hadn't been to a zoo since, either.

"Come on," Tina said, slipping her arm through mine. "Let's check out Africa."

Just inside the gates of the Woodland Park Zoo, only a football field away from my apartment building, was the African Savannah, a wide meadow with zebras, giraffes and a hippo pond. Two hippopotami were submerged in the greenish water, their backs and heads protruding like large wrinkled rocks.

After lingering there for a few minutes, we walked through the bird tent and followed the path alongside monkeys and lions in separate natural enclosures made of rocks and trenches. We passed a laughing hyena in a rare metal cage, pacing silently back and forth behind the bars while a group of small boys called out: "Open your mouth, Mr. Hyena. Open sesame!" And, "Nice ears, bucket head!"

"No wonder zoo animals attack children who fall into their cages," Tina remarked loudly enough for the mothers of the offending juveniles to stare at her askance.

I tried not to laugh and pulled Tina away from the intra-species conflict. Around the next corner, past a spotted jaguar, and that was it—we'd come through the African Savannah. And all without being attacked by lions or contracting some horrible monkey virus.

"It's kind of sad, isn't it?" I said, thinking of my brother. "The animals, I mean. They must hate to be cooped up, especially the ones that weren't born in captivity."

Tina growled at one of the children underfoot. He turned and ran back to his posse. "I know," she said. "They should be out on the real Savannah, with their herd or pride or whatnot. But out there the lions would eat them. Here, at least, they get to die of old age."

In the Elephant Forest, we spotted elephants lumbering about a playing field to the delight of watching children. Beyond a nearby glass wall, we glimpsed siamangs and orangutans in a wide enclosure with rock walls, waterfalls, dense vegetation. We crossed a wooden bridge, Highway 99 barely visible through the trees. The sound of falling water vied with rush hour traffic. Despite the noise, there among the bamboo trees and nonnative flora and fauna, with signs in English and Thai, it really felt as if we'd left Seattle.

We followed the Northern Trail past vigilant wolves and massive grizzlies, circled through Australasia and the Tropical Rain Forest, paused to admire kangaroos, emus and gorillas. We prowled the indoor Day and Night Exhibits, spooked by snakes, bats and giant cockroaches. A quick tour of the Temperate Forest, a brief stop at the Family Farm, and we were done.

"Now, wasn't that fun?" Tina asked as we exited through the front gate a little before seven.

"Yes, it was," I admitted. I felt different somehow, knowing that I slept only a few hundred yards from lemurs and Sun bears, Colobus monkeys and Cape Teals, tapirs and pythons. From lions and tigers and bears, oh my. Fortunately, I lived on the top floor, so even if there were to be a break-out, in an earthquake for example, I was pretty sure I'd be safe.

Back at my apartment, Tina and I peered into my cupboards and latched onto the old standby of pasta, French bread and a bottle of wine. When I'd lived with her my first few months in Seattle, we'd had a great time most nights making dinner and sharing wine or an occasional joint. Tina was a bit of a pothead now, though she hadn't been in college. She wasn't a lot of things in college that she had since become in Seattle. I liked to think she was more herself now.

Her increased comfort with who she was might have

explained why she was luckier in lust now than she'd ever been in college. As we fixed dinner, she told me about her latest find, a guy she'd picked up at a bar on Capitol Hill the previous week. His name was Matt. He was the guitarist for an alternative band called the Screaming Monkeys.

I paused in buttering the garlic bread. "No wonder you had a sudden urge to go to the zoo."

She laughed. "You know, I never made the connection. But you should see this guy. He's beautiful, with a goatee and pierced eyebrow and four tattoos in a variety of places, including one not even his mother knows about."

"And you know this because…?"

"Because I took him home and slept with him."

I sighed and didn't say anything about common sense and condom usage.

But she knew me. "Don't worry, Sam, we were safe." She opened the wine and poured us each a glass. "And I made sure beforehand that he doesn't diddle with boys on the side."

"That's right, I forgot—no one you sleep with on the first date ever lies."

"Easy, killer. It wasn't exactly a date. Anyway, don't you think it's about time you rejoined the world of the sexually active yourself?"

"Whatever."

"Come on. You work in a young, hip company. There must be someone there you might at least consider fucking."

Her bluntness no longer made me blush. A statement like that back in college would have turned even the tips of my ears red. "No, Tina. Believe it or not."

"But didn't you say lots of guys in their twenties work there?"

"You don't understand." I leaned against the stove. "The developers lack social skills of any kind, so forget it. The marketers all wear loafers with tassels, and I just couldn't date a guy with tassels on his shoes. The tech supporters are even worse—they're all *Lord of the Rings* and *Star Trek* freaks, though they're quick to insist they like the new *Star Trek*, not the old show. As if being a *Next Generation* fan is somehow more acceptable."

"It totally is. The two shows are completely different. Anyway, LOTRO rocks." As I stared at her, she added, "you know, Lord of The Rings Online? It's a game, Sam. You must know about online gaming."

"More than I ever wanted to, thanks to weekly staff meetings. I'm just surprised you do."

"I've dated my share of gamers," Tina said. "The guys at Xytech don't sound that bad. I'll just have to come to your holiday party and scope one out for you. Do I get to be your date this year?"

"It's six months away," I said, checking the pasta water. "You never know, I might have someone to take by then."

"I'm all for that. But get serious—when's the last time you went out on a date?"

"I went to the symphony with that guy from work."

"Yeah, right before you told him you just wanted to be friends or some such malarkey. Admit it, you haven't been on a real date since that guy in New York, have you?"

I shrugged. "So I've been off the market for a little while. Big deal."

"Multiple years without sex at our age is not natural," she said, and shuddered. "I could never go that long. Tell me you at least practice, you know, self-service?"

I willed the blush creeping up my neck not to rise above chin level. "Not like I'd tell you."

She grinned. "I'll take that as a yes. Seriously, Sam, what am I going to do with you? The sexual revolution ended a long time ago, you know, and we won."

"So you say." The truth was, I hadn't thought much about sex since finding out my brother was dying from the mother of all STDs. It wasn't like I'd been a twenty-first century Erica Jong even before Chris told me about his condition. But my brother's illness had altered the way I thought about getting close to another human being. I wasn't about to risk so much for someone I wasn't sure I would like the next morning. Or year.

"Do you even know what kind of guy you like anymore?" Tina asked.

I tried to picture my ideal mate and failed. "I don't know."

"What about a soccer player?" she pressed. "One of the guys in Matt's band played at Seattle U."

An image of Emily Mackenzie popped into my mind. I swirled my wine, watching the dark red liquid circle the glass. "Maybe. Stir the sauce, would you? By the way, I played soccer over the weekend."

"You're kidding! Sam, that's great! How did you feel?"

"Out of practice. Embarrassingly so."

"I bet you were awesome," she said. "You should have told me. I would have come and cheered for you. We might have even convinced Sarah to leave the computer lab long enough to come watch."

Sarah, another friend from Northwestern, was a doctoral student at U-Dub. She and Tina had attended most of my intramural games in college. They used to say that to really know me someone would have to see me play soccer, since to look at me no one would ever think I'd be capable of such violence. As a criminologist planning a career with the FBI, Sarah spent too much time thinking about violence, I thought.

"That's okay," I said. "I didn't need the two of you witnessing my humiliation. Bad enough the other players had to see me bumbling around."

"I'm sure you were great. How'd you find the team?"

"It was totally random. I ran into that girl from my high school, the one who played at U-Dub."

"The one you went to watch last fall? Where'd you see her?"

"Running around Green Lake. Wild, huh?" I pictured Emily in her running clothes, smiling at me with the sun in her hair, and I had to smile too.

"Very wild," Tina said. "So that's what's different about you. I thought there was something."

"What do you mean?"

"You're like one of those snakes, sticking your tongue out testing the air. Instead of curled up in a corner asleep the way you have been ever since you moved here. You're coming out of your shell."

"Which is it—am I a snake or a turtle?"

"I don't know," she said. "But I like it."

"Yeah, yeah. I think the pasta's ready. Let's eat."

Later we retired to the living room with our wine, leaving stained saucepans and garlic-encrusted plates stacked haphazardly in the kitchen sink. We set iTunes on my computer on shuffle, reclined at opposite ends of the couch and proceeded to gossip and reminisce. It was college all over again as we talked about boys (hers) and work (mine) and where we'd be in five years (neither of us could begin to imagine).

A little after nine, the phone rang. I grabbed it before Tina could snag it and answer with her usual line, "Is this the party to whom I am speaking?" When I heard Emily's voice at the other end, I sat up and looked away from Tina's inquiring glance.

"This is Emily," she said, sounding nervous. "Mackenzie."

"Hey." I'd been thinking about her, looking forward to talking to her even, but now with Tina watching I couldn't bring myself to say so. "When's the next soccer game?"

"Sunday, at four. At the same field."

"Great," I said. "I'll see you then."

Tina gave me a thumbs-up. She'd been bugging me to play soccer ever since I got to town. One of the many things she was always bugging me to do.

"I was wondering, could I bum a ride?" Emily asked. "I don't have a car, and my roommate needs hers, so—"

"That'd be fine. But could I give you a call this weekend? I'm a little busy right now." I hadn't intended it to sound quite like that, as if I had some sort of illicit rendezvous going.

"Why don't you call me back when you have time," she said,

and I knew immediately that I'd hurt her somehow, even though she sounded all tough. "Sorry to interrupt." And the line clicked.

I forced myself not to wince. "Okay, talk to you then," I said, and shut the phone off. That had gone well. Not.

"Was that the girl from Logan?" Tina asked. "Emily?"

"Yes. Now where were we? You were telling me about the tattoo on what's-his-name's butt."

"His name is Matt," she said. "You have to try to remember. I've slept with him four times already and I'm not even sick of him yet."

"You are such a slut."

"I know. Isn't it fun?"

Much later, after the dishes had found their way into the dishwasher and Tina had long since gone, I lay in bed staring up at the ceiling, Chloe a purring mass at my side. Sleeping around wasn't always fun. When my brother first ran away to New York City, he'd spent his nights on park benches with other runaways, he'd told me later, mostly other gay kids. They turned tricks to eat and shot up to escape the nightmare of New York's street life. Eventually, after one of his friends was murdered by a john, a social worker convinced him to go straight, so to speak, and Chris finished his GED and started taking classes part-time at NYU.

A couple of years later he met Alan, his only serious boyfriend. But their relationship hadn't exactly been smooth, my brother told me. Alan was older, HIV negative, and had lost many of his closest friends to AIDS in the early nineties, before HAART—highly active antiretroviral therapy—became available. Chris was not only infected with a strand of HIV that was resistant to several key HAART drugs, but he'd also contracted Hepatitis C during his street days. This combination was why he'd ended up getting so sick and dying at a time when most HIV-infected Americans could expect to live almost as long as those who weren't infected.

Alan hadn't been able to handle Chris's many illnesses or

murky long-term prognosis. He finally announced one day that he was moving home to the Twin Cities. Alone. A short time after Alan left, Chris had called home for the first time in seven years and asked if he could visit. A junior at Northwestern, I took a few days off to meet him in Logan for the big family reunion. Emily was a high school senior then; that was the visit when I learned she had a scholarship to U-Dub. Meanwhile, I didn't yet know that Chris was HIV positive or that he had recently been dumped by the love of his life. He hadn't wanted us to worry, he'd told me later.

I shut my eyes. Why was I thinking about my brother again? Was it because Emily had called? Would I flash back to Logan and my family every time I talked to her? Then again, after the way I'd acted on the phone tonight, there might not be a next time. I wasn't sure why my guard came up so high and so fast with her. Except—soccer wasn't the only thing drawing me out. She was doing it too, only I wasn't sure what that meant and even less sure I wanted to face what it might mean. I needed to call her, to apologize. But I wasn't sure I wanted to deal with the memories even the slightest contact with her seemed to trigger.

Like now. My brain was working overtime, feeding wine-fueled memories to my conscious mind. One night in particular came back to me. Chris had already moved home to die. He and I were hanging out on the back porch watching the sun set when he mentioned our childhood visits to Binder Park Zoo. He'd always thought of New York City as a zoo for people like him who didn't belong anywhere else, he told me. He was glad to be home, glad to be back among trees and grass where he could actually see the sky. He hadn't been able to breathe in New York.

I reached over, touched his hand, and told him I was glad he was home too. We sat quietly holding hands, and it might have been the first time in our lives that we held on to each other like that.

A week later we were out on the back porch again watching an evening thunderstorm work its way through the neighborhood, flinching at the cracks of thunder and then laughing at our own fear. The storm was pretty bad, though not as powerful, we agreed, as the tornado that had ripped through Logan in '89 leaving the city's skyline permanently altered. We started reminiscing about walking around town after the all-clear sounded, inspecting shattered buildings and downed trees and power lines, and it occurred to me that this might be the last thunderstorm Chris would ever see.

"How can you be so calm?" I asked him after a particularly deafening blast rattled the porch.

He knew I wasn't talking about the weather. "How else should I be? My liver is shot and my T cells are below thirty, Sam. I'm not going to get any better. It's okay. I've had a long time to make my peace with dying."

"But we haven't," I said. "I haven't."

"I know. I'm sorry."

His apology didn't change anything. I watched a bolt of lightning momentarily illuminate the evening sky, felt the thunder that followed a second later inside my body like the pulsing sound waves of a speaker I'd stood next to at a dorm party a few weeks earlier. Beside me, Chris shut his eyes.

He died two weeks later downstairs in the rented hospital bed on a lovely spring day. Our mother was holding his hand when he exhaled a last rattling breath and grew still. I stood in the den doorway, the tray of soup I held trembling slightly. She looked up at me, but I knew she didn't see me. "He's gone," she said, her eyes and voice empty.

The hospice nurse, Ben, moved to check Chris's vitals, to stop his IV, to close his eyes. He helped my mother up as her face crumpled and the sobs overtook her. Meanwhile I stood there, still clutching the tray, unable to feel anything. I didn't cry until a week after I'd arrived in Seattle, on a warm June morning when the scent of lilac bushes near my parked truck suddenly took me back to when I was a kid sitting on the floor of Chris's room right before he ran away, listening to him play guitar, the pungent fragrance of the lilac bushes outside his window enveloping us in a warm, sweet-smelling cocoon. That was how I had remembered him all those years he lived apart, and when I smelled the West Seattle lilacs after brunch with Tina, I sank to the sidewalk, wrapped my arms around my legs and finally let go. Tina sat behind me on the cement and wrapped her arms around me, murmuring softly as the sobs tore through me, unrelenting.

I squeezed my eyes shut tighter. Damn him. Damn him for running away, for going off and getting sick, for only coming home to die. We never got to see him healthy and happy, never got to meet the man he loved. I never got to have a real big brother. Instead he left me with parents who couldn't look at me without seeing his ghost.

I ground my fists against my eyes. I was tired of crying.

Chapter Six

~EMILY~

The day after Sam blew me off on the phone, I was at Peloton talking to Lori about seat types when the bell above the door dinged. I glanced up. Kristin, one of my soccer buddies.

Brett reappeared magically from his lunch break and sidled up to her, all charm and virility. From across the shop, I could see Kristin flashing her dimples. Toying with him, probably. She was a major flirt, but had a serious boyfriend who would be a senior at WSU in the fall. Much to the dismay of the U-Dub male contingent.

"Someone you know?" Lori asked.

"Just a friend. I mentioned I was working here, but I didn't know she would stop by." I didn't want to get in trouble already. Time enough for them to learn of my sometime flakiness.

"Don't worry," Lori said. "You can have friends in occasionally. Anyway, you're off the clock."

I checked my watch. Sure enough, it was after one.

"You're doing great, by the way," she added, and slapped me on the shoulder. "Now get out of here."

"Thanks." I grabbed my messenger bag from behind the counter and headed over to where Brett still appeared to be hitting on Kristin.

"Yo, girl," Kristin said, lifting her eyebrows in a way that indicated she thought my co-worker was a dweeb.

"You know Mac?" Brett asked.

"I sure do." She slid her arm around my shoulders and pecked my cheek. "Hi, honey."

"Hi, sweetie." Kristin liked to pretend she was gay when geeky guys hit on her.

"Cool," he said. "Check you ladies later."

Outside, we strolled along Forty-fifth, the Main Street of Wallingford, me pushing my bike (I'd been running late that morning and had to ride the six blocks to work), Kristin smiling at everyone we passed. She was from Oregon and didn't know any better.

"So how's the new job going?" she asked.

"Great." I told her how much I'd learned and about the Wallingford types who frequented the store—the yuppies, hippies and new-fangled yippies, a sect of wealthy, outdoorsy professionals that had flooded the Pacific Northwest in recent years.

"Lori seems cool," she said. "And cute."

"Not my type."

"That's 'cause you only like straight girls like me."

"Get over yourself," I said. "I wouldn't hook up with you in a million years."

"Ditto, pal."

People at school were always speculating about Kristin and me. But our friendship was too close for us to risk crossing that line, even if Kristin hadn't been straight. Anyway, I had sworn to never (again) sleep with anyone on my team. Teammate romances could get ugly, especially if it didn't work out and you still had to play together.

"Speaking of straight girls," she added, "what's going on with you and that girl you brought on Sunday?"

"You mean Sam?"

"Duh, yes, Sam," she said, elbowing me.

"Just someone from home I ran into recently, that's all."

"Wait a minute, is this the famous Sam you used to talk about when I first met you? The one who taught you everything you know and made you the soccer player you are today, yada yada yada?"

Kristin had me and she knew it.

"That's her," I admitted reluctantly.

"Wow." She nodded. "Apparently your crush on her is alive and well."

"Who said I had a crush on her? Anyway, she's probably got a boyfriend."

"Since when has that stopped you?"

"You're funny, you know that?"

"Don't change the subject. I want details."

We stopped at one of Wallingford's many sushi joints and brought take-out back to my house where I filled her in on my initial meeting with Sam and subsequent encounters. I even related how I'd caught her checking me out Sunday as we left the soccer field.

"She totally wants you," Kristin announced, spearing a piece of salmon nigiri with her chopsticks.

"According to you, every guy on the planet wants you and every girl wants me."

"They do. But seriously, she had a gay brother, right? You're the one who told me the homo thing runs in families."

"I didn't mean the Delaney family."

"Why not?"

"Just because. Anyway, I told you, she dissed me on the phone. Nothing's going to happen." The night before, when I'd hung up on Sam, I resisted the urge to throw my cell phone across the room because, after all, she couldn't help it if she was straight.

Kristin didn't buy my claim. "Except she's going to call you, and you're going to ride with her to soccer…"

"Look, I don't need to be hoping for something to happen here, okay?"

Kristin frowned a little. "Okay. I'll stop messing with you."

We watched *Ellen* while we finished eating, then Kristin headed home to the U District to get ready for her waitress job at a swanky Queen Anne restaurant. She didn't mention Sam again.

Lori had given me a couple of books on cycle repair that morning, in case I wanted to learn, she'd said. I did want to learn, and I didn't want to moon after someone I could never have, so upstairs in my sunlit room I opened one of the books and began to read about bicycle maintenance. Only it felt just like college again, and I'd never been good at reading in bed.

My cell, chiming a familiar tune, woke me. Before the previous night's fiasco, I'd downloaded a ring tune for Sam, Queen's "Bohemian Rhapsody." Like many American sports teams—thanks mostly to "We Will Rock You" and the classic poor-sportsmanship anthem "Another One Bites the Dust"—our high school soccer team had been inordinately fond of Queen.

"Is this a good time?" she asked.

"I'm not busy, if that's what you mean." The jibe came out more bitterly than I intended.

"About that," Sam said, her voice soft, "I wanted to apologize. I didn't mean to sound weird. I had a friend from college over, and we get pretty silly when we drink."

"No worries." Didn't want her thinking I cared too much.

"Anyway, I just wanted to apologize," she repeated.

"Apology accepted. You still want to play soccer this weekend?"

"Definitely. You still need a ride?"

"As long as it's no inconvenience."

"It's not. We're practically neighbors, after all." Then she asked, "What are you doing tonight?"

"Me? Nothing. Why?"

"I was thinking of watching the Mariners game and ordering a pizza. You interested?"

"Sure." I held the phone away from my head and grinned. Sam Delaney was inviting me over! The fact that I'd eaten pizza two nights in a row seemed unimportant. "What time does the game start?"

"They're on the road at the Red Sox, but I've got DVR. You can come over whenever."

"Awesome. Hey," I added, "did you know that David Winters from Logan is the new starting shortstop for the Sox?"

"My dad told me. He's apparently the pride of Logan." She gave me directions, told me that her building on Fiftieth Street, across the street from the zoo, was hard to miss. The name was carved in stone over the front steps: Camelot.

"You're kidding," I said.

"I know, kind of cheesy."

"No, I like it. Should I bring anything?"

"Just yourself," she said.

We hung up a minute later and I sat staring at my cell phone. Last time we'd spoken, Sam Delaney had barely had time for me. Now she was inviting me over. I could dig it. I pulled on a sweatshirt over my T-shirt and shorts and left the house whistling.

Have you ever heard that voice in the back of your mind right before you do something stupid, like balance a full glass of cranberry juice over white carpeting, for example? Saying, "Don't do it, man! Certain disaster, here!"

That voice was doing jackhammer impressions in my head as I biked through the park to Sam's house: "Go back, go back, go back!"

But I dealt with the voice the way I usually did—I admired the blue sky overhead and appreciated the strain in my quads as I rode my bike uphill through Woodland Park and across the stone bridge over Aurora Avenue. I hummed to myself and in no time I was pulling up in front of Sam's building, named for a legendary kingdom in a land far, far away.

I locked my bike to a handrail and rang the buzzer. Her disembodied voice floated out from the speaker as she buzzed me in. The lobby was beautiful, with polished tiles, gold-framed Impressionist prints and a gleaming chandelier high above the lobby floor. I waited for the elevator, assuring myself I was really in Sam Delaney's apartment building. And I hadn't even invited myself.

The elevator was old and slow. Eventually it creaked to a stop on the fourth floor. Sam waved at me from her doorway. In black Adidas sweats and a V-neck T-shirt, she looked adorable as ever. Just for a moment, an urge to run away threatened to overwhelm me. Maybe I should have listened to that voice after all. I took a deep breath and smiled back at her and walked down the hallway. One foot at a time, just like that, there was a good girl. Good thing I didn't have a tail to wag or I would have betrayed myself long before.

"Come on in." She held the door wide. "That was fast."

"The elevator?" I asked, looking around. Wood floors, muted rugs and matching grown-up furniture. Plus electronics galore— TV (the screen currently paused on a shot of Fenway Park), DVR, DVD player and laptop computer occupied various stations in the living room. She was a yuppie; here was incontrovertible proof. Except that she drove a truck.

"I meant you made it over here fast."

"I rode my bike. You have a great apartment, by the way."

"Thanks. Want the grand tour?"

"Sure."

She showed me the living room, office space complete with another computer (an Apple, like the laptop, I noted, inwardly cheered that she wasn't loyal to the Evil Empire across Lake Washington), kitchen and bedroom. I didn't pause long in the bedroom doorway, just poked my head in to get an impression of wispy curtains, a real bed and a beautiful wooden armoire.

"That's it," she said, and led me back to the living room. She picked up a remote and hit a button, and the TV screen unfroze. "Can I get you something to drink?"

"What do you have?"

I dropped onto the couch that faced the entertainment center. Her flat panel television looked brand new, the picture sharp the way only HD could make it. I could get hooked on experiencing the Mariners at her place. But I pushed the thought away. Dangerous territory.

"I can offer you juice," she said. "Or beer. Wait—you are old enough to drink, aren't you?"

I looked at her quickly, ready to spew out something cantankerous. Then I caught the smile lingering about her mouth. "I'm legal, believe it or not. A beer would be great."

While Sam was in the kitchen, a gray tabby ambled out of the bedroom. I leaned forward, my hand extended. "Here, kitty."

The cat came right up to me, butted its head against my leg and started purring up a storm. I lifted it onto my lap. This was perfect. I was in Sam Delaney's apartment with her cat on my lap, and I could hear her in the kitchen bustling about.

I'd been right to ignore that voice, I decided as Dave Niehaus, longtime Mariners announcer, welcomed Seattle fans to the broadcast from Boston on a fine summer's night. Definitely right. I scratched the cat's ears and waited for Sam to emerge from the kitchen.

Chapter Seven

~SAM~

In my kitchen Thursday night I hummed as I putzed about. Emily Mackenzie was in my living room. I surprised even myself when I invited her over, and then rushed around the apartment picking up. Not that the place wasn't already psychotically clean. That was one of the things I did when I couldn't sleep: sprayed, wiped and scrubbed. Rather Lady Macbeth of me, but I found cleaning somehow soothing. After I hung up with Emily, Chloe had watched me dust the entertainment center, then yawned and curled up on the couch as I moved on to the coffee table. She'd seen this all before. When the buzzer sounded, though, she high-tailed it into the bedroom, where she would probably remain all evening, boycotting the intrusion.

Beers in hand, I headed back to the living room, only to discover Chloe curled up on Emily's lap as if they had known one another for ages. I almost dropped the bottles—some of my friends had never even seen Chloe, who I'd adopted from a no-kill shelter shortly after moving into Camelot.

Emily, apparently mistaking the amazement on my face for displeasure, quickly set Chloe on the floor. "Sorry, I didn't know if your cat was allowed on the furniture."

I placed the bottles on coasters and took a seat next to Emily. "She's allowed. She's just not usually so social."

My uber-finicky cat approved of Emily. This realization was still working its way through my mind when Chloe jumped up and resettled on the cushion between us, purring. I reached out to pet her just as Emily did, and our hands brushed.

"This is Chloe," I said.

She smiled at the cat. "Nice to meet you."

I looked away from her dimples and remembered that the little brother of a boy I'd gone to school with had recently become the starting shortstop for the Red Sox. "I can't believe that's David," I said as he scooped up a ground ball and threw Ichiro out at first—no small feat.

"Crazy, huh?"

"I remember him from kiddie soccer in Logan." Then again, I remembered Emily from those days, too, and look how much she'd changed. "I dated his brother, Chad, in seventh grade. You know, when people used to 'go' together?"

"Totally. I used to beat David up at recess. Now I wish I'd been nicer."

Emily, I recalled, had been a terror on the playground. I pictured her in elementary school with pigtails, overalls and freckles, cavorting with the boys her age. Back then I wore Gap T-shirts and plastic barrettes and played hopscotch with the other girls. I'd never rebelled like Emily. Or Chris. He wore black, listened to punk and stole vodka from our parents' stash. Meanwhile, I'd kept the peace and blended in, careful not to rock anyone's boat.

All at once, sitting on my couch with Emily, I wanted to pack up my truck and drive somewhere I'd never been. But even as I imagined the perfect escape, I knew I'd never take it. No matter how far I ran, I would still be the same me. Besides, I had Chloe to think of now.

As the first inning unfolded, Em and I ordered pizza and talked about people we knew from Logan. Most of the kids who bothered leaving Michigan had ended up in Chicago or the Twin Cities, though a few others had come out west like us. We were on the topic of Logan High soccer players when I remembered her friend Jenna Anderson. They'd been inseparable Em's freshman year. Back then it hadn't occurred to me, but now I wondered about their relationship.

At a break in the conversation, I asked, "Whatever happened to your friend Jenna? Did she play soccer in college, too?"

Emily took a swig of beer, dimples suddenly absent. "She went out east somewhere. Connecticut, I think. Division III."

Her eyes were cold, and afterward I wasn't sure why I asked what I did next, when the answer was obvious: "Are you still friends?"

"No."

I looked back at the TV, trying to find a way to ask what I wanted to know—was Emily dating anyone? I knew from soccer that her friends thought she was single, but she could be dating someone they didn't know. Then again, why did I even care? I was just curious, I told myself. I'd never had a gay friend, just my brother, and we never talked much about it. I wanted Emily to know I was cool with it.

"You and Jenna seemed really close," I pressed.

"We were." She looked over at me, hesitated for a moment, and said, "I'm gay, Sam. You knew that, right?"

My eyes were locked on the television, though I couldn't have said what was happening in the baseball game. "Yeah, I knew. My mom..." But I stopped short of admitting that my mother had informed me of Emily's sexuality.

Out of the corner of my eye, I saw her smile. "Moms know everything."

Not always, I thought.

We watched the game in silence for a while. I still didn't know if she was dating anyone, but at least the gay thing was out in the open between us. And yet, I was a little nervous that she knew that I'd known she was a lesbian when we played soccer on Sunday; when I called her earlier to apologize; when I invited her over. The fact that I'd known cast our previous interactions in a different light. Not to mention our current interaction. Didn't it?

The arrival of the pizza kept us occupied for a couple of innings, as did a discussion of our favorite things about Seattle. Many of the things on our lists matched—proximity to ocean and mountain; mild winters that meant you could run outdoors year round; easy access to hiking and snowshoeing trails; three National Parks within two hours.

"Plus it's such a livable city," Em added. "You can bus most places and the hills make each neighborhood feel completely separate."

I had to agree. For a city, Seattle felt remarkably like a town. Which, to a Michigander, was a good thing.

During the seventh inning, we chased Chloe away with a noisy rendition of "Take Me Out to the Ball Game." She slunk back in after we'd finished and deposited herself between us again, though it took some cajoling by Emily to restart the purring machine.

"Do you ever miss Logan?" I asked a little while later.

"Sometimes." She turned her head where it rested on the back of the couch to look at me. "But I haven't been back enough to really miss it. How about you? You've gone back a lot, haven't you?"

"Yeah." Too much.

"Why did you go to Northwestern, anyway? I got the impression your parents could afford to send you pretty much anywhere. You could have played Division I soccer."

She'd thought that much about my college decision? "Maybe, but I didn't get the same offers you did," I said. "And since I wanted to be a writer, Northwestern seemed perfect."

"Do you still want to be a writer?"

I hesitated. "I'm not sure." Since leaving Chicago, I'd been too afraid the words were gone for good to try to get them back. But I didn't tell Emily that. I didn't even tell me that, usually.

"What do you want to be when you grow up, then?" she asked.

"Happy." The word slipped out without my intending it. "What about you? You seem like you've got it all figured out. You've always known you wanted to coach, right?"

"Kind of. But I'm starting to think soccer might have been mainly an escape for me, a way to go someplace entirely new. Someplace I could be new, separate from who I was in Logan."

Sounded familiar, I thought.

"Soccer is over now that I'm out of school," she continued. "Unless I want to go to Europe and try to find a team there to take me on. But that idea doesn't thrill me. I like my life here. I don't know. Maybe by sticking around to coach I'm just avoiding having to figure out what I really want to do. Maybe I'm still just running away."

We were looking at each other, our heads close together on the back of the couch and I was noticing the color of her eyes—blue with little gold flecks in them—and noticing, too, that this was the closest to genuinely happy I could remember feeling in the year since my brother's death. But then Emily looked away, and I wasn't sure if I was relieved or disappointed.

When the phone rang, I checked the caller ID and almost didn't pick up. "My mother," I told Emily.

"Tell her I say hi."

It was late her time, after ten, but my mother was wide awake and chattier than usual. "It's raining here," she told me, "which made me think of Seattle, naturally. I can't wait to see you. I'm looking forward to your visit so much."

"Me, too," I lied.

"What are you doing, honey? I'm not interrupting, am I?"

67

"Watching baseball with a friend. Actually—"

But before I could tell her it was Emily, she rattled on: "Did you finally meet someone? Isn't it nice that you have him at your apartment! I was starting to worry about you. I know I loved dating when I was your age. Or maybe a little younger than you. By the time I was your age I was already married and had your brother."

"Just a friend, Mom," I said when she paused for breath. Again, I was about to say who, but she didn't give me a chance.

"Well, that's all right too. I'll let you go, since you're obviously busy with your own life."

"That's okay," I said, hoping my insincerity wasn't too obvious.

But she insisted on getting off the phone. I told her I loved her and to say hi to Dad for me. She said she would when he got home—he was still at work. I promised to call over the weekend, told her again that I loved her because I thought she might need to hear it.

"I love you too. It's so nice to hear your voice. Why did you have to move so far away?" Then she laughed and said, "Enjoy whatever game it is on TV, honey."

I turned off the phone and set it back on the coffee table. My father never used to work this late. My mother liked to say that relationships went in cycles, sometimes bad and more often, you hoped, good. In a way, I was glad I didn't know what was going on back there in the house they'd bought just after Chris was born. Emily had grown up in that neighborhood, too, street after street of roomy houses with large yards and huge old trees. My mother was probably in the den now, feet up on her favorite recliner, watching rain fall in the backyard where she maintained a garden that would have rivaled some of the best in the Pacific Northwest.

One entire wall of the den was covered in photos, most of which my mother had taken. Ever since I could remember, she always had a camera close at hand to catch me or my brother in some act or another. Neither of my parents was in many of the shots, except the family portraits my mother had made us all pose for once a year at the holidays. Those sessions usually had to be rescheduled multiple times due to my father's work. Legal matters could be unpredictable, he always claimed.

Emily shifted on the couch next to me and reached for her beer.

"She just called to say hi," I said.

"Gotcha." She didn't glance my way.

Probably I should have said who was with me. But my mother had seemed frazzled. Just as well that she didn't know I was with Emily. No need to start her imagining that her lone surviving child was gay too. She'd only blame herself. Or would she? I'd heard her talking to my father one night when I was in high school, when they thought I was asleep, and he'd said it was her fault. That she had coddled Chris too much and that was why he'd turned out the way he had.

I didn't explain any of this to Emily, though. I just watched the game and tried not to think about my parents or Chris or Logan again. After nine innings, the Mariners and Red Sox were tied at eight apiece. Into extra innings we went, and Emily stayed until the Mariners hit a walk-off double. I finally walked her to the door a few minutes before nine.

"Thanks for inviting me over," she said.

"Thanks for coming over. Baseball is always more fun to watch with someone else."

"Shh—don't let Chloe hear you."

I smiled. "We'll have to do this again."

"I'd like that." She stepped back. "Anyway, see you this weekend?"

"How about I call you Saturday about the game?"

"Okay."

We looked at each other a second longer. Then I opened the door and she moved into the hallway. As she headed for the elevator, I made myself retreat into my living room, even though I wanted to stay and watch her walk away. When she arrived earlier in the evening, I noticed that she almost swaggered when she walked, but in an innocent way, like she didn't know she was doing it. Then, in the dim light of the hallway, her cheeks red from the outdoors, her short hair mussed, she'd looked about sixteen. And yet at the same time, so comfortable inside her own body.

I turned the bolt and leaned my forehead against the door. What was this I was feeling? Somehow, I doubted my mother would approve.

Chapter Eight

~EMILY~

The morning after the baseball game, I lay in bed staring up at the tapestry hanging over my bed, trying not to think about Sam. How had this happened? I'd opened the door to her, figuratively speaking, just a little I thought, and now here she was in the front of my mind, no longer a just memory but a full-fledged inhabitant of my Seattle life.

She'd known all along I was gay. She even asked about Jenna, my first girlfriend. Jenna and I had been together for almost two years in high school until she decided she was too old to "play around" anymore. When she'd set her sights on a boyfriend, I'd gone a little out of control, drinking and staying out late and generally getting into trouble. My parents, accustomed to my sister's good girl routine, hadn't known what to do with me. Then college coaches started showing interest, and I realized I had a way out. I focused on soccer, swore off teammate romances and left Logan as soon as I could.

Jenna was just a ghost now from a life I'd long since abandoned. Unlike Sam—she'd looked so cute the night before, and real, curled up on the couch watching me as I rambled on about this or that. Somehow I ended up telling her about the Detroit Tigers game my father took me to when I was ten. Sam would have been thirteen that year, and I could picture her then, still playing soccer with the boys and riding her bike to the local junior high. I couldn't remember when I first learned of Sam's existence. She'd just always been there, until my sophomore year when she wasn't anymore. In my mind, her past self—the single French braid she'd worn forever, the Gap jeans and Logan High Soccer sweatshirt I remembered vividly—gave way to the Adidas sweats and neat ponytail she wore the night before.

I lay in bed too long and ended up having to shower speedily and sprint out the door. Five minutes later I was at the shop, almost on time but not quite. Lori didn't comment on my tardiness, but Brett the Bellevue boy checked his watch pointedly and winked at me.

"Don't worry," he said. "I've got you covered."

Sam remained in the front of my mind all day. During slow moments I stared off into space, replaying the look on her face as I walked down the hall toward her, as we sang the ballpark theme song, as she watched me play with Chloe. I recalled specific moments, like when we were both slouched down on the couch close together talking about Logan and why we'd left. How she'd smiled, kind of shyly, when she said we should do this again sometime. Do this again—as if it had been a date.

I almost called her after work but instead grabbed a nap to catch up on my recent lack of sleep. Now that I had to be at work so early, I was going to have to cut down on some of the partying. I was getting too old for that scene, anyway. I wasn't a kid anymore. But tonight would kick off Gay Pride Weekend, which meant that homos would be out on the Hill in record numbers. Pride Weekend was always a whirlwind of parties and clubs and rallies—all gay people all the time for three days and nights and then back to the straight world on Monday. For now, my sleep-filled, party-free future would have to wait.

* * *

The nap turned out to be a good idea. By ten thirty that night, Liz, Jessie and I had already had a drink at a bar on Broadway, played a couple of rounds of pool, and were looking for a parking space near Diva's, a gay bar off Broadway. Just before we left home, I'd dialed Sam's number. I wasn't even sure what I would have said if she answered. But her voice mail kicked in, and I hit the off button on my cell, wondering where she was.

At Diva's, we joined the line at the bar, jam-packed with happy Pride-goers. Drinks in hand, we paused at the edge of the dance floor and lit up cigarettes. Jessie smoked more than Liz and me, but none of us were exactly chain-smokers, unlike a lot of lesbians I knew.

Liz and Jessie had each other, so I leaned against a pillar and surveyed the crowd. I took a swig of beer, a drag on my cigarette and had to smile. The night was full of possibilities. I might meet someone new, or I might just dance and drink until I was pleasantly buzzed and ride home in the backseat of Liz's Blazer watching the lights of the city flash past.

From my vantage point, I caught sight of a blonde in the middle of the dance floor, her movements fluid and graceful. At first I thought I was just seeing what I wanted to. It couldn't really be her. But as I watched her dance, I recognized that hair twisted into a seemingly careless bun, those shoulders in a tight white T-shirt, that smile she cast at a redhead dancing a few steps away. If it wasn't Sam, it was her twin. And I would know if she had a twin.

She turned, laughing, saw me watching her and stopped dancing. A boy with a goatee and multiple tattoos sidled between us, and I lost her.

"You okay?" Liz asked.

73

I took a long drink from my beer. "Fine. Just thought I saw someone."

"Bet I know who," Liz teased.

"Zip it." I was about to wallop her when I felt a hand on my shoulder. Liz's raised eyebrows confirmed what I knew before I turned—Sam Delaney.

"I thought that was you," she said, smiling.

Despite my daydreams, suddenly I was too shy to do anything except stare at her. What was she doing here?

Liz asked, "Aren't you going to introduce us?"

I made introductions over the music. Sam shook hands with Liz and then with Jessie, and as she did, I noticed that she looked far more butch than Liz's girlfriend. This wasn't all that surprising since Jessie considered herself a girlie dyke. Still, Sam had an edge I hadn't noticed until now.

Just the usual jock edge, I told myself. Didn't mean she would ever consider kissing girls.

"Dancing Queen" by ABBA came on, a perennial queer crowd favorite, and Liz and Jessie excused themselves to dance. Sam watched me take a drag on my cigarette, leaned in and said, "You smoke?"

Her hair tickled my neck. Our cheeks almost brushed as I said, "Socially."

"Can I have a drag?"

"Sure." I watched her borrow my cigarette, suck smoke in, and exhale it in a series of rings. She leaned close again, handing the cigarette back.

"Bet you thought you knew me," she said.

I watched her, slightly bemused. If I hadn't known better, I would have sworn she was flirting with me.

She looked out at the dancers. I did the same and we stood next to each other, bare arms lightly touching. I was having a hard time convincing myself that this was really happening. A hard time breathing normally too. Not even Jenna, the love of my life so far, had affected me like this. Then again, I'd had a

74

crush on Sam before I ever met Jenna.

"Do you come here often?" she asked.

Even in the dim light I could tell her skin was flushed, and all at once I figured it out. "You've been drinking, haven't you?" I said.

"Absolutely. Haven't you?"

"I'm guessing not as much as you."

We were both quiet for a few minutes, facing the dance floor. I barely even noticed the music, too aware of Sam next to me. She borrowed my cigarette once more and killed it, then handed it back. I ground it out in a nearby ashtray and folded my arms across my chest. I didn't want to feel this way about someone who needed to fortify herself with alcohol in order to go to a gay bar.

But my resolve weakened as an old Clash song came on, one we used to listen to on the bus on the way to and from high school games. I could remember Natalie Sipsma, co-captain with Sam my freshman year, belting out the refrain while Sam sang backup into an invisible mike.

"Come dance with me," she said, catching my hand in hers.

I let her pull me onto the packed floor. Liz and Jessie watched us wend our way through the crowd, hand in hand. Sam stopped near them but didn't let go. Instead she leaned toward me and said, "Remember this song?"

I nodded. All around us people were moving to the beat while we were this motionless island in the middle of it all. What was worse, she was looking at me like she wanted to kiss me. Sam Delaney was going to kiss me.

Then the redhead and goateed boy from before drew near. In a flash, Sam let my hand go and spun away with the girl. The boy smiled at me, and I turned and left the dance floor. I headed for the nearest exit, went outside and walked out to the main road. On Pike Street, I squatted down even though it hurt my soccer-aged knees, my back against the window of a darkened shop, and breathed again, finally.

Liz appeared and squatted down next to me. "You okay?"

"No," I said. "She's drunk. I thought she was going to kiss me."

"I saw that. Mac, are you sure she's straight?"

"Not anymore. But it's her opinion that counts, not mine."

After a little while, we returned to the club. Satisfied I really was fine, Liz wandered off to find Jessie while I took up my initial post at the edge of the dance floor, a fresh beer in hand. I hadn't been there long when Sam appeared at my elbow.

"What happened to you?" she asked.

I shrugged. "I wasn't in the mood to dance." I knew I was being inexcusably cold, but I couldn't seem to snap out of it. This was not how I'd envisioned spending the Friday night of Pride Weekend.

We stayed like that through two songs, me stubbornly refusing to look at her. Then she said, "Do you maybe want to get out of here?"

That got my attention. I looked at her quickly, but she was already shaking her head. "Never mind," she said. "I'm going to dance, okay?"

I hesitated, but she was already moving away from me. As I watched her disappear into the swaying mass of bodies on the dance floor, something inside me, some little part I hadn't known existed, shifted, leaving me feeling emptier somehow without her beside me.

After scowling at nothing for a while, I joined Liz and Jessie on the dance floor. Sam and her friends were nearby. I tried not to watch them. Was the boy with the goatee her boyfriend? No, he seemed to be with the redhead. Which meant Sam was there alone, just like me. She wasn't like me, though, I reminded myself. All I needed was to fall in love with her and watch her ditch me for a Seattle boy with dyed hair and a pierced eyebrow. Or, more likely, khakis and a collared shirt.

When Liz went off to chat with friends who had just arrived, Jessie and I dirty danced to a Prince song, grinding our pelvises together, my arm around her neck. Jessie liked to dirty dance with everyone, and Liz knew I wasn't about to try anything. But I thought I caught Sam watching us across the dance floor, eyes slightly narrowed.

Just before one, she tracked me down at the bar to tell me she and her friends were leaving. She looked more sober now, less warm, more wary. And suddenly I didn't want her to leave.

"I'll call you tomorrow," I said. "About soccer, I mean."

"Okay." She watched me for a moment, then reached out and pulled me into an abrupt hug, her hand at the back of my neck.

Goose bumps rose on my skin. I started to pull her even closer, but she stepped back quickly.

"I'm sorry," she said, and disappeared into the crowd near the exit.

After a minute, Liz asked, "What the hell was that?"

"You tell me." I ran a hand over my hair.

"I got no answers for you, little buddy."

I hated it when she called me that—as if I were Gilligan and she the Skipper. "Shut up, dude."

"Make me."

"I'll make you all right."

Soon we went back to dance. But I couldn't concentrate. I was too aware of Sam's absence. I didn't know which was worse, knowing she was only a few feet away and not talking to her, or knowing she'd left.

Chapter Nine

~SAM~

I woke before sunrise in a strange room lit by a night-light. After a minute of confused blinking, I managed to deduce that I was in Tina's roommate Paul's room, rumpled in the previous night's clothing and reeking of smoke. I hadn't smelled this bad in months, probably not since the last time I went barhopping with Tina. Presumably she was the one who put me to bed on top of the covers, an afghan over me. I'd slept over before (Paul traveled a lot for work), but I'd always been able to remember how I got here. Until now.

I lay still for a while, wading through disjointed memories of the previous night's events. Tina, Matt and I had met up for dinner and drinks at the Broadway Grill before moving on to a nearby bar where Matt's band members had told me all about their musical aspirations. I remembered wondering what hardcore music actually was and why I would possibly care what Screaming Monkeys meant to the Eastside. Mostly I just wanted to get to Diva's. Emily was the main reason I'd accepted Tina's invitation to go out on the Hill—I was hoping I would run into her at the dance club. And sure enough, I had. Only now I couldn't remember exactly what we'd said or done. I seemed to remember a long hug at the end, but I couldn't have said how it started or ended.

Even though it was just six, I couldn't get back to sleep, so I scribbled Tina a note and headed home. The sky was already light, but Capitol Hill was strangely empty. I loved driving my truck through Seattle before the city started its day. The air smelled fresh, cleansed overnight of exhaust and heat, and the few people who were up were morning people, happy like I usually was to be awake at this time of day.

Back at my apartment, I showered, slowly washing the smoke from my hair, scrubbing the sheen of sweat and alcohol from my skin. What had I done the night before, and why couldn't I remember? Clean again, I crashed on the couch. Chloe meowed and crawled over me, burrowing her head into my armpit. I hadn't left her alone overnight since my trip to Michigan at Christmas. She finally curled up against my stomach, and I fell asleep to her contented purring.

When I woke up again, the bruised feeling around my eyes had mostly faded. My dreams came back to me, a wash of color and light with Emily and Tina and Matt dancing across my vision. Weird, alcohol-fuddled dreams, just like my memories of the night before. I knew that Emily and I had talked, and I had an image of us on the dance floor. But I couldn't remember much about the rest.

I picked up the phone and dialed her cell, but there was no answer. When her voice mail beeped, I said, "Um, hi Emily, this is Sam. Just thought I'd call and find out what you wanted to do about the game tomorrow. Give me a call when you get a chance. By the way, I did see you last night, right? The evening's a little foggy. I didn't do anything to embarrass myself, did I? You'll have to let me know. Okay, bye."

It was ten thirty on a Saturday morning. Where was she? Maybe she was screening my calls. A memory of her dancing with another woman, a petite blonde, flashed into my mind. Suddenly grumpy, I turned on the TV and flipped from cartoons to QVC to MTV to ESPN. But I couldn't shake the somehow disturbing image of Emily entwined with the other woman under the disco lights at Diva's.

I was in the process of deciding that I couldn't stand to be inside my apartment for another moment when my phone rang. I lunged for it, checked the caller ID, then took a deep breath and waited through a few more rings.

"It's Emily," she said when I answered. "I just got home from work and got your message."

Her voice was soft at the other end, which made me wonder even more about Diva's. But at least she hadn't been screening my calls. Or still in bed with someone she'd met the night before...

"Where do you work?" I asked.

"At a bike shop on Forty-fifth. Gotta have something to pay the bills till soccer starts."

"What time did you have to be there this morning?"

"Eight. It's not that bad. I have my afternoons and nights free, which is nice."

"I'll bet." I hesitated. "Speaking of nights, did you listen to my message all the way through?"

"Yeah."

I waited but she didn't take the hint. "So did I embarrass myself last night or what?"

"You didn't embarrass yourself. Although you were pretty funny."

That didn't sound good. "What do you mean?"

"Just the part where you took your shirt off," she said casually. "I tried to stop you but you said you were really hot from dancing."

"I did not!" My voice squeaked.

She laughed. "No, you're right. You didn't."

"You little creep," I said, but I was laughing too, mostly from relief that I hadn't in fact stripped down in a gay bar. "I can't believe I almost believed you."

"I can't either," she said. "You're not exactly the naked type, Sam."

We were both quiet for a moment. I pictured her in her house in Wallingford, cell phone pressed to her head.

"What are you doing now?" she asked. "Trying to get over your hangover?"

"I don't get hangovers," I said. "I was actually thinking about grabbing some lunch. Have you eaten yet?" I held my breath. What if she didn't want to see me? What if she was just calling me back to be polite? The image of the petite blonde flashed in my head again.

"I haven't eaten," she said. "Do you maybe want some company?"

I smiled at the television, where colorful figures bounced silently across the screen. "Sure."

We made plans to meet at Kidd Valley, a burger joint a few blocks off 99, and then I shut off my phone and jumped up from the couch, startling a sleepy Chloe. Emily and I were meeting for lunch! Why this should be such an exciting phenomenon I didn't know, I assured myself. Suitably mollified, I went to get ready.

* * *

She was waiting for me when I got there and smiled like she was really happy to see me. As I locked my bike to a signpost and turned to face her, an image from the night before swam across my vision. This time, it was clear—Emily and I, standing motionless in a sea of moving people, holding hands.

"I rode my bike too," she said, and held the door open for me. "It's great that we live so close to each other."

"No kidding." I could feel her warmth as I brushed past and

tried not to focus on her body, revealed in athletic shorts and a tight gray T-shirt with stripes on the sleeves. Fashion was such in Seattle that Emily dressed much the way she had in elementary school, right around the time when I first met Beth Mackenzie and learned she had a younger sister.

Early afternoon on a sunny Saturday, Kidd Valley was packed. We joined the throng at the order counter. "How long have you lived in Wallingford?"

"Six months. When did you move into Camelot?"

I smiled at how that sounded. "Almost a year ago."

"That means for six months we've probably just been missing each other all over the place."

"Probably." I could see it—her walking down one aisle at the QFC on Forty-fifth, me walking up the next; her leaving Zeke's on Phinney Ridge through the side door while I entered through the front; me in my truck passing her on her bike on Green Lake Way. Only, I'd been keeping an eye out for her ever since I got to Seattle. If she'd been that close, I would have known it.

"Weird, huh?" she said.

"Very." I touched her shoulder. "I'm glad we ran into each other finally."

"Me, too."

This felt familiar, standing close together in a crowd, me touching her. I pulled my hand away. "About last night—"

"Classic flick."

"You like that movie?" I laughed. "Remember the headphones? Rob Lowe thought he was so smooth."

"Hey, I learned some of my best moves from that movie."

"I'll bet." But the thought of her seducing someone was disturbing, for a couple of reasons. First, I didn't want to picture her with anyone else. And second, I didn't want to think of her in that way at all because it got me pondering things I'd avoided in recent years, ever since my unofficial vow of celibacy. Plus she was a girl, I reminded myself. But that last part seemed less important somehow. She was just Emily, and I was just me.

It was our turn to order. While we waited for our grilled chicken burgers, fries and shakes—Kidd Valley had the best shakes around, we agreed—and watched for a table to open up, Emily resumed the conversation: "So what about last night?"

"Nothing. That's the problem—I don't remember much." Which wasn't completely true but I wasn't about to ask her what had happened between us, if anything.

"Don't worry," she said. "You're a cute drunk, which is much better than being an obnoxious one. Trust me."

Emily thought I was cute. I tried not to glow.

A booth opened up just before our names were called, and we pounced on it. We sat across from one another, elbows on the table as we dug into our non-fast-food burgers and fries.

"You said the other night you like Seattle better than Chicago," she commented as we stuffed our faces.

"I do. It's great, for a city."

"Okay, that sounds totally grudging."

"I didn't mean it like that," I said, drenching a pair of fries in ketchup. "I always thought I'd live in a city. Logan seemed so small and dull growing up. But then I lived in Chicago and New York—"

"Wait, when were you in New York?"

"Right after college. I had an internship at Time, Inc. I was only there for six months before I moved back to Chicago to work for the *Tribune*." A little over a year later, Chris had followed me back to the Midwest. Only he hadn't moved back for his dream job.

"You've lived all over, then," Emily said. "That's so cool. I've only been to the East Coast a couple of times. The main thing I remember about New York is that it was huge. Of course, I was ten at the time, so hopefully I wouldn't be such a chicken now."

"It's hard to imagine you being afraid of anything," I said, and took a sip of my chocolate peanut butter shake.

"I just talk a good game. I'm afraid of lots of things."

"Like what?" I was pushing now, trying to get her to say

something about me. Because every time I looked at her, I got scared.

"Spiders." She took a bite out of her burger and chewed for a minute. "Our house is older and the basement is full of spiders. Whenever I see one I start yelling and my roommate Liz has to come rescue me. She doesn't kill them, though. She puts them outside."

"Good. Spiders are good. They eat all sorts of pests." Jesus, I sounded like the fricking Nature Channel. I rolled the conversation back a bit. "What about you? City or country?"

She tilted her head to one side. "Definitely country. But I'll probably live in a city most of my life. It's not safe for, you know, people like me to live out in the middle of nowhere. Too many rednecks in pickup trucks with gun racks. Not that everyone who drives a truck is a redneck," she added, grinning at me.

"I know what you mean, though. My brother used to say cities are like zoos for gay people."

"He lived in New York, didn't he? Is that why you went there after school?"

"Kind of. I thought you had to live in New York in order to be a writer. But I also wanted to get to know him. And, I have to admit, I knew it would annoy my parents to have us living there together out of their reach." I couldn't even remember now why I'd wanted to hurt them. But that was before we knew we would have Chris back for such a short time.

"Did you like New York?" she asked.

I could feel her watching me. I looked down at the table, dotted with salt crystals and straw wrappers from previous diners. "Not really. I only stayed because I had an amazing sublet near Central Park. This guy Chris knew was out of the country for six months, so I got his place for cheap."

I could sense the question coming before she asked it: "When did you find out he was sick?"

"While I was living there."

"How did you find out, if you don't mind my asking?"

Not many people knew the story, but I found myself telling Emily about what had happened one Sunday morning after Chris and I had gone for a walk around the Central Park Reservoir. Back at my apartment we'd made a big breakfast, and I'd noticed that he seemed unusually tired. I started thinking about how he was so conscious of his diet and exercise, about his daily regimen of pills. Every other time I asked, he told me they were health supplements. But that morning, I just had a feeling it was something else.

"As we were cleaning up the kitchen," I told Emily, my food forgotten for the moment, "I said I knew he was sick. He just stared at me at first, but then he sighed this big sigh and admitted he'd known he was HIV positive for six years. I know he was relieved to finally tell someone in the family, and I'm glad he trusted me. But the thing is," I said, squinting out at sunlight reflecting from cars flashing past on Green Lake Way, "I didn't really know he was sick. I was just bluffing. And once I did know, terrible as it sounds, I wished I didn't."

"That's not terrible." Her hand found mine and our fingers intertwined. "It's totally understandable."

What wasn't understandable was why holding her hand should feel so good. A wave of peace swept over me, dispersing some of the sadness my story had evoked. I hadn't told it in a while, and yet somehow, sharing with Emily the memory of that long-past morning seemed to have lessened the power it had always held over me. Or maybe it was just time to let go and move on. Either way, I would have been quite happy to sit in that booth for the foreseeable future, Emily's fingers wrapped around mine.

Unfortunately, her cell phone suddenly blared a pop song I didn't recognize, and our hands released at the same time.

"Hey, Mel," she said into her phone. "Just having lunch. No, it's cool. Yeah, I'm up for it. The march starts at five, I think. Totally. See you then."

I chomped on my chicken sandwich, looking everywhere

but at Emily. We'd been holding hands, a fact that couldn't have escaped her notice. Not to mention that of the other patrons of Kidd Valley.

"Sorry about that," she said to me, shutting her phone. "That was Mel, from soccer." She paused, and then said seemingly deliberately, her eyes on mine, "We had to make a plan for the Dyke March on Broadway tonight."

Was this her way of reminding me who she was? Of telling me that we both knew I'd just been holding hands with a lesbian? Which made me—what? I swallowed a chunk of chicken and washed it down with half of my shake, avoiding her eyes.

"Cool," I said. "I actually have to get going soon too. I have plans myself tonight." The declaration was out before I could stop it—as if I had a hot date lined up. Probably I'd call Sarah and hang out with her and her grad school friends, like I did every other Saturday night.

A mask slid over Emily's face. "Okay. Can you still pick me up for soccer tomorrow?"

I nodded. She really had grown up. No more heart on her sleeve.

When we were done, we wadded up our wrappers and headed out into the midday sun. As I unlocked my bike, I didn't want to go home. But it was too late to say, "Never mind, I want to stay with you." No choice but to keep going now. I smiled and waved. She did the same, and we rode off in opposite directions.

My actions seemed unmanageable somehow whenever I was with her, I realized as I headed alone up the hill toward Aurora. All of these emotions and senses that had been numb for years were suddenly waking up, waking me up. It was like when your foot falls asleep and you shake it to try to wake it up and at first, all you feel is the painful tingling. I was stuck in the tingling stage.

Except that it wasn't entirely painful. When I first saw Emily waiting for me, when I brushed past her in the doorway, when she held my hand across the narrow booth, I'd felt an altogether different sensation.

I biked home under clouds rolling in from the west. Already I couldn't wait for the next day. Already I couldn't wait to see Emily. And to play soccer again, of course.

Chapter Ten

~EMILY~

The Sunday morning of Pride, Liz and Jessie hammered on my door until I grunted a greeting.

"Wake up, wake up, wake up!" Liz crowed, and pounced on my futon, her thankfully smaller girlfriend close behind.

I peered up at them blearily. Mel and I had partied hard the night before on the Hill after the Dyke March, and I wasn't sure I was ready to be awake. That was the trouble with roommates. They had their own ideas about appropriate rising times.

"Come on, girl," Liz said, pinning my legs. "Wake up. It's GP Day!" GP Day—Gay Pride, the last Sunday of every June.

I tried to shove her off, but she was a big girl. "Get off, jackass."

"Touchy, touchy. Looks like someone's not getting any," Jessie said, heading for the door.

"Whatever," I said, and yawned. "I could if I wanted." The problem was, ever since Sam had dropped back into my life, I hadn't exactly wanted. The night before, a couple of different cute friends of friends had given me appraising looks, but I'd only been able to muster polite smiles. I knew who I wanted to be with, and it wasn't these admittedly attractive strangers.

Liz moved off my legs and sat next to me on the queen-sized futon. "You smell like a distillery. How much did you drink last night?"

"Way too much."

She ruffled my hair. "Tell you what. Take a shower and I'll have Jessie whip up one of her hangover cures. How does that hit you?"

"Couldn't hurt. Could you just try not to be so sickeningly awake?"

"Not a chance. Come downstairs when you're ready."

After a breakfast that included one of Jessie's mysterious blender concoctions, I was feeling better prepared to deal with the bright sunshine leaking in around the curtains. I took a quick shower, and then we piled into Jessie's Miata and headed downtown. The Pride Parade started at eleven at Westlake. At ten forty-five we found a space in the crowd along Fourth Avenue not far from Seattle Center and stationed ourselves on the curb to watch the action. Liz and Jessie held hands and otherwise displayed ownership of each other, which wouldn't stop other women from checking them out—they were both young and in shape, and Jessie at least was decently pretty. But it would keep all but the boldest dykes from approaching, which I knew was Liz's plan. She always told me she wasn't sure why Jessie was with her, as if Jessie were too good for her. But Liz was the good one, as far as I was concerned.

While we were waiting for the parade to start, I reminded myself that this was the first time I'd been single on Pride Day since I came out my freshman year at U-Dub. But I couldn't shake the image of Sam that kept floating into my consciousness. The day before, as she'd told me about her brother, her eyes had taken on this haunted look, and I'd felt a pang, as if her pain were somehow mine. I thought I was taking her hand because I wanted to make her feel better, but once our hands intertwined, I knew the truth—I'd touched her because ever since she hugged me the night before, I couldn't stop thinking about how touching her made me feel, light and heavy at the same time, euphoric and terrified all at once.

The parade finally started. Liz, Jessie and I leaned against each other watching Dykes on Bikes, the traditional parade leaders. They zipped by on their motorcycles, butch drivers in leather chaps and caps, femmy passengers topless or barely clad in leather bras and frilly lingerie. One of Jessie's friends, a gorgeous bisexual woman whose husband looked the other way when it came to his wife's interest in other women, rode down the center of Fourth Avenue in a Wonder Woman outfit. She easily earned more catcalls than all of the motorcyclists combined.

Once the motorcycles had passed, the parade started in earnest, assorted organizations carrying rainbow-bedecked banners through downtown proclaiming their support for their GLBT employees, members, relatives. A Seattle City fire truck full of out lesbian firefighters passed by, spraying water with squirt guns. Liz and I ducked, but Jessie took a hit in the face. Unlucky.

She dried her face on her tank top. "Good thing I have waterproof mascara on."

Liz and I rolled our eyes.

The floats rolled on, dykes and fags as well as friends and parents of dykes and fags walking down the center of Fourth Avenue, waving and smiling at the amassed spectators. Queer people had taken over downtown for the day. All was well with the world, as far as I was concerned.

Over the next hour, the floats and drag queens and S&M contingents came and went, then Liz, Jessie and I were joining the throng heading toward Seattle Center for the traditional post-parade bash. There, we wandered the vendor booths and found a spot on the lawn not far from the giant International

Fountain where children and adults alike ran half-naked through the spray. I pulled a tube of sunscreen from one of the deep pockets in my gray cargo shorts and slathered the lotion over my bare arms and legs. I had to play soccer later, and getting hit by the ball on a sunburn was a most unpleasant sensation. This I recalled vividly from a childhood spent with parents who thought more about the IMF than SPF.

Liz was dressed like me in cargo shorts and a muscle T-shirt while Jessie was Daisy Duking it in cutoffs and a tank top. On a stage to the west side of the fountain near Key Arena, a band played freedom-themed songs, and for once, they weren't bad. Life didn't get much better than this, I thought. And yet, I wasn't thinking about how great it was to be gay or how cool the PFLAG people were. I wasn't even thinking about how embarrassing some of the queer crowd could be, like the middle-aged, overweight hippies who bedecked their naked bodies in bright paints that did little to hide their genitals. Instead, I was watching clouds drift lazily overhead and wondering if Sam had really had a date the night before or if she had just freaked out because we were holding hands when Mel called.

Ever since the night I'd watched the Mariners game at her apartment, Sam had been giving me the look that told me she was attracted to me but not necessarily conscious of that fact. I had a good feeling about her, at least just then lying in the grass at Seattle Center surrounded by queer people. Everything would work out. She and I would end up together eventually, playing soccer and hiking in the Cascades and taking ferry rides to the San Juans...

Whoa. I stopped myself. Best not to get my hopes up. That way if it did happen, I'd be pleasantly surprised. And if it didn't, there were always other fish in the sea.

Despite my distraction, it was fun watching queer boys and girls walking around the fountain half-clothed, showing off tattoos, piercings and bare skin. On this day, the straight folks were the ones in the minority. In nearby booths, canvassers signed people up for various political funds, handed out stickers and safe-sex kits, doled out petitions for civil rights initiatives. Not far from where we sat, a group of lesbians with dreadlocks and tie-dye tank tops played Hacky Sack, calling out and laughing in pot-mellowed voices. Assorted couples wandered the festivities, publicly flaunting their relationships. A pair of twenty-something women walked past us arm in arm, giggling and looking at each other shyly. New love. Behind them strolled two older men, with thinning hair and matching paunches beginning to stick out over their still-tight jeans shorts. Established love. Would I ever have something like that? An image of Sam popped into my head, and I lay on the grass, surrounded by queer people and daydreaming about a straight woman. But was she straight?

All too soon it was time to go—I had soccer, Jessie was headed to the Eastside and Liz had a crew meeting. We put our sandals back on and traipsed across lower Queen Anne to the lot where we'd stashed the Miata. Usually I was a little sad to venture back into the mostly straight world outside of Gay Pride Weekend. And yet, as we drove north over the Aurora Bridge with the Olympic Mountains to our left and Lake Union hundreds of feet beneath us, Liz and Jessie singing badly with the stereo, I was aware of a sense of expectation rising in me. While there were many fish in the sea, I knew which one I wanted. And one way or the other, in the coming days or weeks I was bound to find out if she wanted me back.

Just then, with the blue sky above me and Mt. Rainier standing sentinel over the city skyline behind me, I couldn't help but hope for a happy ending.

* * *

I was stepping into soccer sandals when I heard a horn. Sam was early. I tried not to grin too widely as I ran downstairs. Liz would only give me crap for getting all googly-eyed over another straight girl. Fortunately Liz was in the living room arguing with Jessie about who was supposed to have put gas in the Miata, so she didn't notice my giddiness. I shot out the door, athletic bag in hand.

Sam's Ranger looked huge parked in the driveway behind the Miata. She was fiddling with the stereo and glanced up as I opened the passenger door and slid in beside her.

"Hey, stranger," she said, smiling.

"Hi." I smiled, too, but shyly.

She checked her mirrors and backed out of the driveway. "Sorry I had to take off yesterday."

"That's okay." I hesitated. Did I really want to know? "How was your date?"

As we neared one of those bizarre unrestricted intersections unique to the Pacific Northwest where there were no signs and no one ever quite knew whose right of way it was, Sam slowed and waved a minivan ahead of us. "No date. I just had dinner with one of my friends from college and her grad school buddies."

I knew it! "How many of your college friends live here?" I asked, and listened as she described her classmates from Northwestern, Tina and Sarah, and their attempts to get her out as a functioning member of society.

"You seem pretty social," I said when she paused.

"It's an act. I can't have you telling everyone from home I'm a loser now, can I?"

"I would never call you a loser." Our eyes held for a moment before she looked away, and I realized I was being too serious. "A shut-in, maybe, but definitely not a loser."

"A shut-in?"

"Sorry, was that supposed to be our secret?"

We kept joking around as Sam guided her truck onto I-5, and I thought we were probably both relieved not to talk about anything real. Such as the moment before Mel's call when we were sitting in the booth at Kidd Valley holding hands. Part of me wanted to bring it up (very lesbian of me, I know), but I didn't want her to shut down like she always did when we seemed to get too close. So I kept my distance and enjoyed her company and the Seattle scenery, white-topped mountains to the east and west, sun sparkling off bodies of water that dotted the landscape. A perfect soccer day.

We reached the field early, warmed up and stretched with the rest of the team. Today Sam even talked to a few of the other players before the game. She seemed more comfortable this week in her warm-up touches on the ball, more relaxed as we took a few shots on goal. Good sign.

Then the referee blew his whistle, and I forgot about Sam. I attacked as soon as the other team kicked off and chased the ball back to their center midfielder, who passed it outside. The game was on. I loved the way I felt when I played soccer. I had tunnel vision on the field, but all of my other senses were incredibly alert. The conscious part of me receded and this brutal part leapt to the fore and I was mean, I was strong, I wanted to feel the joy of beating the defense and slamming the ball into the goal past the keeper's outstretched fingers. I wanted a goal, and once I had one, I wanted another.

Ten minutes in, I dribbled through the defense and slid the ball into the far corner of the goal. We were up. But the other team didn't give up easily. We battled back and forth the rest of the half. In back, Sam showed occasional flashes of brilliance and infrequent lapses of judgment while I continued to hammer on the goal up front.

With only a few minutes left in the first half, we earned a corner kick. Kristin, our center midfielder, chipped it in perfectly to find my head for the second goal. She and I had executed this play more than once in the PAC-10. It hadn't entirely sunk in yet that I would have to watch from the sidelines this fall as she set up other players with her spot-on crosses. Aargh.

We went into halftime with a two-goal lead. As we sat around rehydrating and discussing tactics, I noticed that Sam seemed happier than she'd been the previous week at the half.

No wonder—she was playing much better this time around. Just went to show how much of the game was mental. She glanced my way, and I gave her a thumbs-up. When she smiled, I tried not to ogle her too obviously.

Our opponents were one of the weaker teams in the league and didn't have any subs. During the second half, they tired out, at which point the game turned into a blowout. We finished 5-1. No shutout, but it was only rec league.

After the game, everyone returned to the stands to change. Mel was sitting on one side of me, Sam on the other.

"You didn't play like you were hung over," Mel said, clapping me on the shoulder.

"Jessie fixed me one of her shakes this morning."

"Did you guys go downtown for the parade?"

"Totally. What happened to you? I thought you were going to meet us."

"My mom needed me to do some work around the house. Didn't you get my text?" During the summers, Mel lived with her mother in Kirkland. Unlike a lot of local U-Dub students, she didn't come from money.

"I forgot my cell. We missed you, though."

"Bet I missed you more."

Several other people chimed in about the parade and the afternoon's festivities. A couple of people on the team hadn't made the game, and we speculated that they probably didn't want to tear themselves away from Seattle Center.

Sam was quiet through all of this, stripping off her long socks and shin guards and changing into trail runners. I finished changing just as she did. We offered our goodbyes to the rest of the team and headed for the parking lot.

"You looked like you had more fun this week," I said.

"I did. You were right when you said it just takes time. You're going to be a good coach, Em."

"Thanks." I almost said I learned from the best in high school—her—but even in my current bedazzled state, I could tell that this would be inexcusably cheesy.

In the truck, Sam started the engine but didn't back out yet. "Is the team going out for pizza tonight?"

"Probably. Why?"

"I'm your ride. If you go, I go."

"I should probably drag you along," I said. "You know, battle your antisocial tendencies."

"Not you, too."

I actually wanted to have her all to myself. "I'm feeling kind of antisocial myself tonight. I wouldn't mind going home and making pasta or something." I paused. "Want to have dinner at my house?"

"That would be nice," she said, and shifted the truck into reverse.

I rolled my window down and let my arm hang out in the cooling air as Sam drove us home from the Eastside with its wooded neighborhoods and sandy soccer fields, back over the mile-long floating bridge across Lake Washington. A Dave Matthews Band CD was playing on the stereo as red-orange University buildings appeared across the Montlake Cut. I cupped my hand against the wind rushing along the side of the truck just before we merged onto I-5 and leaned my head out the window, air rushing against my face, in my ears, through my hair as we crossed the Ship Canal Bridge at seventy miles an hour.

"You're like a puppy," Sam said when I pulled my head back in. She was gazing at me with The Look again, the one that indicated she would probably be up for making out if I pressed the issue. "Maybe you were a dog in your last life."

"I don't know if I believe in reincarnation," I said as we left the freeway at Forty-fifth Street. "I mean, what happens if there isn't a body available when someone dies? Or, like, could there be bodies walking around without souls? Although that would explain the Republican Party."

Sam laughed. "Spoken like a true professor's kid."

"What about you? Donkey or elephant?" I squinted at the

sunlit horizon, remembering my sister's estimation of Sam back in high school.

"Independent but I vote Democrat. The Republicans are just too greedy for my taste, not to mention socially backward. I have to admit, though, I'm not always a huge fan of the Democrats, either."

Whew. "Same here. My family thinks I'm a traitor whenever I say that."

"Mine, too, but probably not for the same reasons." She slowed the truck as we turned onto my street. "Your family's really liberal, aren't they?"

"That's one way of putting it. Yours isn't, huh."

"Not exactly." She pulled over in front of my house and killed the engine. "By the way, Em, there's something I've been meaning to tell you."

I hesitated, hand on the door. Was she aware of The Look? "What's up?"

"I can't call you Mac. I hope you don't mind."

I breathed again. "I don't mind."

"Good." She opened her door. "You gonna feed me or what? I'm starving."

"Tell me about it," I said, hopping out. "But you'll have to work for it, Delaney. No free meals for the likes of you."

"What kind of payment did you have in mind?" she asked as we headed up the front walk.

"I'll think of something," I said, and held the door open for her. Whether or not she would agree to pay up, however, was the question.

Inside, I took her on a quick tour. Jessie and Liz were both gone still, thankfully, along with their not-so-subtle looks and raised eyebrows. Upstairs, I led Sam down the hallway to my bedroom. She stood in the doorway, surveying my space. My room had high ceilings and the same fancy molding as the living room, but the décor, I knew, was more typical of a recent college graduate: futon pushed up against one wall, thrift-store dresser with matching mirror, overflow clothes in crates along the wall. I also had a small TV and a newish computer with speakers, tall windows with Southwestern print curtains and a matching comforter. It wasn't bad, I told myself.

I caught Sam staring at the colorful tapestry that hung from the ceiling. "Liz helped," I volunteered.

"Your room is really nice," she said.

"Not as nice as the rest of the house. I don't exactly have Jessie's resources."

"Maybe not but it's totally you." She crossed to one of the windows. A tall cedar partially blocked the view. In the distance, Green Lake reflected the evening sun.

"It's a great place to live," I said. "Having the upstairs to myself is almost like living alone."

"Only without the loneliness," Sam said. She closed her eyes, breathing in as the scent of cedar wafted in through the open window.

Was she lonely? I wanted to smooth away the lines around her mouth, protect her from the darkness I sometimes saw in her eyes. I wanted to do a lot more than just protect her, though, and that was the problem.

Downstairs again, we headed for the kitchen, which hadn't been cleaned up since breakfast. I set to work transferring dirty dishes from sink to dishwasher. Sam eyed the blender, stained with the remnants of Jessie's hangover remedy.

"Looks like you left in a hurry this morning," she said, leaning against the counter near the fridge.

Like a lot of people, we kept word magnets on our refrigerator. Not your average magnet poetry, either, but a special queer edition. At a party we'd held a few weeks earlier to celebrate the end of the school year, several people had gone to town with the magnets. As a result, our fridge was littered with phrases like, "Bull-dyke fans the flames of my femme's heart" and "Take me standing, woman" and "Lick my bush." In other words, things I would have preferred Sam not see. But too late. Her eyes had wandered from the blender to the fridge.

I pretended not to notice. "We went to Pride, so we had to be downtown at a decent time."

"Oh." She was still staring at the refrigerator. Heat rose in my face. Now she would associate lesbian sex with me. Not that that was a bad thing.

"That's not my work, by the way," I said. "Some friends of Jessie's were over a few weeks ago."

"Uh-huh." Sam looked over at me, smiling a little. "Don't worry, I won't turn to dust at the thought of sex."

I jammed a glass into the dishwasher. "I didn't think you would."

She opened the fridge. "What should we have to drink?"

"There's juice. Or the beer on the bottom shelf is mine."

She took out a couple of microbrews and rattled around a drawer or two before finding the bottle opener. I dried my hands on a dishtowel.

"Cheers," she said.

We clicked bottles lightly. Sam Delaney was drinking a beer with me in my kitchen. Who would have thunk it?

Chapter Eleven

~SAM~

Sunday evening found me at Emily's house in Wallingford watching her bustle around her well-equipped kitchen revealing meal possibilities. We settled on tri-colored pasta with sauce, steamed broccoli and garlic bread. While Emily pulled out the pots and utensils we needed to prepare our feast, I set to work rinsing off the broccoli.

"Do you go to the Gay Pride Parade every year?" I asked.

"When I can. It's totally fun."

"It's great that you're so comfortable with who you are."

"Not everyone's as lucky as I was," she said, setting a pot of water to heat on the gas stove. "My parents always encouraged us to be ourselves. I think they would have been disappointed if I had turned out straight."

"How so?" I couldn't imagine any parent being disappointed in having a daughter like Emily, particularly if she were straight.

"I'm pretty conventional otherwise. If I weren't gay, they'd probably think I was way too conformist."

"You're kidding."

"No, I'm serious." She wrapped the bread in a sheet of aluminum foil. "My parents aren't exactly sports fans. My dad doesn't even know the difference between the NBA and the NFL. I doubt he knows that NASCAR has to do with racing. He'd probably tell you it stands for something like, I don't know, Native American social customs and rituals."

"He may not be into sports," I said, "but he came to our games. He was one of the regular dads."

She handed me a jar of pasta sauce. Dutifully I poured it into a pot. Unlike Em's dad, my father hadn't been one of the hot chocolate-drinking, cowbell-toting Logan soccer parents who cheered their daughters on through blizzards and rainstorms. He'd had to work.

"How did your parents react when they found out Chris was gay?" Emily asked.

I paused. My family was going to seem like a throwback to the Dark Ages compared to hers. "They took him to a psychiatrist our minister recommended, one who specialized in gay conversion. He suggested a residency program near Detroit that was supposed to make Chris an ex-gay." I shook my head and set the sauce jar down on the counter harder than I intended.

"Is that when he ran away?"

"Yeah. Not that I blame him."

She squeezed my shoulder. "They were probably just doing what they thought was best."

I stared at her. "How can you say that? You must know what my parents think about people like you." Or what they'd thought a decade before, anyway. I didn't know what Joyce and Steven thought about gay people these days. Not exactly a popular topic of conversation in the Delaney household.

"Of course I know. But nothing I do is going to change their minds. I feel sorry for them, to be honest."

"You shouldn't."

"Must be hard to be that angry with your parents," she said, and turned away to cut up the broccoli.

"I'm not angry with them." But at some level, I knew that wasn't true. I looked down at my sweatshirt and noticed several red spots. "Where's your bathroom, again?"

"End of the hall."

Alone in the bathroom, I dabbed at the pasta sauce but only succeeded in smearing it across the lettering on my sweatshirt. I gave up on the stain and checked my appearance in the mirror. My hair was falling out of its ponytail, I had a smudge of dirt on my forehead from the game, and to top it off, I probably smelled bad. How did Emily manage to look so cute still?

Back in the kitchen, we set the table and finished fixing the meal, talking about soccer again.

"You could have gotten a full ride, too," she said, "especially if you'd been my year. Just a few years has made such a difference in the number of programs out there."

"Too bad I'm an old lady."

"Twenty-five isn't old."

"Tell my mother that. She can't believe I'm not in a relationship of any kind."

Emily paused in peeling foil from the bread. "You're not dating anyone?"

"No. What about you?"

"As single as it gets. Grab the colander, will you?"

I set the strainer in the sink. "Look at that, little Emily Mackenzie knows what a colander is."

"You're not the only one who grew up," she said. "Time didn't just stop for me, you know."

"I know." As she concentrated on the pasta, I took advantage of her distraction to examine the evidence of her maturity. Would that I had legs like hers, sleek, tanned, muscled. But there was more to what I felt than envy. I looked away.

When we sat down to eat, the conversation moved on to classes we'd liked, the sorority girls we hadn't.

"You weren't in a sorority, then?" she asked.

"No chance. You didn't think I was, did you?"

"Um, no." She ducked her head but I could still see her smile.

"You totally thought I was a sorority girl. Is that how you see me?"

"I was just teasing. Honest."

"Uh-huh." I shouldn't have been surprised, given my background—attorney father, stay-at-home mother, big house in the beautiful old section of Logan. My mom had joined a sorority at the University of Michigan, my father a frat. That was how they met, at a joint social event their sophomore year at U of M. "Your sister must have gone Greek, right?" I added.

"Right—Beth and her hippie friends. You had to be a vegan pothead and wear Birkenstocks to belong."

"Sounds like Beth hasn't changed much since high school."

"Nope." She paused. "Think you've changed?"

Chris had asked me the same thing once, the day he came home the first time. "I think so. At least, I hope so. What about you? Same or different?"

"Different for sure. I was never that happy in Logan."

"Well, it's nice to see you happy now."

"It'd be nice to see you happier."

"What can you do?" I shrugged.

"I don't know. What can I do?"

Her eyes were serious on mine. We were crossing boundaries I wasn't sure I wanted to because what if we couldn't go back?

"You're already doing it," I said, and stood up. "Want some water?"

"Sure. There's a Britta in the fridge."

I filled two glasses and sat back down. "Where did you say Beth went with the Peace Corps?"

"Benin."

As we ate, we talked about Africa and travel and the encroachment of Western culture on the non-Western world. By the time we'd exhausted these topics, our plates and beer bottles were empty. Together we rinsed the dishes and stacked them in the dishwasher, covered the leftovers and put them in the fridge.

"You don't have to go yet, do you?" she asked as she wiped the stove with a sponge.

"Nope."

"Good. Have you ever played Wii?"

"Um, no," I said cautiously. I was not a fan of shoot-em-up video games. Was our age difference about to show?

She grinned and tossed the sponge in the sink. "You're going to love it. You played tennis in high school, didn't you?"

"Uh-huh." Open your mind, I told myself. If Emily liked it, couldn't be all bad.

"Don't worry," she said, and led the way into the living room where an entertainment center framed a huge flat-screen TV. "If you don't like it, we can stop anytime."

Within fifteen minutes, my avatar was leaping across the court diving and spinning after Emily's lobs. At first I wasn't very good at making the hand control do what I wanted it to, despite Emily's patient coaching. In fact, after losing three straight games, I cursed the control and briefly considered throwing it across the room. I'd forgotten how competitive I could get—I should have warned Emily ahead of time.

"Maybe we should try a different game," she said, her eyebrows raised as she retrieved the control from me. She was trying not to laugh, I could tell, and I briefly considered throwing her across the room. "Wii baseball is easier to learn."

In between pitches, she asked me about other extracurriculars at Northwestern. I calmed down a little as I told her about the tennis and ultimate Frisbee teams I'd competed on. Wii baseball was easier to pick up. I struck her side out completely in the third inning—not that I was keeping track.

My dad was super-competitive, too, which was what made him a good lawyer. Growing up, I had been his official sports buddy. He took me to watch basketball and volleyball at Southwestern Michigan University when he didn't have to work late. We drove over to Ann Arbor sometimes, just the two of us, to attend Michigan football games. My dad considered loyalty to his alma mater a serious matter and occasionally hosted Wolverine-Buckeye football parties for a few old frat brothers who lived nearby.

Emily crowed as the ball went past one of my outfielders. "Damn, did you see that? I faked your guy out of his jock!"

"You what?"

She grinned sheepishly. "Sorry, I learned to play this with a bunch of guys."

"I never would have guessed."

She nudged me and I nudged her back, and then her arm was around my neck, just for a minute. It reminded me of Kidd Valley the day before, sitting with her in the booth holding hands. Then she released me and I proceeded to strike out her last batter.

Two innings later, I glanced over my shoulder as a tall, butch-looking woman banged the front door shut. I remembered her from the day I first ran into Emily—she'd stood a few feet away that morning looking unimpressed by our reunion.

"Oh, hi," she said, looking from me to Em and back again.

"Liz, you remember Sam, right?"

"Of course." Liz smiled and suddenly didn't look nearly as scary. "How was your game?"

"We won by a bunch," Emily said. "How was your meeting?"

"Awesome. You haven't seen Jessie, have you?"

"No, sorry."

"Maybe I'll call her. Nice seeing you again." She nodded at me.

"You too."

She headed down the hallway to the master bedroom and shut the door. Had she gone in there so that Emily and I could be alone? What had Em told her about me?

When I finally won the third baseball game, we decided this was probably a good time to call it quits. Anyway, Em had to pee. As she excused herself and disappeared down the hall, I sat on the couch and stared at the Wii screen frozen on the avatar page. There were a lot of girls on the screen, twirling and mugging for the camera. Not something I really wanted to ponder.

The last baseball game I'd been to was a Yankees game in the Bronx with Chris. Yankee Stadium was not an experience to miss, he said, even though he wasn't much of a sports fan. Except basketball. He and I had watched the NBA playoffs the previous spring after he moved home. But he died before the finals. I wasn't even sure now who had won.

I could hear the water running in the bathroom down the hall. Did I dare ask to be invited up to her room? It wasn't like anything would happen. She was too good to make a move on me. I, on the other hand, was definitely not good, and hadn't felt this close to another human being in years. Would have liked to feel closer. Dangerous thoughts—but nice thoughts too. Warm, fuzzy thoughts.

Emily returned and sat down next to me. "You weren't bad, Delaney. A few more tries, and I bet you'll be kicking my butt at tennis too."

"Right." Here was my chance to suggest we go upstairs. But I couldn't quite bring myself to do it. What if she wasn't interested? After all, I was the one who'd been inviting her to do things so far, not the other way around.

"Want to listen to music?" she asked, picking up the remote.

"Sure."

"What are you in the mood for?"

"Anything."

She picked a station from the TV screen and cocked her head as strands of guitar music floated across the room. "Indigo Girls. Have you heard them before?"

"Of course. They were my first concert. How about you? What was your first concert?"

She tugged at a thread on the cushion. "'N Sync."

I cracked up.

"Go ahead and laugh," she said. "Everyone does. Jenna loved

them, though. What can I say? I was impressionable."

"Obviously."

We talked about music for a while before moving on to books and plays. Emily was clearly more complicated than the simple jock she appeared to be. Which I'd already known, of course.

"I've always wanted to go to the opera," she said at one point. "Have you ever been?"

Beyond the living room window, the light had faded to nearly dusk. "I went a couple of times in Chicago with my college boyfriend." The part about the boyfriend just slipped out.

"Ah-ha, so you have been in a relationship before."

"Ancient history." I waved my hand, dismissing the subject of my short-lived love life.

"Couldn't have been that long ago. What was he like?"

"What do you mean?"

"You know, how did you meet, what was his name, was he the love of your life? Come on, I told you about 'N Sync. Now spill it."

So I told her about David, a fellow journalism student at Northwestern. We met sophomore year in an investigative reporting class, dated for six months, and then Chris reappeared. I had never told David about my brother, and he couldn't understand why I would hold back such an important fact about my family. My deception caused him to withdraw, he claimed. A week later he broke up with me and started dating one of the girls who lived on my hall. The timing was a little suspicious.

"To say the least," Emily said. "He sounds like a jackass. Was it a tough break-up?"

"You know, I don't remember. Tina, my friend who lives out here, was furious when we found out he was dating that girl down the hall—I can't remember her name, either."

"Doesn't sound like you were really in love with him."

"No, I don't think I was."

"Have you ever been in love?" she asked.

"I don't know," I hedged. "What about you?"

"Sure, lots of times. But not with anyone, you know, special," she added. "Not with anyone I could see myself with long-term."

"Oh." I nodded like I knew what she was talking about. She was smiling, and I focused on her lips. I wondered what she would do if I kissed her.

"It's late," I said. "I should get going."

"Do you have to?"

No. I nodded. "Yes." And that was that.

She walked me out to my truck, told me to drive safely. I thanked her for dinner. Then, just before I got in my truck, I hugged her. She felt warm and soft against me in the cool summer evening, her arms wrapped lightly around my waist. We stood together for a long time, maybe several minutes, and I didn't want to let go of her. But finally I did.

"Good night," I said.

"Good night, Sam."

I climbed into the truck, started up the engine and pulled away from the curb. In my rearview mirror I could see Emily lingering on the sidewalk looking after me.

Driving home, I thought of how she'd stuck her head out the window as we crossed the Ship Canal Bridge. Chris used to do that when we were kids. Drove our father crazy. One time on the way home from church, Dad actually stopped the car and made Chris get out and walk the half mile home. I doubted Emily's parents had ever done anything like that.

What would Chris have been like if he had grown up in her family? Her parents certainly would never have tried to convert him to heterosexuality. He would never have run away, never have turned tricks in New York. He might still be alive today. But you couldn't pick your family. Our parents hadn't even been all that bad. They'd just made a terrible mistake that had led indirectly to Chris's death. That knowledge was something they had to live with. As did I.

Another question occurred to me as I rode the ancient elevator to my floor and walked down the dimly lit hall: What would I have been like if I had grown up with parents like Emily's? Would I have asked to go upstairs with her tonight? Would I have kissed her like I wanted to? And if I had, would I still be there now?

Chapter Twelve

~EMILY~

After Sam hugged me longer than was necessary (not that I was complaining) and drove off in her truck, I went up to my room and lay on my bed thinking about everything we'd talked about: families and literature, soccer and siblings. I'd heard about Christian "rehabilitation" facilities before, of course, where families sent their kids to turn them into ex-gays. One of my favorite movies was *But I'm a Cheerleader*, a comedy that played up the irony of a home for queers all trying not to be queer—*Romeo and Juliet* meets *Tales of the City*. But I never thought I would know anyone who believed gay rehab was a viable option.

The other realization I couldn't avoid was that if I were smart, I would stop whatever this thing was with Sam before we did something that couldn't be undone. But my sister was the brainy one. Besides, I didn't want to stop. I'd been waiting for this ever since I found out Sam lived in Seattle. Probably longer.

At one point, just before she left, I thought she might kiss me. And there was that hug, of course. She felt incredible this time, too, the perfect fit. I'd wanted to say, "Stay." But what if she said no? Or, worse, what if she said yes? I closed my eyes and pictured her in her cream-colored bedroom. If I were there with her, I would kiss her softly and trail my hand across her stomach, where the skin would be soft and, I imagined, pale beneath my touch.

I pushed myself up and headed into the bathroom to get ready for bed. My Sam Delaney fantasy was never going to happen. I would have to just accept that. There were other women out there, attainable ones. Maybe I should try daydreaming about them.

* * *

On Tuesday afternoon, I was sucking down Gatorade and preparing to watch *Ellen* on DVR when my cell phone rang. Sam. I smiled at the sound of her voice. "What are you doing?"

"I'm supposed to be working," she said, "but it's too nice out. Want to go for a run at Discovery Park?"

"Heck yeah."

We made plans to meet at her place and I shut my phone, grinning stupidly where I sat on the couch. Looked like *Ellen* would have to wait.

Sam wasn't home yet when I reached Camelot. I locked my bike and sat down on the front steps to wait. Seattle in the summertime was a lot like the Camelot from the musical, I decided—it often rained after sundown, if at all; June, July and August were rarely too hot; and summer almost always lingered through September. I couldn't think of a more congenial spot for happy-ever-aftering. I wondered if Sam planned to stay in the city or if she would eventually move back to the Midwest.

Pretty soon I saw her coming up the street from Phinney Avenue. As I watched her approach, I mentally calculated the number of hours since I'd seen her last: forty-one and a half, roughly. Somehow it felt like longer.

"Come on in," she said, smiling at me. "I just have to change."

I followed her inside. She was wearing khaki capris and a short-sleeved olive green collared shirt that matched her eyes. The ensemble looked a little dykey, in my entirely objective opinion. We rode the slowest elevator in the world up to her floor, chatting about our days. Sam said it was such a gorgeous day that she couldn't stay at work any longer.

"I decided I should learn to be more spontaneous," she said as the elevator opened on the fourth floor. "You know, the whole only living once thing."

Chloe and I hung out in the living room while Sam changed. Only a wall separated us. I forced myself to focus on rubbing the cat's chin rather than picturing Sam half-naked, or fully naked even, one room away. Just because she'd invited me running didn't mean she wanted to sleep with me.

Chloe stopped preening and blinked at me as if she could read my thoughts.

"She really likes you," Sam said from the doorway.

"I get along well with animals."

"Seems like you get along well with everyone."

"Which is useful if you're conflict-averse, according to my mother." Sam's eyebrows rose, and I shook my head. "Forget I said that. Let's get going—you never know how long the sun will stick around."

Her truck was parked on a nearby side street wide enough to fit only one car at a time. She drove us east over Phinney Ridge and down the hill into Ballard, Seattle's own miniature Scandinavia complete with ships and a waterfront prowled by ship workers named Sven. We crossed the Ballard Bridge and wound out along the edge of Magnolia to Discovery Park, which occupied the bluffs northwest of downtown Seattle. On a clear day from the cliffs you could see Bainbridge Island and the Olympic Mountains to the west, Mt. Rainier and the city skyline to the southeast. Despite the views, Discovery was one of the least crowded parks in the city.

Sam parked her Ranger near the visitor's center at the start of a three-mile loop trail and leaned across me to put her wallet in the glove compartment. Her arm brushed against mine, and for a moment, she was close enough to kiss. I held my breath.

"Pardon me," she said.

"You're pardoned."

We slid out of the truck. A couple of spaces away an older straight couple was attempting to coerce a pair of golden retrievers into the back of their SUV. Sam and I crossed to where the trail started.

"I love this run," I said, stretching my right quad, which had been a little tight the last couple of games.

She leaned against a tree to stretch her calves. "Last summer I ran here all the time. My friend Tina brought me here right after I moved to Seattle."

"She's the one you were with at Diva's, right?"

"Right. And you were with your roommate."

"Both of them—Liz, the rower and her girlfriend Jessie, the one who owns everything."

Sam straightened and looked at me. "Is Jessie blonde?"

"Yeah. You met her but you were pretty hammered, if you recall."

She made a face. "I'd rather not. Come on, Mackenzie, let's see what you got."

The beginning of the trail wound through moss-covered woods, past acres of ferns under hanging vines and curving branches. Western Washington was a rain forest, especially on the Olympic Peninsula where some of the only remaining old growth timber in the country perched precariously close to clear-cut acreage. But if you drove east over the Cascade Mountains to the Columbia River Gorge, in under two hours you'd find yourself in the near-desert of central and eastern Washington. There, from the freeway, you might catch a glimpse of a coyote chasing tumbleweed between heavily irrigated farm fields.

But Seattle was nowhere near the desert. The Discovery trail climbed between huge Douglas firs and Western cedars draped with moss, up a hill past a stable that belonged to a nearby military reserve. Sam and I paused to watch a mare and her offspring cavort in the green corral, and then ran on, following the trail up another hill and along the edge of the military housing project. We were almost to the bluffs and picked up the pace in silent agreement, hurrying to see the sun reflecting from the surface of Puget Sound. We crunched over gravel, passed an open meadow beyond the houses, ran right to the edge of the bluff. There we stopped again to catch our breath, staring out over far-off mountains, the sun on the water a hundred feet below us.

"Logan can't compare, can it," Sam said. The sun was a halo in her hair escaping from its ponytail in perfect, seemingly choreographed wisps.

"Not even close." I leaned against the thick tree trunk railing that separated the trail from the cliff. "Do you think you'll stay in Seattle for a while?"

"I hope to. What about you?"

"I'd like to. Seems like a good place to raise a family," I added, watching her out of the corner of my eye.

"Yeah. A family." She turned abruptly and raced away along the trail above the bluff, calling over her shoulder, "Come on, Mackenzie, I thought you were supposed to be fast!"

Laughing, I sprinted after her and finally caught up where the trail emerged from a grove of trees. We ran side by side following the edge of the bluff, passed people stationed on benches overlooking the Sound, paused again to catch a last glimpse of sun and water where the trail veered back into the woods.

"How're you feeling about spontaneity now?" I asked.

"I love it." Her eyes lingered on me for a minute.

"Come on," I said, darting into the woods. "Let's see if you can bring it, old lady."

"It has already been broughten," she said, and we both giggled.

114

We were breathing hard by the time we reached the parking lot. We gulped water and stretched, not speaking much as we recovered from the run. I watched Sam out of the corner of my eye and tried to figure out the last time I'd felt this good. And here I'd thought finishing college and leaving soccer behind would be the most miserable period of my life.

Once we were breathing easier, we piled back into the sun-warmed truck and drove toward home, singing along with Jack Johnson on the stereo, bare arms hanging out open windows. Too soon we were pulling up behind Sam's building on Phinney Ridge.

"This was so fun," I said as we walked slowly to the front entrance. "Thanks for inviting me."

"Thanks for coming."

When I reached my bike, I pulled my keys out of my pocket and jangled them. I hesitated. "What are you doing now?"

"Showering."

"No, I mean, after that?"

She smiled. "Nothing, probably. Why? What are you up to?"

"I was planning to go to the Seattle Storm game tonight. Have you ever been?"

"I've wanted to, but my friends here aren't exactly sports fans."

"What's wrong with them?"

"I know, right?"

I took a breath. "So what do you say? Want to check out the Storm game with me?" It was clearly my turn to invite her to do something. Besides, there were hours upon hours left yet in this gorgeous day. Why not spend them together?

She apparently agreed. "I'd love to."

I was probably grinning too much as we made a plan for the evening, but I couldn't help it. We high-fived and I pedaled home, no longer amazed that Sam Delaney was part of my Seattle life. I'd planned to go to the game with Mel and her friend Beck, who had a couple of extra tickets for tonight's game. Now I would have to buy tickets separately, which given my current depleted cash situation meant that I would have to use a credit card. But Sam was worth a little debt.

Back at the house, Liz and Jessie were snuggling on the couch, a Brandi Carlile CD playing on the stereo. "Hey, girl," Jessie said, looking up from her crossword. She was obsessed with mind games—in a non-scary-lesbian way. "How was your dinner date the other night?"

"It wasn't a date."

"Honestly?" Liz put in, lowering a fat novel. "You made her dinner and introduced her to the joy of Wii. Sounds like a classic Mac seduction scene to me."

I stopped on the bottom step. "This isn't about seduction. Sam and I are just friends. Anyway, I'm not about to be anyone's experiment."

"'Cause you've never done that before," Jessie said.

I ignored the jibe and started up the steps. "By the way, she's coming over a little later, so please resist the urge to interrogate her, okay?"

"She's coming over?" Liz repeated.

I paused again on the stairs. "We're going to the Storm game."

"You're not inviting us along, are you?" Jessie asked.

"Did you want to go?" I bit my lip.

"Not if we're not wanted. It's totally a seduction," she said to Liz, who nodded. "A little beer, a little WNBA action. What woman could resist?"

"I'm not seducing her," I insisted, but they just smirked knowingly. I shook my head and turned away. "Try to act like adults, if you can. I know it's a stretch."

Upstairs I called Mel about the change in plans. She said she understood, then added, "You know, Beck's tickets are courtside. You sure this chick is worth it?"

"Completely sure," I said. "Enjoy it for me, okay? You're totally going to get MD's sweat on you, you dog!"

"I hope not," Mel said, sounding worried. She could be a bit of a germaphobe.

"Just kidding. Take pictures on your phone for me, though, will you?"

"You got it. Hey, maybe Kristin will want the extra ticket. You're still coming to Pasha's afterward, right?"

A Storm outing wasn't complete without a postgame drink at Pasha's, the lesbian-owned bar only a few blocks from the Key. I hesitated, picturing Sam in the packed bar with its usual sports-dyke-infused drama. Maybe it wouldn't be as crowded tonight. After all, it was a Tuesday. "Of course."

After we hung up, I jumped in the shower and sang disco tunes loudly as I washed up. I even shaved my legs—just in case. Clean again, I dried off and slathered lotion all over my body, flexing various muscle groups in the mirror, then returned to my room to search for something suitable to wear. A knock sounded at my door while I was still debating which T-shirt to wear with my cargo pants. Sam wasn't early, was she? I hadn't had time to grab dinner yet.

"Don't worry, it's just me," Liz said through the door.

"Come on in." I tugged an old Logan Soccer Club T-shirt from one of the milk crates on the floor by my bed and slipped it on.

Liz sat on the futon as I puttered around the room picking up dirty clothes and shoving shoes into my closet. I didn't plan to invite Sam upstairs, but you never know.

"Can I ask you something, Mac?"

"Only if you stop teasing me about Sam."

"Okay, sorry. I guess I'm a little worried about this one."

I paused, a turf shoe in hand. "Why?"

"Are you sure you know what you're doing?"

"Of course I know what I'm doing."

"I just don't want to see you get in over your head. Because for all our joking, she has been straight until now, and she did lose her brother last year."

117

"What's that supposed to mean?" I stopped and faced her, arms folded across my chest. The sermon was on its way, I could tell. I was actually surprised she had managed to hold off this long.

"Nothing. It's just, I don't want to see this blow up in your face. Or hers."

On some level, I'd been thinking along the same lines. Sam wasn't in the best place emotionally, even I could see that. But I wasn't ready to walk away from her.

"I'll be fine. We'll both be fine." I turned away and kicked a shoe into the closet, flinching as it crashed against the back wall harder than I'd intended.

Silence settled over the room. Then the futon frame creaked. In the mirror over the dresser, I watched Liz cross the room and stop at the door.

"Just be careful," she said, and walked out.

Whatever. I could take care of myself, and Sam was a big girl. I shook my head and scrolled through iTunes, settling on an Indigo Girls album from high school. Perfect. I hit play and turned up the volume on the speakers. Only the unmade bed remained.

Singing along with Amy Ray and the other Emily, I tackled the bed.

Chapter Thirteen

~SAM~

Tuesday evening, I was putting the final touches on what felt remarkably like getting ready for a date when the phone rang. My mom, probably, calling about my upcoming trip home, which I had managed not to think about since the last time she called. I checked the caller ID and picked up.

"What are you doing indoors?" Tina asked. "It's beautiful out."

"I'm actually going out in a bit," I said, and pulled a microwaveable burrito from the freezer. Stadium food wasn't my favorite.

"What are you up to? No, let me guess—something involving exercise, am I right?"

"Been there, done that. Now I'm off to do copious amounts of drugs."

"Dude," she admonished, "you know you have to watch what you say over the phone. But more importantly, why am I not invited?"

"Because I was joking. I'm actually hanging out with my friend from Michigan tonight. We're going to a basketball game." I turned the microwave on and moved to the window, out of range of the oven's radioactive exhalations.

"Why have I yet to meet this mystery friend? I could have at Diva's if a certain someone had thought to introduce us. I know, why don't you bring her along this weekend?"

"What's this weekend?"

"The barbecue. We talked about it Friday, remember?"

"Apparently not."

"Matt's birthday is Saturday, which is also the Fourth, so we're going to spend the day at Golden Gardens," Tina said. "We reserved a grill on the beach. Even Sarah's coming with some of her U-Dub friends."

"Are you sure? She didn't mention it when I talked to her the other day." The microwave beeped and I pulled out the plate.

"Great—she probably forgot, too. And you guys call me the flake. I better e-mail her. You're still coming, aren't you?"

"Possibly." I wasn't a huge fan of the beach—too much sand—or of drunken Fourth of July festivities—too many drunks—but Golden Gardens was another Seattle beauty, located on the northwest edge of Ballard not far from Discovery Park. The view from the beach was a picturesque marina, the Olympic Mountains and the tree-lined shores of Bainbridge Island.

"You have to," Tina said. "You promised. And bring your friend from home. I'd love to meet her."

"You would?"

"Of course. I have to thank her for getting you back into the human race, however she managed to accomplish it."

"Oh." I was glad we were on the phone as a blush crept across my face. If only Tina had known the kinds of thoughts I'd been having about Emily. Actually, she probably would have been thrilled. Anything to save me from my allegedly tragic (according to her) celibacy.

"You're coming if I have to drag you," Tina said. "By the way, you don't have to work on Friday, do you?"

"No, Xytech's closed for the Fourth. Why?"

"One of the partners at the firm just gave me a pair of tickets to the Mariners game that afternoon. It's a four o'clock start. I thought we could grab some lunch downtown, do some shopping, get caught up. What do you think?"

She probably wouldn't be impressed if I told her I'd rather loiter around my apartment waiting for Emily to call. "I'm in," I said. Two professional sporting events in one week—nice. The games would give me something to talk to my father about. Since I'd moved to Seattle, he had been threatening to fly out for a Mariners game. He wanted to admire Safeco Field's retractable roof in person, he said. Frankly, I doubted he would ever take the time off to come.

"Good. Call me tomorrow," Tina said.

I hung up the phone, paused, then turned it back on and checked my voice mail. Sure enough, there was a message from earlier in the day. I dug into my already cooling burrito and listened. This time it was my mother:

"Hi, honey. Just called to see how you're doing. What are you doing for the Fourth? We can't wait to see you in a few weeks! Are you getting excited? Is there any way you can extend your trip, do you think? It would be so nice to see you for more than just a few days. I feel like we never see you anymore. But then Seattle isn't exactly Chicago, is it? Well, I hope you're doing well, sweetie. Call home soon. We miss you."

I turned the phone off, imagining my mother's reaction if she knew I was going to a professional women's sporting event with an avowed lesbian. Just more confirmation that neither of her children had turned out quite the way she'd expected.

* * *

Just past six, I parked my truck outside Emily's house. The

121

Miata was in the driveway beside a Chevy Blazer. Emily, however, was nowhere to be seen. I waited a minute, then walked up the porch steps and rang the doorbell.

A short blonde woman opened the front door. "Hi. Sam, right?"

I nodded. This was the woman I'd seen at the club Friday night dancing with Em, their pelvises glued together.

"Come in," she said. "I'm Jessie. We met over the weekend."

"At Diva's," I said, and stepped past her. "Nice to see you."

Em came jogging down the stairs, looking newly scrubbed in close-fitting pants and an old soccer T-shirt, a sweatshirt tied loosely around her hips. "Hey, Sam. Have you met Jessie?"

"Just now."

"Cool."

We all stood awkwardly near the front door for a moment. If I weren't mistaken, there was some sort of tension flitting between the other two. Meanwhile, Liz, the perennially unsmiling housemate, was nowhere to be seen.

Em touched my elbow. "Ready?"

"Sure." In fact, I couldn't wait. I'd been to a few WNBA games in Chicago with my friend Jake, a sportswriter at the *Tribune*, but this would be different. For one thing, Jake was only grudgingly a fan of women's sports. For another, I had heard that Seattle led the league in home game attendance. I was looking forward to being immersed in a huge, screaming crowd all cheering for female athletes.

In the truck, I waited for Emily to fasten her seat belt before pulling away from the curb. Soon we were heading down Highway 99 crossing the Aurora Bridge on our way south. Emily held her hand out the open window, current-surfing.

"This is my favorite view of the city," she said, and nodded to where Mt. Rainier kept watch over Seattle's skyscrapers, brilliant in the early evening sun.

"Me, too," I said, smiling over at her. Our eyes caught and held, and I forced myself to look back at the road. The lanes on the Aurora Bridge were notoriously narrow and the traffic fast for Pacific Northwest standards. Not the best time or place to get distracted by the golden flecks in Emily's eyes.

"Who are the Storm playing tonight?" I asked.

"L.A. You're in for a treat—Nadine Johnson, L.A.'s center, and Monique Dixon do not get along, to put it mildly. The Seattle fans, naturally, hate Johnson. She fouls out practically every time the Sparks come to town, which just makes the crowd go after her more."

"Sounds kind of mean."

Em shook her head. "She totally deserves it. I think one of the reasons the male sports community loves her so much is that she's always harping about how a woman can be a professional athlete and still be feminine. But I'm sorry, not everyone cares about fulfilling outdated patriarchal notions of femininity."

I glanced at her. She sounded more like a women's studies textbook than a would-be soccer coach.

"What?" she asked, catching my look. "I am still a professor's kid, you know. We're biologically predetermined to bust out with multisyllabic words here and there."

Eyes back on the road, I teased her, "Brains, looks and soccer skills. No wonder you have a hard time staying single." I wasn't sure why I said it, except that her friends seemed to spend an inordinate amount of time razzing her about her love life. Maybe I wanted to know what all the hoopla was about.

Out of the corner of my eye, I saw her chew on her lower lip. "I could say the same thing about you."

"You'd be wrong, then," I said, "because I don't have any trouble staying single." Not exactly a primo comeback. Who bragged about the fact that other people didn't find them attractive?

Fortunately, we were almost to the Key. Emily directed me to a parking area on lower Queen Anne only two blocks from Seattle Center, and we headed to the Arena on foot. When she leaned into my shoulder as we crossed Queen Anne Avenue,

I slipped my arm through hers. The sun was out, as were the mountains, and I was going to the Storm game with Emily. At that moment, I was happy, and it was mostly because of her.

As we ambled along, I noticed that we weren't the only women walking together toward First Avenue. From every corner and every direction, sporty-looking women in jeans, T-shirts and Keens were converging on the Key. Here was the crowd support I'd been anticipating—all of these women, all supporting a female professional sports team. As a thirty-something couple with short hair and matching green Storm shirts passed us, holding hands, one of the women caught my eye and smiled. I ignored the look, my excitement dimming a little, and slipped my arm out from under Emily's, avoiding the questioning look I knew my movement triggered.

We didn't have tickets yet, so we stopped first at the ticket windows. "It's a weeknight," Em said as we got in line behind a family of four (perfect heterosexual model, I noted, with an older girl in a Monique Dixon jersey and a younger boy in a Jen Ballantine sweatshirt), "so it shouldn't be sold out."

I nodded and scanned the crowd on the nearby steps. Not far away, an older man with a fistful of tickets caught my eye. Leaving Emily in line, I wandered over to him, my voice casual as I asked, "Any extras?"

"A few," he said. "How many?"

"Just two. What have you got?"

He leafed through his tickets and offered me a pair of seats that were fifteen rows off the floor in what he claimed was the center seating section. Face value was thirty-five each, so I offered him forty for the pair. He accepted. Jake, my Chicago sports buddy, had always refused to pay face value for any ticket.

Deal complete, I waved the tickets at Em. "Our seats await."

She didn't appear overly pleased with my illegal ticket procurement. "But I was going to treat you," she said, following me to the arena entrance.

"You can get the popcorn," I said.

"And beer?"

"And beer. What's a sporting event without a Bud Light?"

"You're not in the Midwest anymore, Sam. They have microbrews here. You just have to know where to look."

"Oh yeah?" I asked as I handed a uniformed attendant our tickets. I held my breath and then released it as the tickets scanned okay. The woman waved us inside the arena.

"The Red Sports Club downstairs is the best girl bar in Seattle in the summer," Emily told me. "My sister loaned me an old copy of her license my freshman year at U-Dub. I've been getting in since day one."

Sometimes Emily seemed so mature, like when she said things like "patriarchal notions of femininity." At other times, it was only too easy to remember that she was the little sister of one of my high school classmates.

We headed along the corridor, dodging men, women and children clad in the green and gold of the home team. Groups of tall teenaged girls in matching jackets and sweatshirts stalked the many concession stands, high school teammates come to observe their idols. Television monitors were mounted on the walls every so often, cameras trained on the arena floor where the two teams were warming up. Tip-off was still twenty minutes away. Em suggested we look for her friends in the bar, which was tucked away just below the main concourse. I followed her down the stairs toward the club entrance, wondering what awaited us. Diva's was the only gay bar I'd ever been to, and my memories of that night weren't exactly clear.

A sign outside the entrance proclaimed, "Season Ticket Holders Only." I hesitated as Emily brashly charged inside. She waved me in past the male Key Arena attendant parked at the door.

"They don't check tickets down here at Storm games," she murmured in my ear, her hand warm on my arm. "I think they're scared of us. You know how dykes can be."

Actually, I didn't.

The interior of the club was well-lit and sparsely occupied by small groups of women. A rectangular bar sat at the far side of the room, while the space near the entrance held booths and tables in a tiered area a few steps above a wide, open lounge. I paused in front of a huge television screen that showed the Storm and Sparks warming up and missed the approach of a woman who barreled into Emily and gathered her into a fierce hug.

Em pulled away, coughing exaggeratedly as she smiled at the older woman. "Hey, Beck. What's up?"

Beck was short, stocky and tough-looking in a black leather vest over a collared shirt imprinted with the Storm insignia, her shoulder-length dark hair sprinkled with gray. She looked familiar, but I couldn't quite place her. "Just another opportunity to see my girls go to war," she said, and looked me over, her eyes narrowing. "So this is the reason you're not sitting with us tonight?"

I sensed that her attitude was insulting on several levels, not all of which were immediately obvious. Frowning, I stared back. Took more than a leather vest and a case of Napoleon's complex to intimidate me. "I'm Sam," I said, and held my hand out. "Nice to meet you."

"Beck," she said, and squeezed my hand lightly before letting it go. "What are you two drinking? At least let me spring for your drinks."

Emily cast an amused glance my way as Beck pulled her toward the bar. Before I could feel awkward left alone among the small groups of women animatedly talking in the lounge, I heard my name. Mel and Kristin, Em's U-Dub soccer friends, were waving me over to the table they'd staked out in front of the giant TV screen.

"Hi Sam," Kristin, the pretty blonde, said as I approached. "How's it going?"

"Not bad," I said. "How about you guys?"

"Getting our game on," Mel said, and took a swallow of beer from a plastic cup. Her eyes darted around the room, settling on one small group of women after another. At the same time, she flipped the top on and off her phone, one of those models with an entire mini-keyboard tucked away inside.

Kristin pushed a chair my way. "Have a seat. Mac won't be back for a while. They have the best drink selection down here but not the fastest service. Have you been here before?"

"No," I said. "This is my first Storm game."

"And it's L.A.," Mel said. "Nice."

They started to tell me more about the Seattle-Los Angeles rivalry, and I leaned back, relaxing a little. They were easy to talk to. Or Kristin was, anyway. After a minute, Mel trailed off mid-sentence and bolted off to greet a new arrival who, bedecked in a Life is Good baseball cap and baggy, low-slung jeans, looked more like a teenaged boy than a grown woman. Kristin and I chattered on, discussing our professional sports event history. We each had been to Women's World Cup games in '99, when the American women had hosted (and won in memorable fashion) the penultimate international soccer event. Kristin had witnessed China's rout of Ghana in Portland while I'd watched the U.S. women blow Nigeria away at Soldier Field in Chicago the summer before my senior year of high school.

"Soldier Field?" Kristin repeated. "I think Mac was at that game."

Sixty-five thousand people had made the trip to Soldier Field that day. If I recalled correctly, Em had been part of the Logan Soccer Club contingent that took up most of one section. I'd caravanned to Chicago with a dozen Logan High teammates, squeezing four younger players into my dad's Volvo, including Jenna Anderson. Emily was about to start high school; otherwise, she probably would have been in my backseat with Jenna on that road trip.

I glanced over at the bar where Em was still waiting to be served. Her friend was talking, hands nearly as active as her mouth. "How do you guys know—Beck, is it?"

"Rebecca Carville," Kristin clarified, watching me expectantly.

The name was more familiar than the face. "The Storm General Manager?"

Kristin nodded. "Mel used to date Beck's cousin. Beck still treats her like family. As in blood, not the gay sisterhood thing."

I took in Kristin's neat blonde ponytail, painted fingernails, Adidas T-shirt with pink striped sleeves. She, I was guessing, didn't play for Em's team. Figuratively speaking.

By the time Emily and Beck returned with our drinks, Seattle and L.A. had finished warming up and were clearing the floor. Beers in hand, Em and I said our farewells and headed upstairs, checking the signs for directions to our section.

"You didn't mention that you already had tickets for tonight," I said as we dodged a pair of little girls with painted faces and oversized Ballantine jerseys. "Or you knew the Storm GM."

Em shrugged, half-smiling at me. "There weren't enough tickets for all of us. This way, Kristin got to come, too."

Knowing she had given up her seat with the Storm GM made me feel all warm inside. Or maybe it was the beer, a delicious microbrew, as promised. Either way, the game hadn't even started yet, and already I was feeling like this might be one of the best nights out I'd had in a long time.

That feeling intensified as we stopped to pick up a large bucket of buttered popcorn before making our way to our scalped seats—center court, across from the benches only fifteen rows off the floor. As we made ourselves comfortable, Emily pulled out her phone, typed in a short message and looked down at the court. I followed her gaze in time to see Mel stand up and look around, phone in hand. She gave us a thumbs-up while Beck and Kristin waved. They were seated in the first row of seats at the exact center of the court.

I couldn't speak for a second. Then, "You gave up courtside tickets to sit with me?"

Em shrugged again and took a handful of popcorn from the bucket. "No big deal. Beck usually invites Mel and me along a couple of times each season. Anyway, you're worth it," she added softly.

Gazing into her eyes, the jumble of sound and light and color all around us, I was aware of the warmth emanating from her skin, the scent of buttered popcorn and beer rising between us, the curve of Em's neck vulnerable somehow above her Logan Soccer Club T-shirt. And then the lights went out and loud music began to course through the stadium. It wasn't "Sirius," the Alan Parsons Project song the Bulls had broadcast during player introductions the past two decades, but it started out the same way, low and long and dramatic. I leaned back next to Emily as flashing lights shot chaotically around the stadium and the bass pulsed in my chest.

Was she right? Was I worth it?

Chapter Fourteen

~EMILY~

Storm games always went too quickly. But with Sam beside me, the first half proceeded at record pace. Dixon and Johnson were up to their usual tricks, throwing elbows, bulldozing through the paint and racking up personal fouls. I was in and out of my seat, cheering on my team and yelling at the refs when they failed to make the appropriate call. To my (and the crowd's) delight, Nadine Johnson had to sit down midway through the second quarter with three fouls. Taking advantage of her absence, Seattle, led by all-star point guard Jen Ballantine, went on a 16-2 run to end the half. My voice was hoarse, and it was only half-time.

At the break, we headed up to the main concourse, still nursing our original beers. "Do you want another drink?" I asked Sam as we stopped beside a pillar just outside our section.

She shook her head. "I'm driving, remember? But don't let that stop you."

"I'm good." I scanned the crowd quickly, my eyes flicking over families and lesbian couples of all ages and types. Normally I would have gone back to the Club downstairs during halftime to mingle with the scene. But today I wasn't in the mood. I wanted to have Sam to myself. So when Mel texted, "Where R U?!" I sent her back a note to the effect that Sam and I would not be joining them.

"2 bad," she texted back. "K n i wr gonna trd w u 4 sec haf."

Trade seats with us for the second half? I guess I didn't have to have Sam all to myself. "How do you feel about braving the club scene again?" I asked her, tucking my phone back in my pocket.

She shrugged. "Whatever you want."

Not whatever, I told myself, looking away from her lips.

Downstairs in the club, already packed with lesbians and their friends, we waded through the various cliques forming and reforming. Mel and Kristin were wedged in at a table in the lounge with a couple of sporty dykes I recognized from campus. A woman I didn't know was there, too, tall and thin with multicolored tattoos peeking out from under her shirtsleeves and collar.

"Dude," Mel said as we approached, and gave me a high five. "Did you see Johnson drop when Monique threw that elbow in the first quarter?"

"Totally, man," I said, nodding at the U-Dub girls. "What's up? This is Sam."

Introductions made their way around the circle. Somehow Bree, the tattoo chick, ended up maneuvering herself between Sam and me as I greeted Kristin. "I like your necklace," I heard her say, eyes on the jade stone suspended at the hollow of Sam's throat.

As Sam thanked her politely but unenthusiastically, Kristin and Mel and I traded tickets for the second half. Then Kris leaned in and murmured, "Don't worry. Sam strikes me as the kind of girl who can take care of herself."

I followed her gaze and discovered Sam looking slightly bored as Bree leaned in, talking into her ear. She glanced over and caught me looking, and I could have sworn she winked.

"I can see what you see in her," my straight soccer buddy added. "She's really cool."

"She always has been."

Copying Bree's move, I insinuated myself between the taller woman and Sam. The last thing I needed was a dyke on the prowl scaring her off. My back to the interloper, I asked Sam, "So, are you having fun?"

"Oh yah, you betcha," she said in a heavy Midwestern accent.

I laughed and shook my head. She was hanging out in my world again, just like Friday night, only this time, it felt right. She seemed at ease, even surrounded as she was by homos and tattoo chicks.

"What about you?" she asked, her hand warm on my arm as she leaned closer to be heard above the din of gregarious Storm fans meeting and greeting.

I inhaled the faint scent of lavender rising from her skin. "Oh, yeah," I said. "I'm there."

Beck found us just before the end of halftime. She'd been making her rounds, greeting season ticket holders and old friends. She slipped one arm around my neck, the other around Sam's, and guided us out of the club. "You can't be late when you're with me," she said as we trotted down the corridor toward the entrance to the lower level.

Sam glanced at me inquiringly.

"Mel and Kristin traded with us," I explained.

"I hear this is your first Storm game," Beck said as we emerged into the brightly lit arena and started down the stairs to courtside seating.

"It is," Sam said.

"Think you'll be coming back?"

She nodded. "Definitely."

"That's what I like to hear," Beck crowed, and guided us to

the best seats in the house.

I couldn't have agreed more.

* * *

Life was good, I kept thinking throughout the second half as Monique Dixon jogged past close enough to touch time after time; as I intercepted meaningful looks between teammates and tried to guess at their meaning; as I tried to rein in my usual heckling of the refs who occasionally treated the women players more like high school students than seasoned professionals. But we were sitting with the GM. Best to leave the heckling to her.

Beck didn't need any help on that front—when MD, our all-star forward, drove to the basket and was hacked by three different Sparks players, Beck was on her feet before the refs had a chance to blow their whistles, pacing the sideline, a mirror image of the Storm coach on the opposite side of the court. She didn't reserve her passion for foul calls, either. When Ballantine drained a long-range three-pointer to close out the third quarter, Beck leapt up and exchanged high fives with everyone within reach.

Beside me, Sam's cheeks were glowing as the game wound down, the home team comfortably in the lead. When Nadine Johnson fouled out with six minutes remaining, Sam got to her feet with the rest of the crowd and chanted, "Beat L.A.!" at the top of her lungs. This from the woman who'd thought before the game that the Seattle crowd sounded "kind of mean."

"You should see this place during the play-offs," I told her during a time-out.

"I'd like to," she said, her eyes lingering on mine again. With her face flushed and her hair curling loosely around her shoulders, she looked like the Sam Delaney I remembered from home. In recent years, my Michigan childhood had seemed to belong to someone else, someone whose memories I shared but who was most definitely not me. For a moment, sitting there beside Sam, I felt dislodged from the world I had built for myself in Seattle. But then the Storm mascot started leading the traditional end-of-game kids' Conga line around the court, and I snapped back to reality.

"Why are you smiling like that?" Sam asked.

"I'm just glad you came with me tonight. Are you?" I didn't breathe for a second, even though I was pretty sure she'd been having a good time so far. What wasn't to love about sitting courtside as Seattle demolished L.A.?

"Very glad," she said, and her gaze dropped to my lips. There was The Look again. Did she know the signals she was sending? I made myself watch the game as the time-out ended, trying to focus on basketball rather than the promise I imagined I could read in Sam's eyes. Nothing was going to happen, I reminded myself. Nada.

The stadium was still full when the final whistle blew. The stands started to empty slowly as the Storm Dance Troupe, made up of sweat suit-clad kids, took the floor, dancing and clapping to loud hip-hop music as the two teams shook hands. The Sparks headed straight for the locker room, but the Storm gathered for a team huddle at half-court only a few feet from our seats.

Beck clapped Sam on the shoulder. "So what's the verdict, newbie?"

"Awesome. Better than any other WNBA game I've been to."

"You've been to other WNBA games?" I asked. I'd thought I was introducing her to something new.

"A few. I had this friend in Chicago who was a sportswriter and could get us in to any sporting event. I dragged him to a few basketball games, but the crowds in Chicago were nothing like this."

Him? I frowned and looked back at the court. The Storm huddle had dispersed, and the players and dancers were throwing T-shirts to the remaining fans. While we were standing at the edge of the court, swaying to the music still pulsing through the stadium, Jen Ballantine grabbed a T-shirt and walked over to us. Except, of course, it wasn't really "us" she was coming to see.

"Hey, Beck," my favorite Seattle superstar said, and slapped hands with the grinning GM.

"Nice game," Beck said. "Once again, Johnson fouls out in the Key. I love it!"

"I know, right? Nice crowd," Ballantine returned. And then, as I vainly attempted to formulate an intelligent remark, she reached past both Beck and me to hand Sam the T-shirt. "Thanks for coming," she said, her eyes on Sam. Then she nodded at Beck and me and turned away, heading for the locker room.

"Great game," Sam called after her. I watched Ballantine disappear into the concourse. Had I imagined the flirty look in her eyes? I'd heard through the grapevine that Jen might not be on the straight and narrow, but rumors about lesbians in the WNBA were a dime a dozen. Which didn't mean they weren't true.

"Well, my girl," Beck said to Sam, "looks like you've made a fan there yourself."

Sam looked down, but she was smiling, I could tell.

I gritted my teeth in silence. Jen Ballantine, hitting on Sam right in front of me—what freaking nerve! Except that I knew exactly why someone would cross a basketball court to talk to Sam.

My phone buzzed against my hip, and I pulled it out of my pocket. Mel had texted: "JB gave ur date a T?!"

I glanced up. She and Kristin were standing in front of our scalped seats, clearly laughing at me. I shut the phone and slipped it back into my pocket. I could only imagine the razzing this incident was going to cost me.

"It was good seeing you, Mac," Beck said, engulfing me in one of her signature hugs.

"My pleasure," I said once I recovered my air supply. "Thanks for the seats. And for the Storm in general—you guys are doing an amazing job."

"Can you believe it's been almost ten years? Hopefully we'll be around for another decade, at least!" She reached out and grasped Sam's hand. "You, my dear, I expect to see again sometime soon."

"You've got it. And thanks for the courtside seats," Sam added, her smile slightly cool. Beck's exuberance, I knew, could take some getting used to. Not that she seemed aware of this fact.

"All right, chickies, off to do some business. Give my best to your cohort for me." And with a last squeeze of my shoulder, she was off to work the remaining crowd.

Sam and I followed the masses toward the stairs. I hoped she wouldn't want to call it a night yet. Mel and Kris would have to behave in front of her, and anyway, the day had been so good that I still wasn't ready for it to end.

"Where are you taking me now?" she asked. "Kristin said something about a bar nearby where you guys hang out after every game."

I perked up. "Pasha's. It's only a few blocks away." Then I hesitated. "But, well, it's basically a women's bar on game nights. A lesbian bar, I mean."

She didn't look at me as she headed up the stairs. "Fine with me."

What was fine with her? Lesbianism in general? My homosexuality in particular? I followed her, sighing. As if I would ever have the nerve to ask.

"Hola, chiquitas," Kristin said when we reached the top of the section. She and Mel fell into step beside me, Mel's elbow working its way into my ribs, Kris's grin wider than it should have been. Ballantine hitting on Sam had clearly entertained them more than it had me. Fortunately, as I'd expected, Sam's presence kept my two buddies from blatantly reveling. As we left the stadium and headed north toward Roy Street, Mel texted various friends to update them on our plans while Kristin, Sam and I rehashed the game.

"Whenever I watch a sporting event live," Sam said, "I can

never seem to focus on the actual game. There's always so much going on, I think I actually see more of the game on TV."

"Understandable you'd be distracted, what with Mac spazzing out at the refs every ten seconds," Kristin said, nudging me. "I've sat with her before."

"Hey, I behaved today," I protested.

"Is that true?" Kristin asked Sam.

"For the second half, yes. But I'd have to plead the Fifth about the first."

"Whose side are you on, anyway?" I slipped my arm around her neck and pulled her to my side, pretending to give her a noogie.

Laughing, she grabbed hold of my waist and started to tickle me. Out of the corner of my eye, I saw Kristin roll her eyes at Mel, who was speaking into her phone instead of typing for once. Reluctantly, I set Sam at a respectable distance from me as we walked on toward Roy Street.

Pasha's was already jammed with basketball fans by the time we arrived. As we waited in line at the door to get our IDs checked, I caught Sam looking in the window at the cute dyke clutching a mike in one hand and a beer in the other.

"Karaoke," I said. "What do you think, Delaney? Does the spontaneous thing cover singing?"

"It could, except you really don't want to hear me sing."

"So there is something you're not good at."

She glanced at me, frowning a little. "There are lots of things I'm not good at."

The bouncer checked my ID and waved me in. I stepped into the bright lights of the main room and stopped to wait for Sam. I recognized some of the women right off—Corrie had played soccer at Seattle U a few years back and was now playing beer pong at the table in the back with some of her friends, one of whom, Lisa, was a Microsoft millionaire. Meanwhile, the karaoke crowd included Molly, a girl I'd gone out with a couple of times the summer after my sophomore year. She nodded at me from across the room. I nodded back.

"Who's that?" Sam asked, coming up behind me.

"No one," I said, and smiled at her. "Want to split a beer?"

"Sure. Half a beer couldn't hurt."

The crowd was thickest around the bar. I held my hand out to Sam. She took it, holding onto me as I wound through the tightly packed bodies, nodding hello to familiar faces, ignoring others. I wanted the women in the bar to know that Sam was mine, even if she didn't know it yet herself. I wasn't in the mood to fight off Brees and Ballantines all night. Although Jen Ballantine I probably wouldn't have minded hanging with, even if she did turn out to have the hots for Sam.

Vic, one of the owners, was working the bar. I caught her eye and ordered a Mac & Jack's. Her eyes flicked past me to Sam, and she wiggled her eyebrows suggestively as she slid the full pint glass across the counter. Grinning, I tossed my last five dollars on the bar.

Sam reached for my hand again, and it was her turn to lead the way back through the crowd to Kris and Mel, who had wedged themselves into a space near the karaoke machine. As soon as we reached them, Mel slapped me on the back and headed for the beer pong contest on the other side of the room. If I wasn't mistaken, she had a crush on Corrie, the Seattle U alum. But then Mel usually had crushes on several women at once. A business major, she claimed it was important to diversify.

"Do you want to know who in this room Mac has dated?" Kristin asked Sam, practically shouting to be heard over the duo belting out the Streisand/Diamond classic, "You Don't Bring Me Flowers."

"No!" I exclaimed at the same time Sam said, "Yes!"

Kristin said into my ear, "That's what you get for not bringing me a beer, biatch."

"I'm broke," I told her. "Otherwise I totally would have."

"Right." She projected again in Sam's direction. "Mac says she'd rather fill you in herself. I'll be right back."

As Kris headed toward the bar, Sam said, "We should have brought her a drink."

"Yeah." I held the beer out to her. "Your turn."

She took the pint glass, her fingers brushing against mine, and swallowed a third of its contents. Then she wiped her mouth with the back of her hand, returned the drink and looked around the room. I followed her gaze. The usual post-Storm crowd was here, mostly twenty-somethings on their way to getting drunk: skinny girls in tank tops that showed off their tats, jock girls in Adidas jackets and Tevas, chubby girls with androgynous hair and men's jeans. Lately this scene hadn't held as much attraction for me. Maybe four years of playing around was enough.

Just then a group of thirty- and forty-somethings entered the bar. They crossed the room to where we had adopted our wallflower poses, rolled their eyes at the spectacle and headed for the stairs that led to the darker, quieter section of the pub where the locals usually hung out.

"They were funny," Sam said, her mouth close to my ear.

I turned, and our noses nearly bumped. I stared at her lips for a moment, then looked up into her eyes. She was watching me and didn't seem nervous at all to have me that close. Which was more than I could say. "How so?"

She shrugged and took the pint glass from me again. "Like they were beyond all the fuss." As she took another pull on the beer, I watched her hair fall over her shoulders, revealing the jade necklace at her throat. I wanted to touch it, to feel the stone warmed by her skin. Swallowing, I glanced back across the room.

From the far side, Mel caught my eye. "Come here," she mouthed, pointing at the beer pong table.

I shook my head. No.

"Is that beer pong?" Sam asked, her hand on my shoulder.

"Um, yeah," I said, flashing back to the night I'd taught her to play Wii and she almost blew a gasket.

"Let's go." She grabbed my hand and led me across the room. Reluctantly, I let her.

Mel clapped me on the shoulder when we reached the table. "Dude, awesome," she said. "Corrie and I won the table. You and Sam are on that end."

"Okay, but she's my designated driver," I said.

"She is?" Mel frowned. Then her brow cleared. "No problem. You'll just have to drink for two."

As Mel poured beer into four cups arranged in a diamond at either end of the table, I explained the game to Sam, who had already taken up position at our end of the Ping-Pong table. The idea was to get the ball into one of the other team's cups. If the ball hit the side or a rim, whoever was up had to take a sip from each. If the ball landed in a cup, they had to drink all the beer in it. The first team to empty the other team's cups won.

We were up first. Sam held out her hand and I gave her the ball. I could already tell how this would go. We had better win—otherwise, I didn't want to see the fallout. She took careful aim, drew back her arm and tossed the ball. It landed just in front of the arranged cups and bounced over. "Damn it."

"Nice throw," Mel said, smirking as she took aim at the cups on our side. She shook the ball to the right, then to the left, like maracas. Corrie giggled, egging on the annoyingly macho guy Mel sometimes channeled. Were Sam and I as flirty as the two of them? Mel finally released a high arcing shot that bounced off the edge of one of the outer cups.

"Shit," I said.

"We'll get them back," Sam promised, her eyes narrowing. I knew that look. I'd observed it plenty of times in high school as well as more recently in my living room. It was damn lucky that she was good at so many things—to be born as competitive as she was but without coordination would have made her a monster.

The match went down to the wire, Mel and Sam making shot after shot while Corrie and I missed again and again. When Mel sank yet another shot, the crowd at her end cheered raucously. I downed the next-to-last beer on our side slowly while Sam surveyed the table from every angle imaginable. The next shot could decide the match.

Mel called out, "Quit stalling! Put up or get out, girlie!"

Shouldn't have said that, I thought. After a long pause, Sam aimed carefully and released her shot. The throng around the table inhaled collectively as the ball drifted up and over the net on a near perfect trajectory. As it landed inside the cup with a resounding plop, I breathed a sigh of relief. Whew.

The onlookers near our end of the table hollered while Kristin, who had appeared halfway through the match, pounded me on the back. Sam grinned at me again and we slapped hands. You would have thought we'd just won a conference championship or something. I was still thinking this when she leaned over and pressed her lips fleetingly to my cheek. Just as quickly she pulled away again, not meeting my eyes. Stunned, I stayed where I was as she shook hands with Mel and Corrie, who had come to our end to extend grudging congratulations.

"Good game, dude," Mel said to me. Then she leaned in and murmured, "Did she just kiss you?"

Corrie and Kristin were chatting up Sam about her "mad skills," and I could have sworn I heard something about a founding role in Northwestern's Beer Pong Club.

"I think she did," I told Mel.

"Sweet." So that the others would hear her, she loudly added, "Now you guys own the table. I think those two called next." And she pointed at Bree, the tattoo chick from the Red Sports Club, and her sidekick, a pierced skateboard type.

"I don't know," I hedged. I was well on my way to inebriation and rattled by the kiss. I wasn't in the proper state required to keep an eye on Bree, who was blatantly ogling Sam.

Turning to me, Sam said, "You have to be at work pretty early tomorrow, don't you?"

Behind her, Kristin shot me a look. She, too, it seemed, had observed the kiss, which after all had taken place in the middle of a crowded bar.

I glanced at Mel. "I do have to work in the morning. The

table's all yours, dude. Kick their asses."

She nodded. "With pleasure."

"Loser," Kristin said, and gave me a hug. "Be good."

Usually it took a while to get out of Pasha's. But tonight, the feel of Sam's lips pressed against my cheek still with me, I skipped the usual social niceties and beat a direct path to the door, Sam's hand in mine as we wound together through the masses. Once we were outside in the cool evening air without the press of the bar crowd or the lights and sounds assaulting us, I couldn't think of anything to say. I let go of her hand, and we walked down the sidewalk together quietly, traffic speeding past on Roy only a few feet away.

My tongue felt heavy, a sure sign I'd imbibed too much. But Sam had kissed me! The thought pounced on my unsuspecting brain. All at once I had to run, had to feel my body moving through space strong and fast. I sprinted down the sidewalk toward First Avenue, the summer sky twilit overhead. Behind me, I heard Sam laugh and call, "Hey, wait up!"

I turned and ran back to her, sprinting as fast as I could over the uneven pavement. She put her arms out and I crashed into her. Her arms went around my neck, my hands ended up on her hips, and we were both laughing. "You really are like a puppy," she said, but it sounded like she thought that was a good thing. Then she stopped laughing, and so did I. We were standing close together on the sidewalk across the street from Seattle Center, my hands on her hips still, her arms around my neck. She was giving me The Look, and I wanted to kiss her so badly that I couldn't remember why I shouldn't. I leaned forward. Our breath mingled and I closed my eyes. My lips touched hers, and after a moment, her grip on me tightened. Her breath was beer-sweetened, her lips soft. I pressed my mouth against hers, wanting to taste more of her. She opened her lips to mine.

But not for long—my eyes flew open as Sam shoved me away, and the world I'd managed to set aside momentarily came rushing back. She was staring at me now, her brow furrowed. It occurred to me that I might just have ruined everything.

"I have to go," she said, backing away. "I-I have to go home."

I held my hand out. "Wait, Sam. It's okay."

"No, it's not," she said. And then she spun around and started to walk away, leaving me standing there alone. This had never happened to me before. Always before I had let the straight girls make the first move. This reaction, apparently, was why. Sam picked up her pace as I hesitated, and soon she was running down the same sidewalk I'd sprinted across a minute before. At the next stoplight, she crossed against the red, turned a corner and disappeared from sight.

"Fuck, fuck, fuck," I said, running a hand over the buzzed hair at the nape of my neck. I was sweating a little, both from Pasha's—all those bodies—and from my recent headlong run. I rubbed my eyes to clear the alcohol fog from my brain and turned back toward the bar. I could always bum a ride from Mel, assuming she went home anytime soon. Then I pictured walking alone back into Pasha's, where only moments before Sam and I had traversed the masses hand-in-hand, and I knew I couldn't do it.

Instead, and for the second time in a week, I caught a bus north to Wallingford. The taste of hops-flavored bile rising in my throat, I rode with my forehead pressed against the cool glass window as the lights of Seattle passed me by.

Chapter Fifteen

~SAM~

I didn't mean to run away. One minute we were entwined there on the sidewalk on lower Queen Anne, kissing each other, and the next I was pushing her away and trying to breathe through the tightness in my chest. But while I might not have intended to run away, that was exactly what I did, my mind empty as the sidewalk fell away beneath my feet.

In the lot off Queen Anne Avenue, I started my truck and pulled out into traffic. But driving, I soon found, was nearly automatic and couldn't stave off the thoughts twisting through my mind. As I headed north up 99, I was suddenly back on the sidewalk with Emily, holding her against me, shaping my lips to hers. As we kissed, I'd noticed an unfamiliar coiling low in my belly. She was touching me without even touching me. This realization was what had made me shove her away. What had made me turn tail and run.

Back at my building, I parked and headed inside. Apparently

it wasn't only emotional attraction I was feeling toward Emily, I thought as I waited for the elevator. I didn't have an innocent crush on my former teammate. I was attracted to her both emotionally and physically—which meant that I wasn't entirely straight, after all. I couldn't be.

When the elevator doors dinged open, I stepped inside. Chris had been gay, and look what had happened to him: disowned and sent to live among strangers and nearly die that way too. Not that I was necessarily gay. Maybe I played for both teams, as Tina liked to put it. Either way, by deserting my Chicago life, I'd exiled myself already. And I wasn't a teenager in a high-HIV risk group. Other than the non-straight thing, my situation and Chris's weren't even close.

When the elevator doors opened on my floor, I headed into the hallway, keys clenched in a hand that didn't feel entirely steady. I walked to my door, fumbled with the lock and stepped inside my apartment. Chloe ran out of the bedroom with the trill of greeting I loved.

"Hey, sweetie."

She purred her contentment against my shins, followed me to the couch and jumped into my lap as soon as I sat down. Light from the street outside illuminated my apartment. It seemed so obvious now. How had I fooled myself into believing otherwise? I closed my eyes, remembering back to high school when I used to stay after practice and coach Emily while Jenna sat on the sideline, watching. Or sometimes I'd see her waiting for the bus in the morning, and I would stop and offer her a lift, happier than I should have been to have her in the seat next to me on our way to school, the Michigan morning dark still outside the car.

Emily wasn't the only girl who'd made me feel that indefinable elation. Sophomore year at Northwestern, Cat Sullivan moved onto my floor. Tall and blonde and smiling, she was an ultimate Frisbee player from California. For the first few months of fall term, much to Tina's disgust, I spent nearly every night hanging out with Cat in her single listening to Van Morrison and talking

145

about the meaning of life, which we were certain we could reliably identify given the year of undergraduate study under our belts. Then she got a boyfriend, and our friendship took backseat.

There were others I could name too—Rebecca Hanson from ninth grade biology, smart and cute with freckles and a crooked smile; Gloria Mendes, a fellow cub reporter at the *Tribune*, whose fearlessness I longed to emulate, or so I told myself; even, if I thought about it, Sheri Tyler, a woman in marketing at Xytech who had a pixie cut and always looked well put together. I had noticed women more than men my entire life. This wasn't any revelation. The only thing different now was the physical component. Until now, I could tell myself that I was just one of those women who preferred the company of other women. Such a preference didn't make me gay. But kissing Emily—and wanting to do more than kiss her—did. Or, at least, bi. Though sex with either of my boyfriends, one in high school, one in college, hadn't been particularly earth-shattering. Certainly not the kind of sex Tina liked to describe in more detail than was truly necessary. I had thought I just wasn't wired that way, but now I wondered. What would it be like with Emily?

Chloe butted her head against my chest, and I scratched her head dutifully. To hell with humans. Chloe didn't care about my ambiguous sexual identity. As long as I fed her, played with her, loved her, she would continue to love me unconditionally in return. And wasn't that how relationships should be?

But my relationship with my parents had never been unconditional. What would they say if they knew about Emily? Not that there was anything to tell. But if my mother asked me if I was seeing anyone, what would I tell her? I didn't want to lie anymore than I wanted to battle her. And if I admitted I had been hanging around with the eminently gay Emily Mackenzie, a fight was likely what I'd find.

The more I thought about my upcoming trip home, the more I wished I weren't going. Only a couple of weeks away now and I hadn't mentioned it to Em. I didn't quite know why, except that I wasn't sure how to blend our present with our Logan past. Seattle was finally starting to feel like home, especially now that she and I had reconnected. As long as I kept the two parts of my life separate, everything would remain manageable, I had somehow convinced myself.

I didn't want to have to think about seeing my new life through my mother's eyes. Ready or not, though, I would soon be home sleeping under my parents' roof. In the meantime, I would have to sort out what I wanted. I couldn't picture seeing Emily ever again, not after the way I'd acted. But I also couldn't imagine not seeing her. I was hooked. Wasn't I?

* * *

That night, I slept fitfully, assailed by technicolor dreams. I woke up when it was still dark and lay in bed, reliving the only dream I could remember. In it, I was with Emily, standing on a street corner, my arms around her neck, her hands at my hips. She kissed me and I kissed her back, only this time when I panicked and pulled away, she collapsed, blood streaming from a gash on her forehead. I dropped to the ground beside her and pressed my fingers to the cut, trying to stem the flow of blood. I wanted to scream for help but my voice wouldn't work. Her blood just kept coming, warm and sticky on my hands.

Then, all at once, in that way unique to dreams, I wasn't holding Emily anymore. Instead, it was Chris who was bleeding, Chris who lay unconscious on my lap. Quickly I pulled my hands away, but I knew it was already too late. I had exposed myself to my brother's blood, and now it was only a matter of time until I got sick too. He opened his eyes and saw his blood on my hands but was too weak to pull away. He fell back. After a moment, I put my arms around him.

"It's okay," I said. "Everything will be okay."

He knew I was lying, but he closed his eyes and leaned against

147

me. And the dream ended.

Tears came as I lay in my bed, the comforting warmth of my cat pressed against me. In the predawn darkness, it all seemed real. But slowly the leftover dread waned and relief seeped in as I realized I wasn't sick, Emily wasn't hurt. At least, not physically. I turned on my side and curled around Chloe, who purred sleepily. Burying my face in one of my pillows, I tried to blot out the memory of Chris's eyes when he saw his blood on my hands. Didn't take a genius to figure out what my subconscious had been telling me: To get involved with Emily would be to risk hurting and being hurt, dual risks I wasn't sure I wanted to face again.

* * *

I didn't make it to work that day. Instead, when my radio alarm clicked on, I shut off NPR and listened to the sound of rain pattering on the roof. A gray day in Seattle, finally, after day upon day of unrelenting sunshine. In a way, it was almost a relief. I didn't have to feel that pressure so familiar to Pacific Northwesterners to take advantage of every moment of sunlight before the clouds descended again. I could stay inside if I wanted and not feel guilty. Which was exactly what I would do, I decided, turning over to go back to sleep.

When Chloe began to pounce on the hump of my unmoving feet under the comforter, I finally dragged myself out of bed. I fed her, called in sick to work and considered toasting a bagel. But I just wasn't hungry. In the living room, I opened the blinds and looked out over gray and green Seattle. The rain had stopped. Maybe I should take a ferry to the Peninsula, I thought, the habit of summer hard to shake. Instead I gave in to my mood and lay on my couch watching TV all morning, flicking from channel to channel. Later I put on sweats and walked to the high-end grocery store down the block, where I blew cash on a stash of junk food the likes of which I hadn't tasted since college. The cashier placed my purchases in the reusable bag I carried, her eyes sympathetic.

On the way home, I stopped at the neighborhood video store and picked up a couple of DVDs—a French film I'd read about and *Victory*, the old World War II soccer standby featuring Pele and Sylvester Stallone as Allied prisoners who take on the German national team and, as the title implies, win. I hadn't seen this movie in a while, and it seemed like just the thing to get me to stop feeling so sorry for myself. A group of people working together for honor and justice in the face of the genocidal Nazis—I was lucky, and I would do well to remember that.

At home again I parked myself back on the couch with junk food and beverages close at hand, Chloe curled up on my lap, and proceeded to watch the movies one after the other. The French film was hilarious, in a darkly cynical sort of way, and *Victory* was as exciting as ever, even though I knew the story by heart. I watched on edge until the final scene. To my mind, Pele was still the best soccer player in the world—better than Maradona pre-drugs, Beckenbauer in his prime, Cristiano Ronaldo now, and any of half a dozen other Brazilians, Ronaldinho included.

After the final scene of *Victory* faded away, I turned off the TV and sat in the gathering gloom of my living room. Outside, the sky was now leaking the kind of gentle spray that collected on tree leaves and dribbled in unsteady rhythm onto cars and pedestrians below. The thought I had been avoiding all day crept in: What was Emily doing? She would have been home from work for hours, maybe done watching *Ellen* even by now.

The last time I'd watched *Victory* was my senior year of high school. The entire team had packed into Natalie Sipsma's den to watch inspirational sports films (*Hoosiers* rounded out the double feature) the night before State semifinals. As co-captain, I'd earned one of the limited spots on the couch. Emily, I remembered, had sat on the floor just in front of me. I'd watched both movies with her leaning against my legs, and I could still remember questioning my urge to smooth her shoulder-length hair off her neck. Even then I felt something for her. And then, like now, I couldn't handle it.

A Mariners game was on, so I watched, telling myself it didn't matter that Emily hadn't called. By the time the baseball game ended, I was slightly dizzy from too much television and stiff from lying down all day. Chris had been plagued by bedsores, I remembered, terrible ones that had seemed to proliferate no matter what my mother and the nurse, Ben, did. Ben was a gentle man who came recommended by the local AIDS hospice. He was there when Chris died in his sleep at three o'clock on a weekday afternoon. My father, meanwhile, was at work. Life doesn't just stop, I'd heard him tell my mother the weekend before my brother died. She had asked him to take time off to stay with her and Chris during the day, but he refused. He couldn't miss work.

The sky beyond my window was darker now. I turned off the television again and sat in the quiet. Why hadn't Emily called? She was the experienced lesbian here. I was the one who had never kissed a woman before. Didn't she know I was waiting for her to make the next move?

All at once, I couldn't stay in my apartment another second. I pulled on boots and a rain jacket, kissed Chloe and escaped into the cool night. I walked for close to an hour through Woodland Park, watching for shadows in the woods. I walked until the cathode ray spots faded from my vision and my lungs filled with fresh air. Alone in the night, I lifted my face to the sky, squinting through the blur of raindrops that clung to my eyelashes. And when mist turned to warm rain that dripped from my skin and made the ground muddy beneath my boots, I didn't even mind.

Chapter Sixteen

~EMILY~

Wednesday morning at work, I was a zombie. I hadn't slept much the night before. I woke every hour or two, lying in the dark wondering why I was awake. Then I would remember how Sam had stared at me on the sidewalk near Pasha's, her eyes dark, and I would lie awake for another twenty minutes, willing sleep to return. Which rarely worked, in my experience. In the middle of night, sleep had to be wooed gently, approached carefully, in a roundabout fashion. Just like curious straight girls.

I still couldn't believe how stupid I'd been to kiss Sam. Sure, she'd been sending me signals for days now, but a public sidewalk in daylight when I'd been drinking was not an ideal setting. Knowing Sam, she probably would have wanted to talk about things first. Or maybe not. My radar seemed off with her. I'd known her for more than a decade, but that hadn't helped much so far.

Time poked by at Peloton on this, the morning after I might

have scared Sam off for good. Every so often I thought of the way she'd looked at me, the way she'd run away, and I felt my face grow warm. At least none of my friends had witnessed what happened. Mel had texted me a couple of suggestive messages, but I hadn't responded. Bad enough that I couldn't forget the dismay in Sam's eyes as she backed away from me. Had kissing me really been that awful? It seemed impossible that something that meant so much to me could mean so little to her. Impossible—yet likely.

Finally the clock hit one. I skipped lunch and went straight home to crash. Before I fell asleep, though, I checked my messages manually. Verizon confirmed that my cell phone was working correctly. I had no new messages.

Around four, my phone woke me, and I grabbed it before the ring tone sank into my dazed brain—Lady GaGa sounded nothing like Queen.

"What happened last night?" Mel asked. "You didn't text back so I figured you must have gotten lucky."

"Nah," I said, brushing her question aside. "I told you, Sam is straight. We're just friends."

"You hold hands with all your straight friends?"

"We weren't really holding hands," I lied. "It was just crowded. Anyway, I was going to call you later. I feel like going out. Want to check out AP?" It was karaoke night again at Aster Place, Seattle's lesbian bar where Mel and I had whiled away many a summer evening. I didn't feel like sitting around tonight waiting for my cell to ring. I needed to get out and remind myself that there were plenty of other fish in the sea. Fish who would want to kiss me back.

"Great minds," Mel said. "I was calling to see if you wanted to go out. I thought Liz and Jessie might want to come too. I haven't seen them in forever."

"I'm pretty sure they already have plans tonight," I lied. I wasn't in the mood to face Liz. She'd been a good friend the last couple of years, but sometimes it seemed like she walked around with a habitual look of disapproval leveled my way. Not all of us were lucky enough to meet the love of our life at nineteen and live happily ever after.

"Cool," Mel said. "Want me to pick you up?"

"Totally." A few beers, some bad singing and the reinforcement that I wasn't a sexual deviant (or, at least, I wasn't the only sexual deviant out there), and maybe I would actually sleep tonight.

* * *

My phone remained silent as I ate dinner alone and got ready to go out. I wasn't sure why I expected Sam to make the call. Maybe because she was older or hadn't dated women before. Or maybe because I was too much of a chicken to call up the woman who had fled from my embrace less than twenty-four hours before. The entire day had passed without our talking, and by the time I got home tonight, it would be too late.

Upstairs, I thumped around my bedroom getting ready for the night's festivities. From my closet, where I kept my good clothes, I selected a black T-shirt that showed off my arms and shoulders, tan painter's pants and chunky black shoes. I pomaded my hair and surveyed myself in the mirror. This outfit was like wearing a sign that said "I'm looking."

On my way out, I passed Jessie and Liz in the living room watching a movie. They both stared at me. I hadn't dressed up girl-style in a while, not even for Pride.

"Going out?" Jessie asked.

Liz looked back at the television.

"Yeah," I said. "See you."

Mel pulled up right on time in her ancient Datsun, perfectly preserved like many an older West Coast car that would have rusted out years before on the salt-drenched roads of the Midwest. Her hair was slicked back too, only instead of a black T-shirt she was wearing a white one with faded jeans and a big black belt. We were both in boi uniform tonight.

"You out to get laid or something?" she asked, putting the car in gear.

"You know it." Although, to be precise, I was mainly out to forget the look in Sam's eyes the night before.

We chatted on the way to the Hill, about work and soccer and what we were thinking of singing at Aster Place tonight. During the winter, Mel and I had been regular karaoke participants. But then spring had arrived with its mating rituals and we hadn't hung out as much. Mel's girlfriend had gone home for the summer too. Now she and I were in the same boat—ready to move on. She was hoping Corrie might show up at Aster Place tonight, she told me as we drove across the University Bridge.

"I wondered about you two last night," I said, the beer pong match flashing into my mind. I pushed it away resolutely. That was then, and this wasn't.

"So did I. But she took off right after you did. What about you? There's really nothing between you and Sam?"

"Nah. She dates boys."

"Since when has that stopped you? Anyway, your supposedly straight friend set off Jen Ballantine's gaydar. Not to mention Bree's."

I wrinkled my nose and turned up the radio for the Nine Inch Nails. "I love this song," I said, unsubtly guiding the conversation away from the lesbians who had a thing for Sam Delaney.

We sang—shouted—along with the stereo on our way south over Capitol Hill to Aster Place. We prowled the block looking for parking, settling for a space all of two blocks away. A light, misting rain started as we backtracked to the bar. Summer in Seattle—you had to love it.

Mel and I recognized the woman working the door. She said she didn't need to see our IDs, she knew we were legal. Technically, Mel wasn't—she used her older sister's ID, like I used to do. We strolled coolly unsmiling toward the bar, where we ordered drinks from one of Aster Place's famously grumpy bartenders. I handed over the Visa card my parents had given me for graduation (the balance was mine and mine alone to pay, they had made clear) and asked to run a tab. Beers in hand, we crossed the threshold into the larger second room that held the pool tables, dartboards and pinball machines. In the corner near the front windows, the karaoke folks were setting up their paraphernalia.

After a couple of games of darts, Mel announced, "I'm ready to sing. What about you?"

"Let's do it."

We ordered fresh pints of Alaskan Amber and claimed a table with a couple of empty glasses on it near the karaoke stage. While a gay boy in cowboy garb offered his rendition of a Garth Brooks tune, Mel and I looked through one of the songbooks. When he finished, the crowd gave him a polite ovation. The next performer took the stage, a woman our age with orange hair and tattoos on both arms.

Mel leaned closer. "That's Cat. She's leaving for the army next week."

I'd never understood how Mel seemed to know every lesbian in Seattle. I was fairly social, but Mel had no qualms about talking to strangers wherever she went. Especially if those strangers were family.

We turned in our selections—Pearl Jam's "Daughter" for Mel and Gloria Gaynor's "I Will Survive" for me—and waited our turn, drinking beer and people-watching. The room filled up over the next few songs, so that by the time my name was called there were quite a few people in the crowd. Including many cute girls I didn't know.

I pounded the rest of my beer, bumped fists with Mel, and headed for the stage. Microphone in hand, I blinked into the lights and waited for the song to start. At first my voice was a little shaky, but I delivered the chorus with conviction as the crowd joined in, singing along. I'd learned these words by heart in high school after Jenna left me for the boy. Tonight, though, I was remembering the look on Sam's face when I kissed her. She had run shrieking into the night, literally, and now I couldn't be sure I would ever hear from her again.

I finished the song, smiled a little sheepishly and bowed as the crowd of women clapped and whistled. Another singer took the stage, and Mel and I slapped hands.

"Way to go," she said. "Want to know who was checking you out?"

I glanced around the room, mildly curious as I took my seat. "Sure."

"Katie, the blonde sitting next to the stage with that big group. Her friend Jamie is dating Cat."

"How do you know these people?"

"I've seen them at a couple of parties."

I focused on the blonde and was almost impressed. She was attractive, with longish hair piled casually on top of her head. Not as good-looking as Sam in my estimation, but that was probably to be expected at this point.

"What do you think?" Mel asked. "You're totally her type."

"Not bad." I reached for my beer and realized it was empty. "I'm going to get another pint. Want one?"

"Nah, I gotta drive. You better be back for my song."

When I got back, Mel was no longer alone at the table. Katie, the girl in question, had pulled up a chair. Mel introduced us.

"Nice to meet you." I nodded her way.

She cast me a flirty smile. "The pleasure is mine."

The word pleasure echoed in my mind, and just for a minute I wondered what she looked like beneath her Buffalo Exchange ensemble. Then I smiled back at her, gulped my beer and watched the next karaoke addict take the stage. This was entertaining, better certainly than moping alone at home or hanging around with the world's most perfect couple.

Mel's turn arrived, and she made her way up to the stage. I looked over at Katie and watched her watching Mel. For someone who wasn't Sam, she was quite attractive. Not to mention bold. She pulled her chair closer to mine, leaned across the corner of the table, and said, "Nice singing, by the way."

"Thanks."

"So you just graduated from U-Dub, is that right?"

"Last quarter."

"I have one more year at Seattle Central," she volunteered. Seattle Central Community College was located at the southern edge of Capitol Hill, right on Broadway.

After a moment, I asked, "What are you studying?"

"Communications. I'm thinking about being a broadcast journalist."

This, naturally, reminded me of Sam, who had graduated from one of the most prestigious journalism programs in the country, according to my academically attuned parents. But Sam didn't want to be with me, I reminded myself. Katie, on the other hand, might.

Eventually Cat and her girlfriend Jamie joined Mel, me and Katie, and the five of us sat around the table chatting and drinking. I was pleasantly buzzed and happy to participate in queer-themed celebrity gossip intermingled with stories of women we all knew. After a while, Katie's hand dipped below the table to rest lightly on my thigh, and the intimate contact brought me crashing back into my body. I didn't pull away, though, just smiled and pretended that I had strange women stroking my thighs all the time. I tried to return to the conversation at hand, a debate over which Margaret Cho DVD was the best. But I couldn't seem to focus because as cute as Katie was, Sam was somehow the only woman whose hands I wanted on me. This realization didn't exactly thrill me—Sam belonged to a world that viewed me not as a big dyke on campus but rather as some gender-confused freak. As might Sam herself, for all I knew.

A little after eleven, I leaned over and said to Mel, "What do you think about taking off?"

"It's cool," she said.

We rose and made our excuses. Katie, her eyes on me, said, "We'll be at Torrent on Friday night, if you guys are interested."

157

Mel lifted her eyebrows at me. This was my chance to bow out, but Katie was attractive and had put herself out there. I didn't want to rebuff her in front of her friends. Anyway, hanging out with her might help me get Sam out of my head. "We're interested," I said, aware of the double meaning my words conveyed.

"Good," Katie said, smiling. "See you Friday, then."

And just like that I had a date. Any other time, I would have been psyched to have plans with someone like Katie. But this wasn't any other time.

Mel didn't know that, though, and congratulated me as we made our way toward the bar to close out our tab. "Way to go, champ. I had a feeling one of us would score tonight."

If only Katie were the one I wanted to score with.

The grumpy bartender handed my Visa back along with a receipt for an amount that momentarily stopped my heart. I tucked the slip of paper into my wallet out of sight as Mel and I headed for the door. My first paycheck was due to arrive on Friday—none too soon.

When we stepped outside, we discovered that the mist had turned into a downpour.

"Last one to the car's a rotten egg!" Mel called, and sprinted away, laughing.

I lifted my face to the rain and followed her into the night.

Chapter Seventeen

~SAM~

After work on Thursday, I thought about calling Emily, but the phone seemed too remote, too cold. I'd awakened that morning from restless dreams knowing I wanted to talk to her. I just wasn't sure what I might actually say. That afternoon at Xytech, I'd wasted hours staring out the window at the clearing sky over Puget Sound, trying to figure out what to do. Emily, apparently, wasn't going to call me. If we were going to see each other again, it seemed I would have to be the one to grab the bull by the horns. Courage, unfortunately, had never been one of my strong points.

Back at my apartment, I changed into shorts and a tank top, grabbed my bike from the walk-in pantry off the kitchen and rode east toward Wallingford. She would want to see me, wouldn't she? Of course she would. Assuming she was home.

But as I walked my bike up her front walk and leaned it against the side of her porch, I wasn't so sure. I climbed the steps slowly, my pulse racing from the brief ride over. It wasn't too late. I could still leave without ringing the bell. But before I could make up my mind, the front door opened and Emily's roommates stepped out onto the porch. When Liz saw me loitering on the front stoop, her eyebrows rose. Then she leaned back in through the open door and called, "Mac! You've got company!"

Jessie smiled at me. "Hey."

"Hey." I forced a smile back. I had caught Em at home. Good thing, I told myself.

"We were just on our way out," Jessie said as she and Liz brushed past me. I gave them a little wave and sat down on the steps, watching Liz guide the Miata down the driveway and out into the street.

Soon I heard footsteps inside the house. I kept my back to the open front door as the footsteps stopped abruptly, then resumed more slowly. I didn't turn even as Emily sat down next to me, just kept staring down the road after the Miata.

After a minute, she said, "This is a surprise."

I nodded, watching her out of the corner of my eye. I had rehearsed my lines on the way over, but now my throat was dry and I couldn't quite remember what I'd planned to say. What if she didn't feel the same? She had kissed me, so I didn't think I could be all that wrong.

"I wasn't sure I'd see you again," she said into the silence.

At this, I turned quickly to face her. "Of course you'd see me again."

"Apparently," she said, and smiled a little.

I took a deep breath, trying to figure out how to get the old Em back, but words continued to elude me. I looked down at my athletic shorts, rubbing at a grease spot.

"So…?" she said, and glanced over her shoulder at the house, as if she'd rather be doing something, anything than talking to me.

"So." I chewed my lower lip and looked at the steps. I could do this. I took another breath and blurted, "I'm sorry," just as she started to say, "Look, Sam…"

We both broke off, and she stared at me. "What?"

"I said I'm sorry," I repeated, rubbing the toe of my running shoe against the splintery wood of the middle step. "You know, for the other night."

"Which part?" she asked, deadpan.

"Do you really not know?"

"No, I do." She sighed and rubbed a hand through her short hair until it stood on end. "Look, I was about to apologize myself. I didn't mean to make you uncomfortable the other night. That's the last thing I wanted."

"You didn't," I assured her.

"Couldn't tell from where I was standing."

"It wasn't you, honestly. It was me. I freaked myself out."

She frowned. "How?"

I paused, wondering if I could actually say the truth out loud: "By wanting to do more than kiss you." There it was, and my voice had even sounded reasonably steady.

The words hung between us until the last hint of ice in her eyes melted and she was my Emily again, smiling at me across the narrow space that separated us. "You did?"

Shyly, I nodded. "Well, yeah. Couldn't you tell?"

"It was kind of hard with the disappearing act. Plus I was drinking for two, remember?" She leaned closer, her eyes warm on mine now. "I'm glad to hear it, though. The whole unrequited thing sucks."

Which meant… I smiled back at her, a giddy rush making my heart beat faster. "Tell me about it."

We sat there, both smiling slightly stunned smiles, until I said, "Are you doing anything tonight?"

"No."

"Would you like to come over for dinner?" I wanted to spend time with her, now that we'd both admitted to—to what, exactly? I put the question out of my mind. Plenty of time to figure that one out later.

"I'd love to," she said.

Seated there on her front porch, we came up with a plan that included stir-fry, among other things. Before we parted, Em reached out and took my hand in hers. "I'm really glad you came over," she said.

"I am too." I squeezed her hand, wishing she could feel how happy I was to see her. Then she let go and we both stood up and I walked my bike down the path, grinning back over my shoulder at her. She waved, and I took off toward home, pedaling hard. One of us was always sprinting away, it seemed. Only this time, I thought with a goofy smile still plastered across my face, it wasn't such a bad thing.

* * *

An hour and a half later, everything was ready. I'd stopped at the grocery store on my way home, in a far better mood than during the previous day's shopping excursion, and picked up veggies, rice and a bottle of wine. Then I headed home to get cleaned up, debating for several minutes—a long time for someone whose favorite clothes were sweats—over what to wear. I finally settled on a pale blue sundress I'd worn only a couple of times. It was a date, after all. At least, I thought it was.

As ready as I would ever be, I carried my laptop into the kitchen for musical accompaniment and worked on getting dinner started. If only I stayed busy enough, I wouldn't have to worry about not making a fool of myself in the next several hours. My elation had faded somewhere along the way, and the butterflies I usually associated with soccer had begun to dance about my stomach. What had I been thinking?

The doorbell rang a little before seven—Emily was running early too. I buzzed her in, smoothed my hand over my hair and dress, took a deep breath. This was it. I just wasn't sure what "it" would turn out to be.

With a last glance around at my apartment, I opened the

door to wait. Down the hall the elevator doors creaked open, and I watched Emily move toward me with that walk that was singularly hers. Dressed in olive cargo pants and a tight-fitting black T-shirt, her bike helmet tucked under one arm, she looked considerably older than sixteen this time.

"You look great," I said as she reached me.

"So do you." She hesitated, then shyly pecked me on the cheek.

Was it possible that she was as nervous as me? I held the door open wider. "Come on in."

Chloe jumped down from her perch on the back of the couch and ran to greet Emily, who squatted to rub her head.

"Can I get you something to drink?" I asked. "Beer? Or wine?"

"I'll have whatever you're having."

I retreated to the kitchen to open a bottle of pinot grigio. From the way she was dressed, the way she was acting all polite and almost formal, it appeared that Em was treating this as a real date too. We were alone together. Now what?

She followed me into the kitchen and accepted the glass of wine I handed her. "To former Loganites in Seattle," she said, holding up her glass.

We clicked glasses and sipped our wine, Indigo Girls playing on iTunes in the background. I turned away from the warmth in her eyes, checked the rice cooker and resumed my vegetable chopping.

"So how do you like your job at the bike shop?" I asked, hoping that mundane conversation might slow my overactive heart rate.

"More than I thought I would," she said. "By the way, is there anything I can do?"

"Let's see—the portabella needs to be sliced."

She joined me at the counter. I gave her a cutting board and knife, and soon we were paring vegetables side by side. I tried not to think about how cozy the kitchen seemed with her there beside me.

"What exactly do you do at work?" I asked.

She told me about the bicycle shop business, selling bikes and gear to serious riders and weekend warriors. "I like the people I work with, which makes it fun. How about you? Do you like your job?"

"It's not anything I ever thought I would do," I admitted, "but it's interesting. I could see getting bored in a year or two, though."

"What'll you do then?" she asked, pausing in her chopping to take a sip of wine. "Go back to writing?"

"I don't know if I could."

"What do you mean?"

"I don't write that much anymore," I said. "I just can't seem to get into it. It's hard to explain."

She paused, and I could feel her watching me. "Do you think it's because of your brother?"

I didn't meet her eyes. "I don't know. Maybe. Probably. By the way," I added, forcing myself to sound cheerful, "did I mention I'm going to Logan at the end of next week?"

She paused. "No, you definitely did not mention that. For how long?"

I described the conference in Chicago and my plan to catch the train home afterward. "I'm not entirely looking forward to it," I said. An understatement. I set my knife down, poured olive oil into a pan and set it on a burner to warm.

"Why didn't you tell me about the trip before?"

"I don't know. No reason."

"Right." She frowned into her wineglass.

"I'm sorry," I said after a moment. I knew I should apologize.

"It's okay," she said, but she still wouldn't look at me. "When's the last time you were in Logan?"

"Christmas. You?"

"Same—Christmas."

"Wouldn't it have been wild if we'd been on the same flight?"

I asked. "I kept an eye out for you, just in case."

"Yeah?" She finally lifted her head. "So did I. I've kind of been keeping an eye out for you ever since I heard you were out here."

"I have a confession," I said. "I actually saw you before we ran into each other. I...I stopped by some of your games last fall." All but one home match, but I didn't mention that.

She frowned again. "Why didn't you come down to the field and say hi?"

"I wasn't sure you'd want to see me."

"Of course I would. I'll always want to see you, Sam."

The warmth in her eyes again was exactly what I had been hoping for, but now I wasn't quite sure what to do with it. "Can you check the rice?" I asked. "I don't want to start the vegetables if it isn't close."

She checked. "Looks close to me."

I scooped the vegetables into the pan, and for the next few minutes, the sizzling and crackling of the oil prevented conversation. Emily wandered out of the kitchen. I could hear her in the living room, talking to Chloe in a low voice. I wasn't doing a very good job with this date thing. Still acting too scared, still sending mixed messages. If I wasn't careful, I'd push her away and she'd end up with someone else. There was a reason Emily didn't ever stay single for long.

When dinner was ready, we piled our plates high and carried them over to the small dining set by the window. I rarely ate at the table. Usually I sat on a barstool at the counter with a book or took my plate into the living room to watch the news or sports or *Friends* reruns.

"This looks great," Emily said, and dug in.

The stir-fry was good, I had to admit. We polished off our first helpings and went for seconds, chatting about Logan and vacations we'd spent there since high school. Emily told me she'd stuck around Seattle for Thanksgiving the previous year for the first time. Staying had made her feel like a genuine adult, even though all she did was go to her friend Mel's house in Kirkland.

"What did you do for Thanksgiving?" she asked.

"My friends from college had an orphans' dinner."

"I wish I'd known you lived so close."

"Me too." I took a sip of wine. "I should have gotten in touch with you sooner, but it was just too soon after Chris. It felt like it would have been too hard to see someone who knew my family."

Emily nodded. "I think I know what you mean. That's how I felt when I came out my freshman year at U-Dub. I didn't want to see anyone from home at first."

Danger, my brain flashed like the robot from *Lost in Space*. "Oh, yeah?" I said, stalling.

"Yeah—it was still so new, I wasn't sure I could explain it to myself let alone anyone else. Like, I was finally dealing with this thing that society didn't want me to acknowledge, and now I had to face all the people who'd always assumed I was straight. Who wanted me to keep pretending I was just like them."

She had put into words one of the reasons I didn't want to go home right now. What if I told my parents about Emily and they refused to accept it? Would I waffle and come back asexual again? I had never done anything knowingly against my parents' wishes. Except move to Seattle—but even then, they'd been so caught up in their grief over Chris that they never thought to ask me not to go.

"You okay?" Em asked.

"Fine. Do you want more wine?"

"I'm okay for now." She smiled at me, reached across the table and covered my hand with hers. I smiled back at her, relaxing as a familiar peace spread through my body. Whenever she touched me, I had this overwhelming sense that everything would be all right. No one had ever made me feel like that before.

We finished the meal and lingered at the table talking. Then we moved into the living room. The previous night's *Daily Show with Jon Stewart* was on Comedy Central, and we watched for a while, laughing and nudging each other. When it was over, we listened to more music and talked about work and our soccer team and past and future World Cups, including the Soldier Field game we'd both attended nearly a decade before. When these topics had been exhausted, we finally fell silent.

Emily was sitting slouched down on the couch, her stocking feet up on the coffee table. She looked over, caught me watching and leaned her head against the back of the couch, her eyes on mine.

Now or never, I thought. Reaching out, I pushed her hair off her forehead, my fingers drifting down to caress her cheek. Her skin was soft and warm.

"What are you doing?" she asked, her voice low.

I didn't answer, just took her hand and lifted it to my lips. I kissed her palm softly, turned her hand over and kissed each finger.

"Sam, are you sure?"

"I'm sure," I said. The butterflies had long since vanished, and the serenity her proximity elicited was radiating through my body along with the glass of wine. I moved closer, leaned across the narrow space between us and pressed my lips to hers. She was softer than I remembered, and her mouth tasted like wine as she, after a moment, began to kiss me back. I was kissing a woman, I thought, closing my eyes and running my hand along the back of her neck. But I wasn't kissing a woman. I was kissing Emily.

Soon we were stretched out on the sofa, my leg over hers. Her lips felt amazing against mine. So did her body. She pulled her mouth from mine and began to kiss her way down my neck, pushing me gently onto my back. I shivered at the feel of her lips on my neck then froze as her fingers skimmed the top of my dress. Was I ready for all of this?

Above me, Emily stilled. "Are you okay?"

I nodded but didn't open my eyes. The butterflies were back along with the same low stirring I'd felt when she kissed me standing on the sidewalk outside Seattle Center. Only this time, it was more insistent. Running away at this point, I knew, was not an option.

She rested her forehead against mine. "Maybe I should get going."

My eyes flew open. "What? Why?"

"It's late," she said. "And anyway, I think we should wait until you really are okay."

I remembered how she'd looked at me on her porch that afternoon, cautious, uncertain. I couldn't blame her. How could she know I wouldn't change my mind again? I couldn't even be sure. "But I am okay. I think."

"And with that ringing endorsement…" She sat up on the edge of the couch and stretched, rubbing her neck. She did look tired. Maybe she hadn't gotten much sleep the last couple of nights either.

I sat up beside her and rested my chin on her shoulder. "Don't give up on me."

"As if I could," she said, and pressed her lips softly to mine. "Can I see you tomorrow?"

"Yes, please." Then I remembered. "No, wait, I'm going to a Mariners game with Tina."

"Oh. Actually, I'm supposed to be someplace too."

She picked at a nonexistent spot on her pants, and my earlier worry returned. Was she seeing someone else? Then again, why wouldn't she be? I turned her face to mine and kissed her again, not as softly this time. Any uncertainty had vanished at the thought of her with someone else. She kissed me back, matching my intensity. I banished thought and concentrated on the feel of her mouth on mine, the heat of her hands at my back, the press of her ribs against my breasts.

But she pulled away again, blast her. "Wait, wait a minute. What about Saturday?"

"Saturday?" I closed my eyes. What was Saturday? "I'm going to a barbecue at Golden Gardens. Actually, Tina invited you."

"She did?"

"She says she wants to meet the person who's brought me

back into the human race." I rolled my eyes at my drama queen friend's word choice.

Emily smiled and ran a finger over my lips. "I think I like how that sounds. I have to work until one, though."

"That's okay, I'll pick you up afterward."

She was staring at my lips, and in another minute I was sure we would be making out again. But instead she stood up and walked to the door where her shoes and bike helmet were waiting.

"You sure you'll be okay riding home?" I asked, following her. We had, after all, consumed half a bottle of wine.

"I'll be fine."

We stepped forward at the same time and hugged each other tightly. I closed my eyes, my cheek pressed against hers, and touched the short hair at her neck again. I liked that spot best.

"Thanks for dinner," she said softly.

"You're welcome." We stood together until Chloe meowed and wove between our legs. Then I pulled back, laughing, and Emily started kissing me again.

"I really do have to go," she said a few minutes later.

"I know."

"Take care of her, Chloe." She patted the cat's head and kissed my cheek. "Sweet dreams." Then she smiled at me and slipped out the door.

I stayed where I was for a moment, staring at the spot where she'd been as if I could will her back in through the door. But it was no use. I was alone again in my apartment and wouldn't see Emily for two whole days, during which time she may or may not have a date with someone else. I headed into the kitchen and piled our dinner dishes in the sink. When in doubt, clean, was my motto.

I picked up Emily's wineglass and thought about the lips that had sipped from it, then laughed at my own silliness. I was smitten. I only hoped the feeling was mutual. As Emily had pointed out, the unrequited thing sucked.

Chloe came in to sit on one of the kitchen stools while I

washed dishes. "I kissed Emily," I told her, as if she didn't already know. She meowed and licked her shoulder.

Probably she approved.

Chapter Eighteen

~EMILY~

Friday morning, I whistled as I walked to the bike shop, summer sun shining down through tree branches. The night before was still with me, though I couldn't quite believe it had actually happened. As unlikely as it would have seemed earlier in the week, Sam Delaney and I appeared to be dating.

Which meant I was dating two women at once, I realized, the spring in my step abating somewhat. I'd forgotten my plan to meet Katie tonight at a gay bar on Capitol Hill. I didn't have her cell number. I would either have to make an appearance or stand her up. Since Sam would be at the Mariners game with her college buddy, looked like Mel and I would be clubbing it on the Hill again tonight. Rough life, being wanted by two women. Except that I didn't want to start things with Sam on the wrong foot. Assuming we were really starting something—maybe in the light of day she would reconsider. Maybe she had already reconsidered.

Chewing my lip, I arrived at Peloton early for once. Brett shot me a thumbs-up, I resisted the urge to roll my eyes, and the work day was on. As the morning progressed, my initial euphoria faded, replaced by trepidation that only grew when I checked my cell messages on the way home. Nada. Hadn't Sam said she would call me? I ate lunch and waited a while, tossing a tennis ball against my bedroom wall, but she still didn't call. Had she changed her mind? Was she going to ditch me again? Damn it.

I lay back on the bed and looked up at the ceiling. I couldn't remember being this worked up about anyone in recent memory. Usually my relationships developed organically and predictably, like with Katie—I would meet an attractive friend of a friend, and if we clicked, we'd hook up. Usually we would hang out for a while before one or the other of us moved on due to circumstance (the rhythms of the school year, the presence of another love interest), and we'd stay casual friends. Assuming the parting hadn't been overly acrimonious.

But with Sam, I had no idea what to expect from one day to the next. First she blew me off when we ran into each other at Green Lake, then she started inviting me to hang out all the time. Then she kissed me at Pasha's and ran away when I reciprocated, admittedly somewhat less innocently. Finally she showed up on my doorstep and announced that she wanted me, an admission I had definitely not seen coming. Conflicting emotions, hers and mine alike, threatened to sink me. Did I really want to date a woman I'd admired most of my life and worshipped for a good chunk of it? This would be no casual relationship. Once we started, we couldn't just stop. But I guessed we'd already started. The night before had been our first official date.

I smiled, remembering the feel of her skin beneath my fingertips, the look in her eyes when I kissed her on the couch. Sam wanted me. And, at last, she knew it too.

* * *

My cell woke me up a little while later. I grabbed it, blinking at the sunlight streaming in my window. "Peloton. I mean, hello?"

"Are you sleeping?"

"No. I mean, yes," I said. It was Sam.

"Do you want me to call back later?"

"That's okay." I was careful not to sound too eager. With women you had to maintain mystery or else they took you for granted. "I'm awake, really."

"How are you today?" she asked.

"Good. How are you?"

"I'm good. How are you about, you know, last night?"

"Fine," I said, cautious again. "Are you okay with everything?"

"I'm okay if you are."

"I'm okay."

We were both quiet. I could hear voices in the background at her end and wondered where she was. Meanwhile, the only sound on my end was a couple of birds singing outside my window.

"Do you still want to go to the barbecue tomorrow?" she asked.

"If you still want me to."

"I'd love it if you did. What did we say, one-ish?"

"Yeah. Oneish." She'd love me to go. I tilted my head back and smiled up at the tapestry overhead.

"Guess I'll just have to wait until then to see you," she said.

"Guess so." I hesitated. "Blows, doesn't it?"

"Completely." Someone called her name in the background. "That's my friend Tina," she said. "This is her cell phone. I have to go. But I'll see you tomorrow, right?"

"Right."

"Have a good night, Em. Don't do anything I wouldn't do," she added.

The line went dead and I was left holding my cell, half-smiling. Somehow Sam had guessed I had a date tonight. I knew

173

she was bright, but I hadn't realized she was that perceptive.

Poor Katie. I turned over on my stomach and buried my face in a pillow. Little did she know she was just in the picture to distract me until I could see Sam again.

* * *

Torrent occupied an unassuming brick building on Eleventh Street between Pike and Pine, not far from Broadway at the south end of Capitol Hill. Inside, the downstairs space provided booths and couches for conversation while the VIP room upstairs offered a second bar and a dance space where cute boys could see and be seen. Every other Friday was Girls Night at Torrent. Tonight the lesbians would outnumber the gay boys.

Katie and her friends had already claimed a booth downstairs by the time Mel and I showed up. I ended up wedged onto the end of the bench next to Katie, a situation that didn't thrill me. I didn't want to be tempted to cross the line of Sam's parting comment. I wasn't sure how successful I would be fending off the not entirely unwanted advances of a cute lesbian.

Over nachos and pints of Dos Equis, Katie asked me about myself. I didn't feel much like talking, though, so I turned the conversation back to her and sat back as she told me about her family in Issaquah: little brother the soccer player, father the software engineer at a local company, mother the tax accountant. Her parents had been disappointed when she turned down offers from a couple of East Coast schools. They hadn't understood why she would want to take a year off before college. But she had stuck to her guns, moved to Seattle, and come out a month later. Her parents were less than supportive of her "lifestyle choice," which was how she'd ended up at Seattle Central. They wouldn't help her pay for school as long as she was in this "phase."

My coach at U-Dub had counseled at least one of my teammates not to come out until after college for the very situation Katie had encountered—some parents held their child's college tuition ransom and used it to ensure that the kid behaved "appropriately." I was lucky, I knew, to come from a family where not only was being gay not considered a transgression, but education was valued for its intrinsic worth rather than its power as a bargaining chip.

When the nachos and beer ran out, our group moved upstairs to check out the dance scene. Corrie was in line at the bar with another Seattle U soccer alum, and Mel made a beeline for them. I hesitated. Mel was my ride. If she and Corrie hooked up, I might be stranded.

Katie touched my arm and leaned in to be heard over the music. "I feel like a beer. Can I get you one?"

"Actually, I have to be at work pretty early in the morning," I hedged. "I can't stay out too much longer." Alcohol and dance music had the potential to weaken my resolve. Then I pictured Sam as she'd looked beneath me on the couch the night before, her eyes half-shut as I ran my fingers over her collarbone, her skin hot to the touch. In a little under fifteen hours, we would be together again with an entire weekend stretching ahead of us. I wasn't about to risk that.

"That's too bad," Katie said. "Do you work all weekend?"

"Just Saturdays," I admitted.

We hung out for another hour, dancing and chatting. I spent much of it wishing time would cooperate and speed up during the duller moments in life, slow down during the happier periods. But of course, time rarely cooperated. After I checked my watch for the fifth time, Katie asked, "Do you want to get going?"

"I probably should," I said, figuring bus schedules in my head. Mel and Corrie were slow-dancing to a fast song, a sure sign that I was on my own in the ride department.

"My car is parked nearby," Katie said. "Why don't I take you home?"

"That's okay," I said. "I can bus it."

She frowned. "It's really no problem."

I didn't want to hurt her feelings. Anyway, the sooner I got home and went to sleep, the sooner morning would come and the sooner I would see Sam. I caved and let Katie drive me home in the car her parents had given her before she came out. We chatted on the way, talking about Pride and other people we both knew from the scene. She was easy to talk to. I wondered what might have happened if I'd met her before Sam popped back into my life.

When she pulled the Accord to a stop before my house, I paused, hand on the door handle. I knew she wanted me to invite her in, but Sam's parting words echoed in my mind.

"I had a great time tonight," I said.

"Me, too."

"Give me a call sometime."

"Well, okay," she said as I slipped out of the car. "I will."

I smiled in at her, closed the door and headed up the walkway. After a moment, Katie started the car and pulled away. I'd made it. I was alone. Whew.

Or almost alone, anyway. Liz and Jessie were sprawled on the couch in the darkened living room watching a movie. They looked up and waved as I came in the front door. I nodded at them, grabbed a glass of water from the kitchen and retreated upstairs to get ready for bed and watch the late news.

My leg jumping a mile a minute, I waited through stories about contaminated lakes, crippled ferries and railway routes damaged by the spring's mudslides. Finally, my patience was rewarded—a recap of the Mariners game Sam had gone to tonight. The Mariners won big, I learned. Who had Sam rooted for? I almost picked up my cell to call her, but it was late. And anyway, I didn't want to seem too whipped. Time enough for that later.

Chapter Nineteen

~SAM~

On Friday, I met Tina at the market downtown for a late lunch. The usual teeming hordes of Mariners fans (Tina called them lemmings) had yet to descend on downtown, which was quieter than usual on the day before the Fourth of July. Since the Fourth fell on a Saturday this year, most businesses in the city were closed. Except restaurants. At the Athenian Inn, a Pike Place eatery that overlooked Puget Sound, Tina and I ordered food and drinks and watched pier traffic, the sun a shimmering orb above the Sound.

"So, anything new?" she asked casually, toying with the salt shaker on our table.

I paused. Was I glowing visibly from my date with Emily? "Not really."

"You sure? You seem different."

"I've just been thinking about my trip home next week, that's all," I lied. I hadn't decided yet if I wanted to tell Tina about

Em. It was still too new. For all I knew, Emily had changed her mind overnight. Probably not, but it was possible. Anyway, she had that date tonight. Things could still change.

"Last time we talked, you said you weren't looking forward to going home," Tina reminded me.

I picked at the label on my bottle of locally brewed root beer. "I'm not."

"Do you want to talk about it?"

"Not really."

Tina reached over and touched my hand. "You can talk to me, okay? About anything."

I looked at her, considering. She really did seem to know. Apparently I was just that transparent.

When the food arrived, we munched and chatted about the usual—our college days, mutual friends, her latest escapades. She told me she and Matt might be together for a while.

I pretended to choke on my salmon burger. "Excuse me? This from the woman who once said she could never see herself staying with anyone for more than a month?"

"You're not supposed to remember things like that. Anyway, at least I date."

She looked at me expectantly, as if waiting for a confession. I just shrugged and asked how she liked her temp job. Occasionally Tina took a break from waiting tables and slummed it in corporate America. The zoo pass and tonight's Mariners tickets were fruits of her latest foray into downtown Seattle assignments.

After lunch, we wandered downtown, window shopping at the art galleries on Western Avenue, shoe and dress shopping at Nordstrom's Rack on second. Tina loved clothes, and I didn't mind living vicariously through her sometimes. While she tried on half a dozen outfits, I borrowed her cell without asking and called Emily, who sounded adorably sleepy when she picked up. I pictured her at home in Wallingford and knew from her voice that she hadn't changed her mind. I couldn't wait to see her—despite her evening plans.

"Who was that?" Tina demanded suspiciously when I hung up.

"No one," I said. "That dress looks fabulous on you. Which shoes would you wear with it?"

Distracted, she forgot about the phone call and launched enthusiastically into a description of potential footwear options. Tina had way too many shoes. She hated it when I called her Imelda, but even she knew her shoe fetish was out of hand.

An hour before the game, we joined the pedestrians headed toward Pioneer Square and Safeco beyond. We reached our seats a few minutes before the first pitch—box seats only ten rows off first base.

"No wonder so many people sell out and become corporate whores," Tina commented, surveying the field from our impressive vantage. She had never been to a baseball game before and seemed intrigued as one of the Seattle players hit a home run with two men on in the first inning. From then on it was a slugfest, with the Mariners going on to score again and again against the Detroit pitcher, whose name was none other than Kenny Rogers, a fact Tina snickered at each and every time he took the mound.

We snacked on hot dogs and pretzels, drank beer, sang "The Gambler" and cheered against the Tigers despite our Midwestern ties. Tina declared the people-watching priceless—mostly software geeks and marketing executives in our section jumping out of their seats and screaming in voices unaccustomed to such displays of passion, then sitting back in mild embarrassment afterward. Rednecks flanked the computer executives, fake-tanned women with gold jewelry and red-faced men in Jay Buhner jerseys who subjected the visiting players to heartfelt heckling. I had to explain the Wave to Tina, but once she understood the concept she dragged me out of my seat every time it traversed our section. By the end of the game, we were both slightly sick from the rigors of overeating and cheering on the home team.

"I had no idea it would be so much fun," Tina said as we filed out of the building with the rest of the crowd.

"Live sporting events are more exciting than televised ones," I said. "You should have come with me to that Women's World Cup game in Ohio senior year. The U.S. may never host again in our lifetime."

"Too bad," she said, making her voice sound as if she realized now that missing the Women's World Cup had been one of the worst mistakes of her life.

I glanced sideways at her. "Nice try, Hoffman. You forget I can tell when you're acting."

The buses were running late, so we decided to walk to Tina's building on Capitol Hill. The evening was warm and clear, the sun shielded by buildings as we headed northeast through downtown. We were on Madison crossing over the freeway when I finally decided I should confide in Tina. I needed to talk to someone about Emily, and she seemed like the best bet. "So something happened last night with Emily," I said, unbidden.

She stopped, her hand on my arm. "What did you say?"

I stopped too, glanced at the cars below and the fading light above before finally looking her in the eye. "With Emily. Something happened."

"What sort of thing?"

"I kissed her," I said, and started walking again.

"You kissed her?" She fell into step beside me.

"Yep." I looked sideways at her. "Bet you didn't see that coming."

"Actually, I did."

"Did not," I said. We reached the other side of the bridge. The freeway noises receded as we walked on.

"It was obvious, Sam, the way you talked about her. I'm happy for you, hon. I really am. And I'm glad you told me." She wrapped one arm around my neck, kissed the top of my head and let go.

"Oh. Well, thanks," I said, and shoved my hands into my jeans pockets.

"I've always wondered what it would be like to kiss another woman."

"You have?"

"Uh-huh. I bet women's lips are softer. And you wouldn't have to worry about razor burn."

"You never told me that before," I said as we stopped at a corner to wait for the light to change.

"You're not exactly the easiest person to talk to when it comes to sex."

"What do you mean?"

"I mean," she said, "you've been hung up on the subject since I've known you."

"I'm not hung up on sex."

The light changed and Tina started across the street. When she realized I wasn't following, she came back. "I didn't mean that in a bad way."

"How exactly am I supposed to take the fact that you think I'm repressed?" I never challenged her like this. Usually I let everything roll off of me.

"I didn't say repressed," she pointed out. "You just don't seem that comfortable talking about it. I get why. You watched your brother die of AIDS. That's enough to turn anyone off for a while."

The Don't Walk sign started to flash. I crossed the street, not waiting to see if Tina was following.

She was. "Hey."

I didn't look at her.

"Sam, I'm sorry." She made her voice soft. "I didn't mean to be so blunt, okay?"

"Fine." I stared straight ahead. It was just Tina being Tina. She had blithely trounced on my feelings a thousand times before, but somehow I seemed to be all jangling nerve endings at the moment. I wasn't used to feeling like this. Would it pass, or was this how I would feel from now on?

We walked on in silence for a bit. Eventually I let her know she was forgiven by asking who would be at the barbecue. She told me about Matt's friends, the guys in his band and his buddies from high school. Matt was two years older than we were. He'd grown up in Bellevue. Up until a few months before, he'd still lived in the basement of his childhood home. Tina didn't know that I knew.

We took our time walking up the hill and didn't reach Tina's apartment until after eight. Twenty minutes later, she stopped her mother's hand-me-down Volkswagen in front of Camelot.

"I'm sorry about before," she said as I unbuckled my seat belt. I looked at her quickly. It wasn't like her to circle back to an earlier conversation. Usually she charged brashly ahead, living in the now the way her mother had trained her at an early age to do.

I touched her arm. "It was just hard to hear, you know?"

"I know. I didn't mean it that way. Are you still bringing Emily tomorrow?"

"I think so. But please keep what I told you to yourself," I said. "I'm not sure I'm ready for everyone to know yet."

"Don't worry, it stays between us. Matt's friends would all get hard-ons if they knew you were together. You know how straight guys are."

Actually, I didn't. "Thanks for tonight." Then I surprised us both probably by reaching out and giving her a quick, awkward hug. I couldn't remember the last time I'd hugged Tina of my own volition. Maybe it was the day I arrived in Seattle. Or was it after graduation when I left for New York?

"You're welcome," she said.

I slipped out of the car. "See you tomorrow."

"Ciao, bella."

She waited at the curb while I unlocked the front door. Then I waved and the VW darted away into the night. Tina was a good friend, I thought, heading for the elevator. I was glad I'd moved to Seattle—for more reasons than one.

* * *

Just before one the next day, I threw beach gear into a bag and packed up the food I had promised to bring. Maybe Emily would be ready early. Even if she wasn't, I could always lie on her bed and watch her change. Then again, if we were alone in her bedroom at this point, both of us scantily clad, we might not get out of there anytime soon. Tonight, I promised myself. Waiting would make it that much better. But make what better, exactly? I didn't even know what two women did together, despite owning the latest edition of *Our Bodies, Ourselves*. Fortunately, Emily had that part covered.

I had spent the morning pacing my apartment and washing every window I could reach. Despite our phone conversation the previous day, I knew Em had gone out the night before with someone else. Would she still want to see me today? Would she still want to be with me?

She was waiting on the porch when I stopped my truck in front of her house. She smiled when she saw me, leapt down the steps and strode down the front walk. I watched her, smiling too. There was my answer. And yet I couldn't believe she was really mine. Almost mine. Assuming nothing had happened the night before with her mystery date.

She slid into the seat next to me, leaned over and kissed me on the cheek. "You're early."

"So are you." I took her hand in mine. There was that sense of peace again. I squeezed and let go, put the truck in gear and pulled out. "How was your night?" I asked after a minute.

"Fine. I didn't get lucky, if that's what you're asking."

I concentrated on the road. "Well, kind of."

Emily touched my hand where it rested on the gearstick. "You have nothing to worry about. Honestly."

I relaxed a little. "Good."

We rode through Fremont and down the hill into Ballard. Emily asked, "How was the game?"

"Awesome. The Mariners trounced the Tigers. The buses were a mess afterward, though, so Tina and I ended up walking back to her apartment on Capitol Hill."

"Sounds nice. It was a gorgeous night."

"It was." I stopped the truck at a red light and looked over at her. "I told her about you."

"You what?"

I couldn't tell if the expression on her face indicated a good surprise or not. "Um, I told her that we kissed." The car behind us honked. The light was green. I hit the gas. "Is that okay?"

"Of course it's okay," she said. "It's better than okay. What did she say?"

"That she already knew anyway and was happy to see me happy."

"Wow. That's amazing. I'm glad you have such a good friend."

"So am I. Have you told any of your friends?"

"A couple."

I wanted to know what they'd said, but her silence wasn't exactly promising.

"Anyway, I couldn't wait to see you," she added, smiling at me.

"This morning took forever." I wanted to suggest that we skip the party and go somewhere we could be alone together all day. But I kept driving. If I didn't show up, Tina would never let me live it down.

The clouds had been clearing all morning. By the time we reached the west side of Ballard, blue sky had broken out overhead. Emily and I sang along to Fleetwood Mac's *Greatest Hits* as we neared the beach. Could she tell I was nervous? I hadn't brought a date to a social event since college.

Soon we were pulling into the Golden Gardens parking lot, packed with minivans, SUVs and every conceivable Subaru model. Families and couples littered the beach, kids and adults with miniature American flags, sparklers and firecrackers playing at the edge of the Sound. The water was still pretty cold, Emily said. The Sound didn't really "warm up" until August. Like Lake Michigan, only colder.

Tina, Matt and the rest of the group were crowded around a cluster of picnic tables at the edge of the parking lot. Emily and I headed toward them, food bag held out before us. I surveyed the group—Tina and Matt; several boys I vaguely remembered from the previous weekend with dyed hair of various colors, tattoos and girlfriends; and Sarah, our other Northwestern soon-to-be-FBI buddy and her friends from grad school.

"There they are," I heard Tina say. Like in a scene from a movie, everyone turned to watch us approach.

Emily smiled and held a hand up. "Hey," she said, breaking the pause that had fallen over my friends and their respective others.

Tina made the first move. She stepped forward and held out her hand, smiling. "You must be Emily. It's nice to finally meet you. I'm Tina."

"Hi Tina," Emily said, and shook her hand.

Watching them greet each other, I noticed just how androgynous Em looked. She had a black motorcycle T-shirt and baggy shorts on over her bathing suit, a baseball cap perched backward on her head, sunglasses masking her eyes. Everyone except Tina had probably been trying to figure out who the guy was with me.

I set the bag of goodies on the table and wished Matt a happy birthday. Then I returned to Em's side and slipped my arm through hers. I wasn't nervous anymore. To me, these guys with their green hair and dreadlocks and tattoos were more freakish than preppy-grunge Emily could ever be. I introduced her to the people I knew, got introduced by Tina to the ones I didn't. Sarah eyed Emily suspiciously. I hadn't expected a look like that from her, but then again, I saw her most weekends and had only mentioned Emily in passing.

Matt fired up the grill, and I added our turkey burgers to the pile. Emily chatted him up about charcoal and starter fluid while

I wandered away with Tina.

"She's adorable," Tina said as we sat down at one of the picnic tables.

"Isn't she?" I watched Emily flip a burger expertly—grilling was practically a competitive sport back in Michigan. Matt took the spatula from her and copied her move, only his burger landed on its side. They both cracked up.

"And social," Tina added.

"Much more so than me." Tina was so cool. She was treating us completely normally, unlike certain other people.

Speak of the devil. Sarah sat down next to us. "Hey."

"Hey, yourself," I said.

"So that's your Michigan friend?" she asked. "I didn't realize you two were so—close."

"Well, we are," I said evenly. I wanted to tell her that it was indeed what she was thinking, but the look in her eyes as she watched Emily was almost hostile. I held my tongue.

"Where's George's wife?" Tina asked, guiding the conversation away from the object of my affection.

Sarah told us that her classmate George was separating from his wife of five years. He only had one more year left in his Ph.D. program, but they just couldn't keep it together. He was thoroughly depressed, Sarah said. She and her friend Casey had brought him along thinking that the fresh air might do him good. "So far, though," she added, "he keeps seeing couples everywhere he looks. Maybe we should have taken him out on Broadway. At least everyone there is gay." She looked at me pointedly.

I tried to remember if I had ever heard Sarah make a comment about Capitol Hill or gay people. Nope, this was the first. I glanced at Tina. She was watching Sarah with a sour look she usually reserved for old white men in business suits. The three of us sat quietly for a minute there in the shade at the edge of the beach.

Then Emily walked over balancing two half-full plates, sunglasses on top of her head. "Soup's on."

Sarah stood and brushed past her without a word. I exchanged a look with Tina as I stood up to take one of the plates. "Thanks, Em. Want some chips?"

"Sure." She followed me to the other picnic table. "Are you guys okay, by the way?" she asked as I opened a bag of chips and a bottle of pop. "Looked a little tense over there."

No need to alert her to the apparent bigotry of one of my oldest friends. "Sarah and Tina butt heads sometimes." Which was completely true.

"They seem really different," Emily said, glancing over her shoulder. Tina had followed Sarah to the grill, and the two were deep in conversation. I could tell from the scowl on Tina's face that Sarah was not winning any diversity awards.

"They probably wouldn't still be friends if it weren't for me," I said.

"I have friends like that. By the way, this is great, Sam. Thanks for inviting me."

"You're welcome." I forgot about my friends and smiled into her eyes. She was so cute, and the sky was clear, the shade cool, the breeze off the water just right. Even Sarah's uncharacteristic narrow-mindedness couldn't ruin the day.

We piled our plates and filled our cups and took them back to the other table as Tina stalked away from Sarah.

Emily's eyebrows rose. "They really don't get along."

I murmured agreement and concentrated on spreading ketchup across my bun with a plastic knife.

Soon the others joined us, even Sarah, food in hand. Native Washingtonians asked the rest of us about our differing points of origin and how we all knew each other. Tina, Sarah and I ended up reminiscing about Northwestern and Chicago like we always did when we got together. The rest of the group moved on to a different topic without us, but Emily and Matt both listened as we teased each other about ex-boyfriends and ex-friends and ex-classmates.

"What was Sam like in college?" Em asked at one point.

"Pretty much the same," Sarah answered. She'd been brusque to Emily throughout the meal, and I was nearly ready to strangle her. I'd always known she could be overly analytical, critical, even, but she'd never before acted like that toward me.

"I think she's different," Tina said. "She was a lot quieter in college, more reserved."

"Right, 'cause now I'm a social butterfly," I put in.

Emily and Tina both laughed, but Sarah didn't seem to get the joke.

Once our food had digested somewhat, Emily and I took to the beach with towels and sunscreen. She asked me to put lotion on her back and I obliged, rubbing the liquid in slowly. Her skin, tanned and dotted with an occasional freckle, was smooth and warm beneath my fingers.

I leaned forward and murmured, "It'll be nice when we're alone."

"No kidding. How long do we have to stay at this shindig?"

"We'll see."

She offered to return the favor. I sat back, unable to talk at the feel of her hands on my skin. The peace was there, along with something else. I shivered a little and heard her laugh quietly from behind me.

"Hey, now," I said, and took the bottle away from her.

She sat back beside me and watched Matt and his drummer, Tyler, tossing a Frisbee nearby.

"Do you want to join them?" I asked.

"You don't mind?"

"Of course not."

"Cool." She leaned toward me then backed off. "Whoa. I was about to kiss you." She rocked back on her heels and touched the top of my head as she walked away. "See ya."

I watched her walk across the sand. Her one-piece racing suit and shorts revealed her body nicely. I was looking forward to peeling that suit down her stomach, over her legs, past her toes. Then she'd be naked and all mine—to do what with? I sighed and lay back on my towel. The question of the day.

As the afternoon progressed, I napped in the sun, played beach volleyball, tossed the Frisbee and walked on the beach with Tina and Emily. Bainbridge Island and the Olympic Mountains were visible across Puget Sound. White sails dotted the water between Golden Gardens and Bainbridge, and the day was clear enough to make out details on the distant, snow-topped mountains. Seattle could be home for a while, I thought at one point as Emily and I walked along the edge of the water together, close enough that our arms brushed with each step. Not far away, a two-person slip glided into the harbor at the southern edge of the park.

"I love sailing," Emily volunteered. At my look, she added, "What—don't I look like the yachting type?"

"Not exactly."

"Jenna's family had a vacation house in Holland. I used to go out there with them in the summers and do the beach thing."

I hesitated. "You and Jenna were together in high school, weren't you?"

"Yeah." Emily squinted at a boat moored near shore.

"What happened?"

"She wanted to be straight and I didn't. It's weird to think you'll be back there next week."

"I know." I looked down at our feet, moving in unison across the packed sand at water's edge.

"I don't think I'm going to like having you gone," she said. "I just got used to having you around."

I smiled over at her. "I know what you mean."

"Do you need a ride to the airport?"

"Tina's taking me," I said, "and checking in on Chloe while I'm gone. But you could pick me up. My plane comes in on Sunday night."

She leaned into my shoulder. "It's a date."

We walked on until we reached the southern edge of the beach then returned the way we'd come. The sun was still high in the western sky, and light skipped across the water's rolling surface. Just before we reached the others, Emily checked her watch. "It's almost six. I have an idea."

"Let's hear it." If she was thinking what I was thinking, her idea would involve leaving Golden Gardens very soon.

"How about we make our excuses and head back to your place?"

And then...? "Sounds like a plan." I reached over and pecked her on the cheek. "Race you," I added, and sprinted away.

She caught up to me right at the end. Tina, Matt and Sarah watched us collapse giggling on our towels. Tina and Matt were smiling, but Sarah didn't appear amused. I stopped laughing and looked at her, but she wouldn't meet my eyes. What was her deal?

Emily elbowed me unsubtly.

"Thanks for everything," I said to Tina. "I think we're going to hit the road."

"But we're going to have a bonfire and watch the fireworks later," Matt said.

Tina ignored him. "I'm glad you could come. Emily, it was really great meeting you."

We packed up our things and said goodbye to the rest of the group. Various people waved. Tina said she'd call me. But Sarah didn't say anything at all as Emily and I shouldered our bags and headed for the parking lot.

"What an awesome day," Em said when we reached the truck. "Wasn't it?"

She waited until the key was in the ignition. Then she leaned in and said, "Thanks for bringing me, Sam. It means a lot." She kissed me softly.

I closed my eyes against the world outside my truck and kissed her back. She was starting to taste and feel familiar, and I didn't want to stop. But the gearshift was digging into my hip, and sounds beyond the truck were seeping in through the open windows. Emily pulled away and we grinned at each other so widely that my face hurt.

"What do you want to do about dinner?" she asked as we left

the parking lot.

"I still have leftovers from the other night. There's salad stuff, too, and some wine." Half a bottle—just enough to get me brave enough to do whatever it was we would end up doing together.

"Sounds good to me."

I drove home faster than I usually did, Emily's hand in mine. Outside my building I stopped the truck and hopped out of the cab. Em circled around to my side. "You okay?" she asked.

"Better than okay." I guided her toward my building.

Chloe was waiting just inside the door. She saw us and meowed, rolled over on her back and exposed her tummy for someone, anyone to rub. Emily sprawled headlong on the living room rug to oblige. I could hear the cat purring as I pulled my key from the door. I turned the bolt and stood there, watching Emily play with the cat. Now what?

I needed to relax. I flopped down on the floor next to them. Emily stopped petting Chloe and turned on her side to face me. She lifted her hand and touched my cheek. "So...?"

"So." I moved closer to her on the rug, glad I had vacuumed recently, and slid my hand along the curve of her waist. She was soft but firm, too. I was starting to get used to this.

She caught my hand and intertwined it with hers. "Here we are on your living room floor."

"Yes." I stared at her, wishing I could slow the pounding of my heart. Why was I so freaked out?

She leaned forward and pressed her lips lightly against mine. She tasted of suntan lotion and beer. I kissed her back, hoping I didn't have Dorito breath. Then I forgot to worry about my breath as her hand slipped down, following the outline of my body from shoulder to hip.

"You have great legs," she said, resting her palm on the outside of my thigh.

My stomach fluttered. "So do you."

She pulled back a little. "Do you remember the first soccer game you came to? I could have sworn I caught you checking me out afterward when we were walking to the parking lot."

I nodded. "I was still trying to convince myself I wasn't attracted to you."

"Not trying to convince yourself anymore?" she asked.

"No." I met her eyes. "Not anymore."

"When did you realize?"

"High school."

"What?" She pulled back further and stared at me.

"Okay, I guess I didn't really admit it to myself until recently."

"How recently?"

"I don't know. Earlier in the week, I guess."

"This week? Wow." She sat up and stroked Chloe, who purred in appreciation.

I sat up too. "Did I say something wrong?"

"No, I just don't want you to do anything you're not ready to do."

"I won't," I said. "I know what I want."

"What's that?" she asked, her eyes on mine.

"You," I said, ignoring my unsteady stomach.

"You're sure?"

"Yes, Em. I'm sure."

She moved closer then and started kissing me again. Softly at first, then more and more insistently. I wrapped my arms around her and held on. But Chloe, apparently miffed at being ignored, meowed and butted her head against us. We both started laughing. Emily leaned away to pat Chloe on the head.

"It's okay," she told the cat. "I'm not going to hurt her."

I hoped not. "So. Dinner?"

"Sure."

Emily and Chloe followed me into the kitchen and hung out together while I bustled about, nuking leftovers and whipping up a quick salad. I poured the wine, set out plates and silverware and checked on the stir-fry. I had just hit the start button on the microwave when I felt Emily behind me. She slid her arms around my waist and kissed the back of my neck. I leaned into her, covering her hands with my own. I had never felt this good before. Was this what my brother had felt with Alan? I hoped so. I hoped he had had at least a few years of happiness.

We ate quickly, perched at the bar. Gulped down wine, swallowed leaves of lettuce nearly whole, grinned at each other over the stir-fry we had made together two nights before. I watched her movements, admired the ripple of muscle in her forearms, imagined her hands on my body. The idea that she had been with other women was disturbing and reassuring all at once. But what if I was terrible in bed? Would I even know?

Neither of us finished dinner. We left the dishes in the sink and headed into the living room. I stopped near the coffee table. Em was already close and moved closer still, her hands on my waist.

"Thanks for feeding me," she said.

"My pleasure." I felt myself blush. "I feel kind of gross from the beach. I was thinking maybe we could shower."

"Together?"

"Um, I don't know." My blush deepened.

"Just kidding," she said. "A shower sounds great."

"Do you want to go first?" I offered.

"Okay." Backpack slung over one shoulder, she disappeared into the bathroom.

While she cleaned up, I selected the playlist I'd compiled that morning on iTunes—Ella Fitzgerald and Louis Armstrong, Enya and Loreena McKennitt, Indigo Girls and Sarah McLachlan—and hit shuffle. By the time I picked out clean clothes, Emily had emerged from the bathroom dressed in a T-shirt and shorts, her skin rosy from the shower, damp hair falling across her forehead.

"I used some of your toothpaste," she said. "Hope you don't mind."

"Not at all." I brushed past her. "I'll be right out."

I showered almost as quickly as she had, taking a little time afterward to examine my body in the mirror. I didn't have much upper body in terms of bulk, not like Emily, but I was toned all over. I hoped she would like me, even if I didn't have the same body I'd had last time we were naked together in the Logan High locker room.

I brushed my teeth and pulled on my clothes. Good to go. I paused, hand on the doorknob, and took one last look at my reflection. Here went...something. I opened the door.

Chapter Twenty

~EMILY~

At her apartment Saturday night, Sam showered after I did. I almost asked if she needed help scrubbing her back, but I didn't think she was in much of a joking mood. Not that I was. Laughter just sometimes helps ease tension. And there was definitely tension, on both our parts. I'd done this a thousand times (okay, not literally) but had never cared about anyone as much as I cared about Sam. I wanted everything to be right.

While she showered, I distracted myself with a book from the coffee table, a beautiful, glossy collection of excerpts from the works of various women journalists. Inside the front cover an inscription read, "To Sam, my favorite writer. Happy Holidays! Love, Tina."

The date of the inscription was Christmas a year and a half before when Sam had still been working at the *Tribune*. I leafed through the book and studied the essays, which ranged from political exposés to depictions of homeless women and children.

I hadn't known Sam all that well in high school, but I did know she wanted to be a journalist when she grew up. Everyone knew that. So why had she given up her dream job to move to a city she'd never even seen? I still didn't get it.

She did have friends here, though. I liked Tina, a smart, semi-punk Seattle girl with bright hair and clunky glasses. Sarah, their other college buddy, I wasn't so sure about. She'd watched me all afternoon as if I were a parasite attached to Sam. I'd ignored the looks. They came with the territory.

I was reading an essay on Thai sex slaves when Sam came out of the bathroom clad in shorts and a T-shirt, damp hair loose about her shoulders.

"Hey," I said, setting the book back on the coffee table.

"Hey." She stopped between the entryway and the living room looking like she might bolt at any moment, eyes wide and hands restless at her sides.

I decided to offer her a way out. "I never asked, did you want to go somewhere to watch fireworks?"

She shook her head. "No, I don't want to go anywhere."

I stood up and moved across the room toward her, slowly. I felt like I was approaching a flighty animal. Stopping before her, I held out my hand. An Ella Fitzgerald song was playing. "Would you like to dance?" I asked.

She hesitated, then took my hand. "Okay."

Drifting closer, I rested one hand on her waist. She put her other hand on my shoulder and we moved together to the music, shuffling slowly around the room. After a minute her hand shifted to the back of my neck, and I felt her fingers smoothing my hairline. My cheek brushed against hers. Dancing had never felt quite like this.

We swayed together for a while, Chloe stalking our legs. After we tripped over her a third time, Sam laughed and shooed the cat away. "I knew she'd be jealous."

"She just loves you."

She squinted at me as if she were trying to figure something out.

"You know, nothing has to happen," I said. "It's your call. Whatever you decide is fine with me."

She nodded.

Backing off, I wandered over to the desk in the corner, checking the iTunes playlist on the computer. I hadn't heard this Ella CD before, one of the Best Of series. Sam had good taste. As if I hadn't already figured that out.

She came up behind me and rested her chin against my shoulder. "I'm sorry. I'm just nervous. I don't really know what to do."

"It's okay. Just do what you want."

"Yeah?"

"Yeah." I turned and kissed her, gently, slowly. Didn't want to scare her off. But somehow she didn't seem as scared now. She kissed me back and ran her hands down the length of my body. If I hadn't known better, I would have thought she knew exactly what to do.

We stayed in the living room for a while. I discovered that Sam wasn't wearing a bra; neither was I. Her breath caught audibly when I brushed one hand lightly over her breast. Then she slid her hand under my shirt and kissed me harder.

Eventually she pulled back. "Do you want to go into the bedroom?"

"Okay."

I let her lead me into the other room where she lit a candle on her dresser. Chloe jumped up beside it and watched us, her tail flicking spasmodically. Sam turned out the overhead light and faced me. "Emily."

I moved closer, slid my arms around her waist and buried my face in her damp hair. She smelled so good. "Are you sure?" I asked one last time.

"Yes." And she kissed me so that I would feel just how certain she was.

Afterward, I held her close, our naked bodies entwined on her bed, and murmured softly to her as she cried. "You're okay," I said, kissing her hair. "I've got you." Then it occurred to me that I might have hurt her. It had been a while since anyone had touched her, and though I had tried to be gentle, it was hard to keep myself in check. This was Sam, after all, the woman I'd wanted since before I knew what sex was. "Did I hurt you?"

"No," she said against my neck. "No, I just—I've never..." She stopped, then said, "I got your neck all wet."

"It's okay. I'm waterproof."

She rolled on top of me, rising up on her elbows. In the candlelight she was very serious and so beautiful I couldn't keep from staring at her. "I'm sorry," she said. "I just didn't know it could feel like that."

"You don't have to be sorry."

She eased down on top of me, her face near mine. "I want you to feel it too. Tell me what you like."

Soon I was lost in the feel of her hands and mouth on my body. *She's new at this?* was my last clear thought before I gave myself over to her in a way I was certain I had never done with anyone else. I just let go, and at the end of it she was beside me kissing my forehead, my eyes, my cheeks, my lips.

"I love—" she started.

I looked at her quickly.

"—being with you," she finished, and kissed me again.

"I love being with you too," I said against her lips. I cradled her against my side, rested my cheek on her shoulder, shut my eyes. I was so sleepy. And so friggin' happy. This was perfect. She was perfect.

"Are you smiling?" she asked.

"Um-hmm."

"Are you asleep?"

"No." I lifted my eyelids with difficulty.

"That's what I thought." She blew out the candle and slid down on the bed beside me again. "Good night, Emily."

I moved closer. "Good night, Sam."

Chapter Twenty-One

~SAM~

The first thing I was aware of when I woke up was Emily. I was holding her from behind, our bodies curved together in the half-light, naked beneath my comforter. The next thing I noticed was Chloe meowing in the hallway outside the bedroom. No doubt she was the alarm clock that had awakened me.

The night came back to me—Emily's gentleness, my tears, the way she had opened to me. I hugged her tighter and she stirred, murmuring something unintelligible. I kissed the warm skin at her neck and pulled away. The feeling of peace was transforming into something else, something closer to need. I just wasn't sure I was ready to need Emily Mackenzie. She was so young. By her own admission, she hadn't had any serious relationships since high school. Not that I was exactly an expert. But these days I often felt closer to a hundred than twenty-five. What if Emily was looking for something casual? I didn't do casual.

Slipping from bed, I tucked the covers over her and pulled

on a T-shirt and boxer shorts. I tidied up the room, opened the door as quietly as possible and picked up Chloe. It was early still, too early to wake Emily. Sunday was the only morning she got to sleep in.

I carried my purring feline into the kitchen, fed her and stood at the kitchen window looking out over Fiftieth Street. Soon minivans would swarm the block, transporting families from all over Seattle and the outskirts to stroll among the caged animals that lived across the street from me. I turned away from the window and stretched. My body felt different today, not quite my own. My muscles seemed longer, looser. For once, I had awakened feeling more serene than not.

I turned on the coffee machine and jogged downstairs for the Sunday newspaper. On the elevator back up, I skimmed the headlines. I was unlocking my apartment door when I heard my phone. Hurrying into the kitchen, I caught it on the second ring.

"Sam, honey, it's Mom."

I set the paper on the counter and glanced at the clock on the wall—not even eight yet. I hoped she hadn't disturbed Emily. "Mom, do you know what time it is on the West Coast?"

"I'm sorry, sweetie, I forgot again. Half the day is already gone here. Did I wake you?"

"No." I slid onto a bar stool and swung around to look out the kitchen window. "Chloe woke me up a little while ago."

"Chloe—oh, your cat," my mother said.

I wanted to ask her who she thought Chloe was if not my cat. I had an urge to confirm her worst fears, to inform her that there was in fact a naked woman in my bed. "What's up?"

"I wanted to run an idea by you. I was wondering if maybe I could come meet you in Chicago. I thought I could take the train in, you know how I love that ride, and spend a night or two there with you. Just the two of us."

It was news to me that she loved the train ride between Logan and Chicago. She had never visited me on her own, not when I was at Northwestern, not even when I lived in Chicago after college. Then again, I didn't know that I'd ever invited her. "It should be okay. I think my hotel room is a double."

"Are you sure? I don't want to intrude."

"You wouldn't be intruding," I said, even though I'd been looking forward to spending some time in Chicago by myself. "I'll just be working a lot. I won't be able to hang out with you much."

"That's fine. Now, what day should I come in?"

We worked out the details—she would join me in Chicago Wednesday night and stay through the end of my conference on Friday. Then we would take the commuter train together to Logan. I gave her my hotel information and offered to meet her at the train station Wednesday evening, but she insisted she would catch a cab to the hotel. She didn't want to put me out.

"You're not putting me out," I assured her.

"Good." She paused. "You're talking awfully quietly, Sam. I'm not interrupting anything, am I?"

"No, Mom. You're not interrupting." And, technically, she wasn't. Everything that might have happened between Emily and me had already happened.

"You still haven't met someone? I hear Seattle's quite the young city."

Just when I thought we could have a normal conversation, she had to go and ruin it. Again, I was tempted to tell her the truth. But maybe coming out wasn't something you did over the telephone, especially not when your parents had lost their only other child to the "Gay Plague," as AIDS had been called in the beginning. "No, Mom, sorry to disappoint you. No one's here. I was just about to read the paper over coffee by myself."

"Well, I'll let you get back to your breakfast, then. Call me Tuesday and let me know when you get in, okay, Sammy?"

My hand tightened on the phone. Only Chris ever called me that. "Uh-huh. I'll talk to you soon."

I hung up first, set the phone down next to the newspaper and stared out the window. She was so desperate for some sort of involvement in my life. She hadn't been like this before Chris ran away or after he reappeared. It wasn't until he died that she turned her attention back to me. Not that I was jealous of Chris. I was happier when our mother wasn't focused on my life.

The coffee had finished percolating. I turned toward the counter and caught sight of Em standing in the kitchen doorway. She was watching me, and I smiled at seeing her, I couldn't help it. She looked so cute with her messy hair, blinking at me like Chloe always did when she first woke up. "Hey you. How did you sleep?" I asked.

"Fine," she said, but looked away from my smile.

Something was clearly wrong. And I wondered: How long had she been standing there? "You heard that, didn't you?"

She didn't answer at first. I couldn't believe she would consider lying to me, but she did have a fairly decent reason. I could only imagine how it must have sounded. "Look," I said, "I'm sorry but my mother and I aren't close. I don't share anything personal with her as a general rule. It has nothing to do with you."

Emily just nodded, her eyes flat like the other day on her porch before we made up. I sat quietly for a moment, wishing I could step back ten minutes and miss my mother's phone call. Why did she have to call this morning?

Our standoff ended when Chloe crossed the kitchen floor and twined herself around Emily's legs. This reminded me that, really, all I wanted to do was follow my cat's lead. "Would you like some coffee?" I asked.

But Chloe had not succeeded in softening up Emily, who shrugged off my question.

"Juice?" I asked, borderline panicking.

"No, thanks."

I considered dropkicking her across the kitchen. But that didn't seem productive either. "I apologized already, Em. What else do you want me to do? I haven't done any of this before, you know."

At this, she relented, crossed the room, and hugged me finally.

203

"I know," she said. "I'm sorry." Some of the tension drained from her when she touched me, I could tell, but she wasn't the same Emily I had fallen asleep with. She wasn't even the same person I'd awakened to this morning. And it was all my fault.

When I invited her to stay for breakfast, for some reason—pity?—she agreed. Over coffee and bagels and the Sunday *Times*, she was polite but not entirely present. I could only sit back and wait out her withdrawal. She deserved to be with someone who was comfortable with her identity, someone who didn't flinch away from the word "lesbian." Someone, obviously, who wasn't me.

After breakfast, she went to stand next to the living room window, beyond which another busy day had commenced at the zoo. Turning abruptly, she fixed me with a slight frown and announced, "I have to get going."

I tried to make my eyes go flat like hers, but I thought she could probably see the effect her words had on me anyway. I smoothed a hand over my boxers. "All right." Maybe she had plans. And then I remembered—Friday night she'd gone out with someone else, probably a woman who was more comfortable being gay than I was.

As I stood silently by, she slipped on her Tevas and shouldered her backpack. "I guess I'll talk to you later, then," she said.

After a second, I walked over to her. "Is it okay if I hug you?"

"Of course."

As soon as I put my arms around her I felt her body loosen like before, and her arms came around me as if she didn't want to go, as if she wanted to stay here with me in my apartment, Chloe nestled on the couch between us. In my arms, she was mine again.

But then she pulled back. I didn't want to let her go, but if she stayed any longer, it would just get ugly. Uglier.

"Bye," she said, barely looking at me, and let herself out.

With the closing door, I felt a small, acute loss click into place in my chest. Emily was gone. Until now, I had managed to forget about the woman she was with on Friday. But as I looked back on the previous night's events, upon the disaster this morning had turned into, I couldn't ignore reality. Maybe Emily simply wanted to be with this other woman more.

Chloe sat with her back to me, licked her paw and brushed an ear with it. Then she spun around and sauntered down the hallway toward the bedroom. I turned back to the newspaper, but I couldn't focus on the words. Nothing had sunk in since I'd started reading. I lay down on the couch and shut my eyes, remembering what it had felt like to wake up with Emily in my arms. I wanted her to come back. I wanted her to want to be with me. I could have sworn she'd felt it the night before. Why couldn't my mother have called while I was downstairs picking up the paper? Then she would have left a message and I never would have talked to her and Emily never would have heard me lying about her presence in my apartment. In my life.

I fell asleep on the couch and dreamed restless dreams, woke up later and turned on the TV. I channel-surfed for a while, until all at once I couldn't stand being in my apartment another second.

I called Tina. "What are you doing?"

"Sleeping," she said, and yawned.

"Take a shower. You have half an hour. We're going shopping."

"Good morning to you too. What if I don't want to go shopping?"

I knew she was teasing, but my sense of humor was missing in action. "You have to come. Things kind of fell apart with Emily this morning."

"Oh. Well, that's different," Tina said. "Come get me."

I hung up the phone and looked around my apartment. There on the floor at the edge of the living room was where Emily and I had kissed the night before. There by the entertainment center, too. Not to mention what had gone on in the bedroom... I had to get out.

A little while later I pulled up in front of Tina's building. She was outside, sitting with Matt on the front steps. They kissed, and he waved at me and strolled off down the sidewalk.

"I'm sorry," I said when Tina slid in beside me. "Did you guys have plans?"

"No." She leaned over and half-hugged me. "Anyway, he knows my friends come first."

I guided the truck through the narrow, car-jammed streets of the west side of Capitol Hill and down onto I-5.

"Where to?" Tina asked.

"I was thinking the Supermall. Sound okay?"

"Fabulous. Have credit cards, will spend. But what happened? You two seemed great yesterday."

So I told her about going back to my place and Emily spending the night, leaving out details, of course, despite her prodding. I explained how I had let Emily sleep in and how my mother's phone call had wrecked everything.

"She left?" Tina said. "Just like that?"

"Yeah, but I don't blame her. She deserves someone, you know, further along than I am."

"Sounds to me like she freaked out. She didn't say anything about never wanting to see you again, did she?"

"No, we didn't fight at all."

"This is not irreparable," Tina announced. "Trust me. This is just a little speed bump on the road to love."

The metaphor made me smile, though only a little. "What makes you say that?"

"I saw how you were with her, Sam. I haven't seen you that happy since, I don't know, maybe not ever. And I saw how she was with you. The feeling is entirely mutual."

We were on I-5 south of the city now, nearing Boeing's airfield. "I don't know," I said. "What if I'm not good for her, though? I have all this baggage, and I'm new at the whole gay thing."

"Everyone has baggage. Matt has this ex-girlfriend who really fucked him up. She stole a couple of his guitars and sold

206

them for drug money."

"What kind of drugs?"

"Coke and speed." Tina patted my arm. "Don't worry, nothing with needles. Anyway, my point is that no one is going to come undamaged into any relationship, you know? Emily obviously has her own skeletons."

"Maybe. There's something else, though. I think she might be dating someone else."

"Wait, what?"

"I think she went out on a date Friday night."

"You're kidding," Tina said. "Dang, girl. You must really like her if you knew that and made a play for her anyway."

Hearing Tina say it out loud made me realize it was true—I was the one who had made all the moves. Emily had just gone along. Oh, God, what if she had slept with me because I practically begged her to? She had said more than once that nothing had to happen. Had she felt sorry for me? Was that why she'd been hanging out with me?

"Let's talk about something else," I said.

"I didn't mean—" Tina started.

I held up my hand. "Please? I can't think about it anymore. Let's just, I don't know. How did Matt like his party? Let's talk about the party."

She hesitated but let me change the subject. We rehashed Matt's birthday bash the rest of the way. He loved it, Tina told me, and she'd felt as if the blending of their friends had occurred seamlessly. Almost.

"You know what Sarah said to me?" she asked as we pulled into the parking lot of the Supermall, a huge indoor mall of discount stores.

I stopped the truck, not sure I wanted to know. "What?"

"She basically blamed me for you hooking up with Emily. She said I'm always trying to convince you to do things that aren't good for you."

"You are," I said. "Just not this time."

"Whatever. Come on, girlfriend. Let's go get you some retail therapy."

I locked the truck, and Tina slipped her arm through mine. As I let her lead me across the parking lot, I wondered what Emily was doing. Whatever it was, she had made it pretty clear this morning that she didn't want to be with me. Apparently I would have to accept that we weren't going to be together after all.

That idea would take some getting used to, I thought as Tina and I entered the cavernous, air-conditioned expanse of the Supermall.

Chapter Twenty-Two

~ EMILY ~

When I left Sam's apartment, I didn't wait for the elevator but ran down the emergency stairs and out into the cool morning. Clouds had blown in, blocking the sun. Chilled in my shorts and T-shirt, I jogged across Fiftieth Street to the zoo and ran through the park to Green Lake. There I slowed and walked around the south end of the lake, trying to figure out how the elation of the previous day and night had turned into the trepidation currently twisting my stomach. Maybe it had started when I woke up alone in her bed, my clothes still on the floor where they'd fallen the night before. Her clothes, like Sam herself, were nowhere to be seen.

I'd stayed in bed for a little while, waiting to see if she would return. But no sound leaked through the bedroom door. For all I knew, I was alone in her apartment. So I dressed in my discarded clothing, shivering in the cool morning air, and pulled the comforter up over the tangled sheets. Now there was no trace of me left in her room. Maybe that was what she wanted. Liz and Jessie's warnings about straight girls came back to me then, and I remembered my own assurances that Sam wasn't like other women. Sam was different.

Then the phone call and the sourness in my gut when I heard her talking with her mother on the phone, denying anyone was there with her. I'd tried to let it go, tried to recreate the feeling I'd had earlier that morning when I first woke in the dark to find Sam holding me from behind, our bodies connected from shoulder to knee. But all through breakfast I couldn't shake the ice that had me in its grip. What was I doing? Why did it matter that she had lied about me to her mother?

But it did matter, just like it had the first night when I came over and she didn't tell her mom on the phone that it was me watching the Mariners game with her. Sam couldn't help that up until now she had thought she was straight, but I also couldn't help that I had busted out of my closet four years before and had no intention of going back in now. If Sam and I were going to be together, it was going to have to be all the way. And that was why Liz had been right.

Rollerbladers and Sunday morning walkers passed me, moving with purpose around the lake, laughing together and holding hands. That could have been me, I thought. If only I could fall for an actual lesbian.

At home again, I crept upstairs, stepped out of my sandals and flopped across my comforter cover. Exhausted from the morning's melodrama, I fell asleep, cedar tree beyond my window quietly creaking.

* * *

When I woke up again it was past noon. I lay on my back for a little while, staring up at the tapestry overhead. Life sucked. Sam sucked. And yet in a way I was relieved to be alone. The night before had been wonderful, but I hadn't relinquished control like that since Jenna. I'd sworn not to get that wrapped up in someone ever again—it only left you vulnerable to getting dicked over.

Of course, it also brought happiness of a degree I'd never managed to feel alone, I had to admit. I liked life. I liked soccer and dancing and nature and sunny days. All of those things made me happy. But the feeling I had when I was with Sam was unlike anything else.

I rolled off my bed and changed T-shirts. This one smelled too much like her. I threw it in the dirty clothes basket, hesitated, then plucked it from the pile and set it on a shelf in my closet. I pulled on a clean shirt and padded downstairs. Liz was lying on the couch, watching tennis on TV.

"Hey, dog," she said. "How did your night go?"

I dropped onto the recliner. "Great."

"What happened? You look like shit."

"Thanks, I feel like shit. Who's playing?"

"Venus Williams and Maria Sharapova. I swear, tennis players keep getting better looking."

I glowered at the TV screen. Good-looking women only caused problems.

"You okay?" she asked.

"No."

"Want to talk about it?"

"Nope."

We watched the match in silence. Even Sharapova's pout and Venus Williams's lithe body didn't interest me today.

"I slept with Sam last night," I said finally.

"Yeah?"

"Yeah. But then this morning I heard her tell her mother on the phone that no one was there, that she was having coffee alone. She lied practically in my face."

Liz considered this for a moment. "That's rough. But correct me if I'm wrong—you are the first woman she's ever slept with, aren't you?"

"Well, yeah. I mean, I think so."

"And last night was your first time together?"

"Yes." I could see where she was headed. I waved a hand, hoping it would shut her up. "Let's just watch tennis."

"You started this, little buddy. Tell me, when did you come out to your parents?"

"You already know that."

"Exactly—you were seventeen. And you and what's-her-face had been together for, what, two years before that?"

I sat up straighter. "Look, I get it, okay? I'm a shithead for not being more understanding. But I can't do it, Liz. I can't live in a closet."

"You wouldn't be living in a closet. She took you to meet her friends yesterday, didn't she?"

Another good point. Sam had even told Tina about us before anything really happened. Turned out I was just an asshole. But we already knew that.

Liz let me brood on this one before adding, "Nothing is ever going to be perfect. And just because Sam has taken a tumble from her pedestal doesn't mean you can't salvage this. You just have to figure out what you want and be happy with it. You know?"

"I get it," I said, and stood up. "You're right, I'm a jackass. I'm sorry, not all of us can be perfect."

"Come on, Mac."

I shook my head and retreated upstairs. I wasn't really angry with Liz. I just wanted to rewind to when I'd woken up in Sam's bed the first time, to get back that feeling of perfect well-being, smashed by her mother's phone call. I should have been able to get over it, should have been able to let go of the moment when I heard her lie and my stomach turned over. Liz was right; nothing was ever going to be perfect. But hearing Sam call me "no one" had hurt. I so wanted her to feel about me the way I felt about her. With Jenna, I'd practiced invisibility for so long that eventually I had become invisible even to myself. Shortly after she left me, I'd walked out onto a bridge over the freeway near our high school and stood at the edge watching cars rush past beneath me, imagining what it would feel like to climb over and let go.

Besides the fact that I could never have done that to my family—not to mention to some unsuspecting freeway driver—I didn't really have it in me to give up like that. But I still remembered the desperate need to escape I'd felt when I lost Jenna, and my utter inability to do so. I didn't ever want to feel like that again.

I lay on my bed watching tree branches from my window wave in the afternoon breeze. I should eat lunch, but I wasn't hungry. Sam must hate me by now. No one had forced me to come out. Of course she should take the time she needed to figure out how to talk to her parents. I'd just wanted to wake up beside her and kiss her and know that she wanted me there as much I wanted to be there.

Suddenly I wanted to be back at her apartment, to hold her and tell her everything would be okay, and mean it, like I should have done that morning. She was leaving for Chicago on Tuesday. I couldn't let her go without telling her I hadn't meant to be such a jerk.

Mind made up, I hurried downstairs, climbed on my bike and raced the short distance to her building, arriving out of breath and sweating. I leaned on the buzzer and waited, but there was no answer. I went and stood under her window.

"Sam!" I shouted. "Sam Delaney!"

But the only response I received were frightened looks from people headed into the zoo parking lot. Apparently Sam wasn't home.

I sat down on her front stoop to wait, remembering how she had come to my house a few nights before. What was wrong with us? Why couldn't we seem to move forward without retreating? I pulled my cell from my shorts pocket and dialed her number. The machine picked up.

"Hi, it's me," I said, and paused. I should have thought through what I wanted to say. "Um, I just wanted to call and apologize for the way I left this morning. I just, I don't know, I guess I was uncomfortable. Anyway, call me, will you? I'd really like to talk to you. Okay, bye."

I ended the call, wishing I could retract the message. Uncomfortable? What the hell was that? I sounded like an idiot. And I hadn't managed to say what I felt. I should have kept it simple—an "I'm sorry" and a "Please call me," and not much more. Aargh.

After forty-five minutes, I had chewed down all of my fingernails and was starving. I biked home through the park, debating what to do next. My only option seemed to be to wait and see if she would call me back. If she didn't—well, I could cross that bridge if and when I came to it.

The rest of the day crept by as I waited for Sam's call. Kristin picked me up at three for our soccer game. Unsurprisingly, Sam didn't show up, and I muttered a random excuse when Anna asked me where she was. I left my cell on during the game and manually checked voice mail at halftime, but no dice. Also unsurprisingly, I played like crap. We won anyway. Not surprising as we were the only team in the league stacked with Division I college players.

Kris wanted to go to Pagliacci's afterward with the team, so I was stuck going. Cell phone on the table in front of me, I moped through dinner as my teammates chatted and laughed. Back home, I lay on my bed for a while looking at nothing and replaying in my head every painful moment from the morning. After an hour or two of this, I carried my cell into the bathroom. I needed a shower but didn't want to miss her call. Of course, she would have had to call for me to miss it. Clean again a little while later, I tried to read my bike repair manual, and still Sam didn't call. I wandered downstairs, phone in my sweatshirt pocket, and hung out with Liz watching a baseball game. Sam liked the Mariners. Why hadn't she called?

During the seventh-inning stretch, I headed back upstairs.

I was thinking about hopping on my bike and heading up to Phinney Ridge when my cell phone rang. I almost dropped it, then punched the talk button before my brain could register the ring tone.

"Mac? It's Katie."

Not Sam. Fortunately, I had call waiting.

She asked how my weekend had gone, and I told her fine but didn't offer any details. While I wasn't exactly looking for anything to happen with Katie, it was still bad manners to tell a woman who is interested in you that you'd slept with someone else since the last time you saw each other. I asked about her weekend and she told me she had gone windsurfing with friends the day before at Lake Washington. "Have you ever tried it?" she asked.

"No." I was on my side facing the window now. The sky had been cloudy all day with what Seattle meteorologists liked to call sun breaks. Now the clouds were moving on and the sky was the blue I loved just before dark. Why didn't she call?

"Well, you should try it some time," Katie said.

"Definitely," I said. "Actually, I'm sorry, I have to go. Can I talk to you in a day or two?"

"Oh, yeah, okay."

I could tell from her tone that she thought she was being blown off, and who could blame her? But I didn't want her to think that, even if it was true. So I said, "Are you planning on going to Aster Place for Taco Thursday? Maybe I could meet you there."

"Really?" Her voice perked up. "That'd be nice, Mac. Give me a call and we'll figure it out."

As soon as we hung up I checked my voice mail, just in case she'd called at the exact same moment Katie had and call waiting wasn't available. But no messages. No Sam.

Obviously I was going to have to either go over there or call her again and hope she picked up. The latter option seemed less scary, so I listened to some Queen Latifah to get psyched and

215

went over what I wanted to say ("I'm sorry, why haven't you called, why don't you love me"—or something like that). It was getting late. If I didn't call soon, I wouldn't be calling tonight at all. I opened my cell phone and stared at the glowing wallpaper, a picture of me, Mel and Kristin from the previous season, my last at U-Dub. Did I really want to do this? I wasn't convinced.

I found her number in my call history and hit Send. She picked up just before voice mail kicked in, her voice cool and remote. This wasn't going to be easy.

"Did you get my message earlier?" I asked.

"Yes."

"Why didn't you call back?"

"I didn't know what to say."

"Say what you want. Say what you're thinking." I looked out the window and listened to the sound of Sam breathing over the phone. She was so close. I could be at her house in five minutes, sitting on her couch, Chloe purring between us. It would be different from this morning. I would be different.

"Say something, at least," I said, unable to stand the silence.

"I don't know," she said, and her voice sounded like a stranger's. "Maybe this isn't going to work out."

I swallowed hard. "What do you mean?"

"It's okay, you don't have to worry. I'll be fine."

What was she talking about? "Sam, I said I was sorry."

"I know. I am too."

We sat quietly at our respective ends of the line, and I could imagine her in her fourth-floor living room, the window open to the cool evening, lights glowing on various electronics stashed throughout the room.

"Are you still dating that other woman?" she asked.

I hesitated, thinking of my earlier conversation with Katie. "Not really."

Her voice went from cool to cold. "I have to go."

"Wait, don't hang up," I said quickly. "It doesn't mean anything, okay?"

"Yes, it does. Just like what I said on the phone this morning means something. Maybe we should just take a step back, you know? Maybe we're getting ahead of ourselves."

There it was again—one step forward, two (at least) back. I pictured her the day I'd first seen her on the trail at Green Lake, when she ran past me and would have kept running if I hadn't called after her. I couldn't blame her now. I had pushed her away this morning when I should have taken her in my arms and told her how much she meant to me. To make matters worse, I couldn't deny that I was seeing someone else at the same time I was seeing her. What must she think?

"Maybe we should," I said quietly. "Step back, I mean."

"Fine," she said, her voice devoid of emotion.

I paused. "I guess I'll just talk to you when you get back from Chicago, then?"

"Sounds good."

But it didn't sound good to me, not at all. "Okay, then," I said, forcing my voice to remain steady. "I'll talk to you later. And Sam?"

"Yes?"

"Have a good time at home."

"Thanks. I will."

The line clicked, and I dropped my cell, rubbing my eyes. I hadn't cried over a girl since Jenna, a distinction I often congratulated myself on. What was it about women from Logan? How did they possess this power, this sway over me?

Soon enough Sam would be back in our hometown, sleeping under the same old trees that had watched each of us grow up and move away. I wondered what she would decide while she was away, how she would categorize our short-lived relationship. It wasn't too late to ride my bike over to Camelot, I told myself. But I wasn't sure she would see me now. And if she refused, what then?

I lay on my bed unmoving as the summer sun set and the streetlights flicked on outside my window one by one.

Chapter Twenty-Three

~SAM~

Chicago was not the same city I remembered. I had forgotten how big it was, how dirty, how hot. Usually when I thought of Chicago, I pictured the winter wind whipping off the lake, slicing between buildings to cut through even the heaviest outerwear. But now with the humidity making my shirt stick to the backseat of the cab I'd caught at O'Hare, winter seemed impossibly remote.

At my request, the taxi driver headed down Lake Shore Drive, past Lincoln Park and the zoo, past Navy Pier and over the Chicago River, which ran green every St. Patrick's Day. He dropped me in front of the Best Western Grant Park Hotel, within walking distance of McCormick Place Convention Center. It was mid-afternoon. I could check in, drop my stuff in my room and still have a few hours to check out the exhibit hall.

On the flight from Seattle, I'd read the first book of the *Chronicles of Narnia*, a series I liked to reread every few years, to keep myself from staring out the window obsessing about my last conversation with Emily. She'd seemed resistant to slowing things down and confused by my assertion that I would be fine. Was it possible I had misread the situation? Maybe Tina was right and Emily had just gotten scared Sunday morning. Maybe she wasn't in love with someone else. Regardless, I wouldn't be back in Seattle for nearly a week now. And anything could happen in a week.

For the next twenty-four hours, I would submerge myself in the Web convention, attending workshops and seminars on social networking sites, Web-based procurement systems and CMS, all the while dreading the moment I would have to return to my hotel to await the knock at the door announcing my mother's arrival.

* * *

That moment arrived, of course, too soon. And when it did, I opened my hotel room door and smiled. My mother enveloped me in a swirl of her orange cape, nearly knocking me over with her small wheeled suitcase. The scent of her flowery perfume reminded me of my last visit home. On Christmas Eve, she and my father had gotten loaded on eggnog. I came to regret my own abstinence when they started bickering about who had promised to pick up stocking stuffers for me. Needless to say, my stocking was only half-full Christmas morning. Good thing Chris had told me the truth about Santa when I was four.

"Come in," I said now.

"Thanks, sweetie." She deposited her bag on one of the beds and looked around. "This is nice. Your company is paying for all of this?"

"They better be." Now that she was here, the room felt different. To me, the plush carpeting, flat-panel TV and oversized tub with Jacuzzi jets represented luxury. But my mother had likely never stayed in a Best Western in her life. She was more of

219

a Marriott girl.

"You look wonderful," she said. "You've done well for yourself in Seattle, haven't you? I don't pretend to understand why you had to go so far away, but I am glad your life is working out so well. There's something enthralling about the West Coast, isn't there?"

"Um, sure," I said, and really focused on her for the first time. She looked older. Her hair was still the same ash blonde (she dyed the gray), her skin still as smooth (or at least, made up to appear so), her frame petite as ever beneath the orange cape and tailored pants. But she looked older about the eyes, with lines and shadows there I hadn't noticed before.

"How about we grab a quick drink at the hotel bar?" she suggested.

"I haven't eaten dinner yet."

"Neither have I." She laughed, a brittle sound that reminded me of breaking glass. That was new too. "I suppose we should take care of that first. You used to live here. Where should I treat us to dinner?"

We caught a cab to a Thai restaurant in Lincoln Park, an old favorite of mine. Yanisa, the owner's wife, still remembered me.

"Where have you been?" she asked as she seated us in a booth with a view of the street.

"I moved to Seattle," I told her, aware that my mother was watching the exchange closely. "Last summer."

Yanisa tsk-tsked me. "You went too far away. This is your sister?"

My mother laughed. "You're too kind. I'm her mother."

"Welcome to Thai House. I will bring you Thai salad while you look at the menu."

"Thanks, Yanisa," I said as she moved away.

"You're popular," my mother said, glancing over the yellow laminated menu. "You'd better order for both of us. I'm not that familiar with Oriental cuisine."

"Asian food," I corrected her.

She waved a hand. "I'm also not very good at political correctness. Your brother gave up on me long ago."

I discreetly checked my watch. We'd been together for close to an hour before she brought up Chris. Had to be a record.

Yanisa returned, and I ordered for both of us, nothing too spicy because my mother had lived all of her life in Michigan. After Yanisa approved the order and took our menus, my mother eyed the salad in front of her and delicately speared a piece of iceberg lettuce with her fork.

"What's new with you?" she asked. "Tell me all about your life in Seattle."

"It's pretty much the same as it was at Christmas."

"Well, then, tell me something I already know. What's a typical day like for you in Seattle?"

So I told her about my job, even though she had heard it before. She nodded and smiled in the right places. I told her I saw Tina and Sarah at least once a week, usually more. Then the appetizers arrived, chicken satay and vegetarian spring rolls. I dipped a strip of marinated chicken into peanut sauce and took a bite. The food was even better than I'd remembered.

"Your friend Sarah is still in school, isn't she?" my mother asked, picking at the chicken on her plate.

"She's almost done. She's planning to join the FBI when she finishes," I said, munching a spring roll. I should learn to cook Thai food. Maybe Emily—but I stopped the thought before it could fully form. A month before, my life had felt full enough. Now there was an Emily-shaped hole in it.

"The FBI." My mother shook her head. "I admire that girl for going after what she wants. What does your other friend do again?"

"Tina's working as a receptionist for a law firm, just until her acting career gets off the ground."

"Acting? Not the steadiest work, is it," my mother said. "Then again, after growing up in such a radical household, is it any wonder she has a hard time committing to a career?"

I experienced a sudden urge to pocket the appetizers and walk out, but I couldn't desert my mother in a neighborhood she didn't know. Besides, Yanisa would never forgive me. "Tina is going after what she wants, too, Mom. Which is more than I can say."

"Maybe being a journalist just wasn't the right path for you," she said. "I read that a person your age will likely have four different careers before he retires. You've already had two." She smiled at me and sipped her plum wine.

My mother's careers had been homemaker and serial volunteer. Over the years, she had served on the boards of more organizations than I could keep straight. And speaking of straight... I took a deep breath. "Guess who else I've been seeing in Seattle?"

"Not the Fitzgerald boy. I told you their oldest moved out there, didn't I? We're all losing our children to the West. One would think it was the pioneer era."

"Not Colin. Actually, Emily Mackenzie."

"Is that the soccer player?" my mother asked. "Or the smart one?"

I tried not to bristle at this characterization. "The soccer player. She was a freshman when I was a senior. But she's actually quite smart herself," I couldn't resist adding.

"You know she's, well, gay, don't you?"

"Yes, you already told me." So am I, I almost added. But I wasn't that brave. Or certain. "She lives near me. I've been seeing a lot of her. She recruited me to play on her soccer team."

"Recruited you?" My mother's eyebrows lowered at my choice of words. Then they lifted. "You're playing soccer again? Why, honey, that's wonderful! How long has this been going on? Why didn't you mention it before?"

"It's only been the last month or so."

"That's the change in you, then," she said, dabbing the corner of her mouth with a cloth napkin. "I knew there was something. I kept thinking you must have met someone, but you kept saying you hadn't."

I bit into another spring roll. She had just given me the perfect opening, but I wasn't ready to dive in just yet. Or to dive out, as the case may be. I still had to spend the next few days with her. It might be best to share the news right before I left. Less fallout to deal with in person.

Our entrées arrived—Pad Thai and sweet and sour tofu— and my mother prattled on about her various volunteer positions as we ate. I told her about the conference so far, we discussed which train to take to Logan, she told me it was good to see me happy.

I wished I could tell her why I wasn't happy, how afraid I was that Emily and I wouldn't be together. A few months before he died, Chris told me that he had tried to talk to our mother about Alan, his ex-boyfriend. She had stopped him, told him he should conserve his strength, said she had to make dinner. He never mentioned Alan to her again.

We finished dinner and caught a cab back to the hotel. I asked the driver to take Lake Shore Drive South. The lights of the city approached, the lake black and silent to our left. Soon we were in among the tall buildings. The skyline was so familiar and yet strange too. I had spent most of my adult life in this city. I'd grown up in Chicago. But I didn't belong here anymore. In the back of my mind was Seattle with its snow-peaked mountains, tree-lined lakes, evergreen hills. And Emily.

At the hotel, I dissuaded my mother from going for a drink at the bar. I was pleasantly buzzed from the wine with dinner, but she still seemed sober. In our room on the eleventh floor, she stood at the window looking out over Grant Park and Buckingham Fountain toward the nearby lights of Navy Pier.

"It's a big city, isn't it?" she said.

"Yeah." I picked up the television remote.

"Think of all of those people, all living different lives." She was holding the curtain to one side and looked so sad, I almost asked what was wrong. If she had been Tina or Sarah, I would have asked. But she was my mother. I flipped through the hotel TV stations.

Terms of Endearment was on. She lay next to me on top of the thin bedspread, and we watched the movie and shared a box of tissues. When Debra Winger's character died, my mother broke into wrenching sobs. I took her hand and held onto it when she tried to pull away. Her sobs quieted. She even seemed to like holding my hand after a while. As soon as the movie ended, though, she got up and went into the bathroom. When she came out again, she was makeup free and looked even older.

"It's all yours," she said.

By the time I finished getting ready for bed, she was tucked under the covers.

"Good night," I offered.

"Come give me a kiss."

My parents had stopped kissing me good night so long ago I couldn't remember the last time. I perched on the edge of her bed and leaned over to kiss her cheek. She smelled of Dove soap as she had at bedtime ever since I was a little girl. I couldn't smell Dove without thinking of her.

She kissed my cheek and held tightly to me. "I love you, Samantha."

"I love you, too."

I crawled between the sheets of my bed and turned off the lamp, plunging the room into darkness. I wasn't tired yet. It was only eight o'clock in Seattle. I wondered what Emily was doing. Was she out on another date? I punched my pillow into shape and listened to my mother breathing only a few feet away. I knew she was awake, just as she had to know I was. But neither of us said a word as the lights beyond the window blinked and flashed, those thousands of other lives my mother had noticed going on all around us, just out of sight.

* * *

My mom and I were in the back of a cab on the way to the train station Friday afternoon when she said, "What do you think about staying in Chicago for the weekend? We could shop and go to museums and have a nice time, just the two of us."

"What about Dad?" I asked, frowning.

"He'll probably have to work this weekend, anyway. There's an important case about to go to trial. There's always an important case going to trial."

I almost asked her what was going on. She wouldn't tell me where she had spent the previous day, and after dinner the night before she had treated me to a drink in the hotel bar and proceeded to rip on my father the entire time.

"I was kind of looking forward to going home," I said. In Logan, I might be able to figure out how my past and present fit together. There was the whole coming out thing, of course, too. I was starting to look forward to that, in some strange way. By the end of the weekend, I would know where I stood with my parents, good or bad.

"Oh. Well, okay, then," she said. "Home it is."

She sat quietly beside me for the duration of the ride. I paid the cab driver and led my mother through the high-ceilinged, ornate section of Union Station always featured in movies into the low-ceilinged basement near the commuter tracks. The four o'clock express was already boarding.

We managed to find a couple of seats facing forward before the train pulled out of the station and wound through the city, over the Dan Ryan Expressway with its southbound lanes stopped dead, out through the south side of Chicago to where the train tracks met the lakeshore. Only then did my mother stop sulking and start chattering again. She kept up a steady stream of words from the Illinois-Indiana border all the way to the Michigan-Indiana border, at which point I pretended to fall asleep.

I didn't remember her talking this much. Or being this down

on my father. But then, I hadn't seen her in a while. I had never lived this far from home before. Even in New York, Chris and I were only a day's drive away. I'd been in Seattle for a year now with only one short visit home. Had I changed, too? Would she have noticed if I had?

My father was waiting on the platform when the train pulled into Logan. He came forward to meet us and gave me a hug and a kiss. "How's my girl?"

"Fine, Dad. It's good to see you." And it was. He at least looked the same: still slim in his suit and tie, still in possession of a full head of hair (which one would expect of the lead counsel of a company whose hair regrowth product was a household name), though he was grayer than I remembered.

He nodded at my mother. "Joyce."

She nodded back. "Steven."

No hug for them, no kiss on the cheek. My dad picked up my bag and rested his arm across my shoulders. "Come on, kiddo. I ordered a pizza and there's a Tigers game on TV I thought we might watch."

Same old dad.

In the parking lot not far from the station entrance, we ran into Natalie Sipsma, my childhood soccer buddy, and her mother.

"Hello, Phyllis," my mother said. "Fancy meeting you here."

"Natalie is just on her way back to Chicago," Mrs. Sipsma said. "She took a few days off from her job as an investment analyst to visit."

"We just came from Chicago," my mother said. "I went in to meet Samantha. She came from Seattle for a computer conference. What a coincidence."

Nat and I rolled our eyes at each other. Luckily, we didn't often have to witness our mothers competing over whose child was more brilliant and successful.

"Hi, Sam," she said, and hugged me lightly.

"Hey, Nat."

A few feet away our mothers continued to engage in

competitive conversation. We ignored them.

"How long have you been in Seattle?" Natalie asked. "I kept thinking I would run into you on Rush Street, but then I heard you left."

"I moved last summer."

"Oh." She was doing the math, and I could see her make the connection. She had an older brother Chris's age. Her whole family had come to the funeral. "How's Seattle?"

"Great. I love it." I felt fake, chatting like this with Natalie Sipsma. We were friends when we were little, but we went different routes in high school and college. She partied and ended up at Michigan State, whereas I geeked out and landed at Northwestern.

"A bunch of people from Logan are out there," she said. "Colin Fitzgerald and Ben Ritchie. Oh, and I heard little Emily Mackenzie went to school out there."

"I live near Emily. We've been hanging out lately."

"Really? I heard she was a lesbian."

My shoulders tightened and I nodded. "Yes, she is a lesbian." Our parents' exchange had just ended.

"Who's a lesbian, dear?" Mrs. Sipsma asked Natalie.

"Emily Mackenzie, from the soccer team. She lives near Sam in Seattle."

I felt my face turn red as we stood there discussing Emily's sexuality. I considered telling the lot of them to go jump in a lake but only said, "We don't want you to miss your train, Nat. Nice seeing you."

"You, too. Have fun in Seattle. Tell Emily I said hi."

I paused. "I will." Maybe she wasn't being critical after all. It was possible I might be a tad sensitive when it came to Emily.

I followed my parents to the Volvo (my Dad's car—my mother bought only American, out of loyalty to her long-dead Ford executive father) and headed home through Logan.

"Did you hear what Phyllis said, Samantha?" my mother asked.

"No, what?"

"She said she thought it was brave of you to pick up and leave Chicago for Seattle when you didn't even have a job lined up. Isn't that nice?"

But it was cowardice that had made me move two thousand miles away instead of staying and dealing with Chris's death. Should Emily and I somehow end up together, I wondered what Nat and her mother would think when they heard the gossip. Not that that would probably happen now.

Later, my father and I watched the Tigers game in the den, accompanied by pizza and beer. He had stocked the fridge with beer from the local microbrewery, he said, because he knew what a micro town Seattle was.

"I saw the Tigers play at Safeco on Friday," I told him. He occupied the La-Z-Boy recliner in front of the TV, remote on the arm, while I got the couch. For a moment I flashed on the room a year earlier when the furniture had been pushed to the edges to make room for Chris's hospital bed.

"You were at that game?" my dad said. "I saw the highlights on SportsCenter. One of your guys hit a three-run homer in the bottom of the first, didn't he?"

"Exactly. It was pretty much a slugfest from then on."

"Sounded like it. Seattle seems like a good sports city."

"It is. I went to my first Seattle Storm game last week."

"How was that?" my dad asked.

I paused, remembering how Emily had shot out of her seat at every big play, how my hand had hurt afterward from high-fiving, my throat from cheering. "Great," I said. "Really fun."

We talked sports on and off during the first part of the game. Then my dad asked about work and we dwelled on careers for a while. Near the end of the baseball game, I mentioned that I was playing soccer again on Emily Mackenzie's team.

"Sam, that's great. Is it a good team?"

"First in our league."

"That's my girl," he said without taking his eyes off the TV screen. "Did you see that pitch? The ump obviously can't see around his belly. I tell you what, these major league umps need to go on a group diet."

My mother used to read beside me on the couch in the den while my dad and I watched sports. But tonight she had settled with her pizza and a book on low-light photography in the living room, opera playing on the stereo. I had no idea she was so interested in the technical side of photography.

I looked at the wall behind the television, covered in family photos. In most, Chris was grinning into the lens, posing in some fashion or other. I was in the background in some, along with my father, milling about apparently unaware of the shot being snapped. The pictures trickled out once Chris hit puberty. The next photos were obviously from the period after he disappeared, mostly shots of me—high school graduation, a club soccer game at Northwestern, college graduation, the day I left for New York in my old yellow VW bug. The annual family portraits stopped when Chris ran away and began again when he came back. We hadn't bothered to take one this past Christmas.

I stood up. "I'm going to get another beer. Want one?"

"Sure. And Sam."

From the doorway, I looked back at my father. He had taken his jacket off, loosened his tie and rolled up the sleeves of his crisp white shirt. His stocking feet looked vulnerable somehow without wingtips to protect them. "Yeah?"

"It's good to have you home, kiddo."

"It's good to be home." And, I guessed, it was.

Later, lying in bed in my childhood room, white stars on the wallpaper glowing in light from the neighbor's garage, I thought about the family photos again. My mother had come to all of my important soccer games, recording wins and losses for posterity even though she hadn't particularly liked sports. One framed photo from my senior season when we won Regionals still sat on my bedroom dresser. Nat and I were out front holding up the trophy, while Emily stood in the middle row, her arm around

Jenna. A few days later, my mother snapped a shot of me hugging Em after our final game, when she cried on my shoulder and said it would never be the same.

That was just the first, I thought now, of so many things that could never be the same.

Chapter Twenty-Four

~EMILY~

On Thursday morning, I woke up thinking that Sunday was only three days away. But it wasn't like Sam was going to come home from Chicago and magically decide to talk to me again. The likelihood of me ever being with her decreased in inverse proportion to how much I wanted to be with her.

That night, Liz and Jessie decided to check out Taco Thursday at Aster Place with me and Katie—dollar tacos and cheap cerveza were hard to pass up. As we cruised down to Capitol Hill, I felt a little better than I had the past few days, ever since Sam had announced that she didn't think things between us would work out. I was on my way with friends to have some fun. I didn't need Sam, I just needed to forget that Saturday had ever happened. Right.

We got to Aster Place early and commandeered a booth on the bar side, ordering tacos and beer and chatting with people we knew who wandered by. The Seattle community wasn't all that big. Once you'd been around for a few years, you got to know the people who went out, sometimes too well. But early on in the evening, I noticed a woman at the bar I didn't know, a woman who looked enough like Sam to rattle me each time she crossed my line of vision. To distract myself, I chugged my first beer and was pleasantly buzzed when Katie dropped by our booth.

"Hey, Mac," she said, smiling.

"Katie! Sit down." I patted the space beside me.

She slid in, and I introduced her to Liz and Jessie. Liz shook Katie's hand and gave me a look, eyebrows raised, as if to say, "Who's this?" I ignored her. As she had done on more than one occasion, Liz would likely counsel me not to start something new until the old thing was over. But Sam was the one who had wanted to "step back," not me.

"So what do you do?" Jessie asked Katie.

"I'm a student at Seattle Central. What about you?"

"I work for a financial services firm downtown in the WaMu building."

"I love that building!" Katie said.

Sam loved the Washington Mutual tower too. She had told me it was her favorite building in Seattle the night I went to her place to watch the Mariners game. Between innings, the producers liked to pan away from Safeco to show the beauty that lay just beyond the stadium. Downtown had been constructed on an angle facing southwest, and in summer, when the sun set over the Olympic Mountains, the buildings turned silver and gold. Sunset was one of my favorite times to drive along the Highway 99 Viaduct downtown, I'd told Sam that night. She'd smiled at me, there on her couch, and said we would have to take a drive at sunset some time together.

The sense of loss crept over me now so that I had to swallow hard against my tightening throat. All the plans I'd been making without meaning to were ruined. Sam wouldn't be in the stands at our home games this fall or hanging out afterward to congratulate or console me. She and I wouldn't help entertain each other's out-of-town friends and family by taking them to Pike's Place Market or the Space Needle. We wouldn't wake up together in her apartment near the zoo or in my room with its distant view of Green Lake. We wouldn't be together, and I wasn't sure why.

Sam's look-alike chose that moment to walk by. I gripped my pint glass tighter and tried to push the real Sam from my mind. I would be fine. A month ago, she'd been nothing but a memory. A month from now, that was all she would be again. In the meantime, I was with friends and a cute girl who fit easily into our group. By this time next month, Katie might be even more important to me than Sam ever had been. Well, she could, I told myself.

I didn't have too bad of a night after all. I ate tacos and hung out with my friends and with Katie, whose gratifying attention eased the knot in my chest a little. She may not have been Sam, but she was a nice alternative. Sam—what if she knew I was here now with Katie? But I didn't have any reason to feel guilty. Sam was the one who wanted to "slow things down," as she had put it. Still, I kept remembering how she'd asked if I was still dating Katie, how she'd suggested we not see each other when I admitted I was. It did matter, she had said.

Eventually Liz and Jessie said it was time to call it a night. Katie pulled me aside and asked if I wanted to come back to her place for coffee.

"I can't," I said, falling back on my old excuse. "I have to be at the bike shop early."

"You work every morning but Sunday, right?"

She remembered. "Right."

"So do you want to maybe get together on Saturday night?"

I hesitated. Sam. But Sam didn't want to see me. "Why not."

As I rode home in the backseat of the Blazer, I wondered what I had agreed to—but I knew. I just kept hoping something would stop me from continuing along this road with Katie. That something, though, was two thousand miles away. Even if Sam had been across town, there was no guarantee she would have wanted me to stop.

Back at home, I'd just changed into a T-shirt and boxers when I noticed Liz standing in my open bedroom doorway.

"Can I come in for a sec?" she asked.

"Sure." Here it was, I thought. Folding my arms across my chest, I faced her as she sat down on the edge of my futon. "What's up?"

"I was just wondering how you're doing."

"You know. Okay, I guess."

"You don't seem okay."

I glanced at her, trying to gauge if she was regarding me with her usual disapproval. But no, her eyes were warm and open. Sighing, I sat down next to her. "I guess I'm not. I miss Sam."

"Is that why you're hanging out with Katie?"

"Yeah, I need to get over her. You're the one who said I should stop going after straight girls."

"That was before you two hooked up. Either way, kind of sucks for Katie."

"I don't think Katie's looking for a girlfriend."

"How can you be sure?"

"It'll be fine. Don't worry."

"Too late." She patted my leg.

"I'm a schmuck, aren't I?"

"No, you're not. I think you're just hurting. It'll get better, little buddy." And she slipped her arm around my neck, pulling me against her side.

For once, I didn't mind the Gilligan reference. "You know, you were right about some of the things you said before," I told her. "Just, not everything. I did feel differently about Sam. I still do. I'm just not sure how she feels about me."

"When does she come back from Michigan?"

"Sunday."

"Maybe you can talk to her then."

"Maybe."

"In the meantime," she added, "do you really want to do

anything that might hurt your chances with her?"

For once, I didn't get bent out of shape by her unasked-for advice. I just nodded, slowly. "I know. You're right."

"Wow, twice in one night. Must be a record," she said. "Friends again?"

"We always were," I said, and hugged her. She pounded me on the back affectionately and I winced into her shoulder. The girl was too strong for her own good. And mine.

"Good night," she said, heading for the door. "And good luck."

"Thanks." Luck was not what I needed, I thought as I went to brush my teeth. Like the Lion in the *Wizard of Oz*, I was more in need of courage. Liz was right about Katie and Sam. I knew what I should do. I just didn't know if I was capable of doing it.

* * *

Saturday afternoon I was watching Dick Van Patten and the rest of the cast of *Eight Is Enough* attempting (vainly) to act when my cell rang. I grabbed it, thinking for some reason that it might be Sam. But the ring tone wasn't Queen, and Katie's name popped up on the caller ID. I slouched back down on the couch. "Hey, Katie. What's up?"

"Not much. Just checking in," she said. "You still up for hanging out tonight?"

She was giving me an out. I could cancel on her right now and not have to deal later. But I was getting a little old for the dump-and-run move I had perfected during my college years. Besides, Katie was a good person. "Actually," I said, "something's come up. Do you have time now? Could we maybe meet for coffee?"

"Coffee," she repeated, and paused. "I guess so. Where?"

We arranged to meet at Revolutions in half an hour. I shut my phone and stared at it for a minute. What was I doing? The old me from college would probably have slept with Katie tonight and still tried to get back in Sam's good graces when she got home. The college me would have known she was being an ass and, frankly, wouldn't have cared. But the time I had spent with Sam had changed me. Or maybe it was just time to grow up and move on. I was no longer a big dyke on campus. Now I had to try my hand at real-world lesbian life.

I was sitting at a table by the window at Revolutions when Katie walked in, looking good in tight shorts and a tank top that revealed her ample chest, hair twisted into a casual knot on top of her head. Doing the right thing blew, I thought, and waved at her.

She bought a bottle of juice and joined me. "So," she said as she sat down.

"So," I said, picking at the collar on my latté cup. I'd been hoping a shot of caffeine would motivate me, but instead it had just revved up my heart rate.

"What's up, Mac? What are we doing here?" She didn't sound annoyed, just a little confused.

"I'm sorry," I said, still not looking at her. "I really am. But, well, I can't date you." This was a first for me. Since arriving in Seattle, I'd rarely said no to any attractive girl who showed interest. What that said about me I preferred not to acknowledge.

"I don't understand," she said. "What does that mean?"

"It means—" I stopped and looked at her, bracing myself for the words that were about to cross my lips. "It means I'm in love with somebody else." This was the first time I had admitted it, even to myself.

"You are?" Katie asked, her perfectly plucked eyebrows lowering.

I bit my lip. "Guess I should have mentioned it before."

"No joke." She shook her head but continued to look more confused than anything. "Why have you been hanging out with me, then?"

I ended up telling her the abridged story of Sam and me,

starting with Logan High and finishing with the previous weekend, while the espresso machine whined and whirred and coffee shop patrons came and went around us.

"Damn, Mac, you finally get this girl and you just walk out?" she asked when I finished. "You've got to get in touch with your feelings. Maybe you should try meditation."

"Maybe." I leaned back against the metal chair. "You're being cool about this. Anyone else would have walked out by now."

"Well, it's not as if we confessed our undying love," she said, smiling a little. "Anyway, I haven't been entirely honest, either."

"You haven't?"

"I was in a pretty intense relationship until a few weeks ago. You were supposed to be my rebound."

"Ah." I smiled at her. "You were supposed to be mine."

"What can you do?" She leaned forward and kissed me on the corner of the mouth. "Tell you what. If it doesn't work out, give me a call sometime."

We parted outside the coffee shop. I watched her go, shaking my head a little at my own folly. But it was the right thing to do and I knew it. Caffeine still coursing diabolically through my bloodstream, I rode my bike west, down to Fiftieth Street and up along the edge of Woodland Park. I passed Sam's building and turned down the side road where her truck was parked. I stopped beside it, thinking of the last time I'd ridden in it—almost exactly a week before on our way back to her place from the barbecue. Walking from the truck to the building, she had placed her hand at the small of my back and told me she was better than okay.

If I had a car now, I would go for a long drive out some road off I-90 in the mountains with the sun shining overhead, evergreens looming against the sky. In Logan, there was a road behind the high school that was a straight shot, thanks to the Northwest Ordinance of 1787, with few houses and little traffic. I used to cruise along it at ninety miles an hour after soccer practice my senior year, the road rushing past beneath the car, my body hurtling rapidly across the land. I couldn't wait back then to escape Michigan. I knew there was something better for me, unknowable as yet, out beyond the farm fields and forests of the immediate horizon.

But I didn't have a car in Seattle, so I rode my bike away from Sam's silent truck and down Fremont Avenue. I flew down the hill amid sparse car traffic, turned onto a side street and pedaled to where the north side of the Aurora Bridge met the steep hillside. There under the bridge stood the statue of the Troll, a Fremont landmark, its giant concrete hand wrapped around an actual VW Bug. I paused on my bike near the Troll, listening to traffic roar overhead on the bridge. A car full of tourists drove slowly past, occupants ogling the Troll. I heard Katie again: "You've got to get in touch with your feelings." And she was right. But I knew what I felt. I loved Sam Delaney and wanted her in my life. Needed her, even. Here in Seattle, back home in Logan, wherever. I wanted to be with her. It was that simple.

I started pedaling again and rode slowly down one hill and up another, back to my house in Wallingford. No more cowardice, I decided as I went inside and made my way upstairs. I would give Sam a day or two to settle in when she got back, and if she didn't call me, I would stake out Camelot and wait for her to appear. She was the one who had been reaching out all this time. Now it was my turn.

I lay on my bed planning my next move. Soon.

Chapter Twenty-Five

~SAM~

On Saturday morning, as my mother had predicted, my father went into work "for just a few hours." I made French toast with Mom, getting her shiny kitchen good and dirty. We used to cook together all the time, mother and daughter bonding, but after Chris had moved home she never had the time. Usually I would come in from Chicago on the weekends and make lasagna or turkey casserole, something she could heat up during the week. My father ordered in at the office on weeknights. I'd taken a longer leave from work than he had.

After we cleaned up the kitchen, my mother offered to take me shopping at the mall in Baxter, a wealthy suburb of Logan. Shopping with my mother was always entertaining because we had the exact opposite taste in clothes. I liked faded jeans and muted colors, shirts bordering on ugly, nothing too frilly. My mom went for capes and flowered skirts and tight, bright shirts. When I came downstairs after breakfast, she eyed my cargo shorts and white T-shirt with obvious disdain. She wouldn't be caught dead in such an ensemble.

"When was the last time you and I went shopping together?" my mother asked as she paid for a skirt at the Limited.

I didn't shop at the Limited anymore. Value Village, the used clothing store on Capitol Hill, was more my style these days. "God, Mom, I don't know."

"Was it when you left for college?"

"That sounds right."

"Cute skirt," the salesgirl chimed in, smiling at me. "I'm sure you'll love it."

"I'm sure she will," my mother said, even though the skirt was for her.

We ran out of purchase gas after that and decided to catch a matinee of a chick flick about which I knew next to nothing. The story was set in the Detroit suburbs and featured a troubled mother-daughter relationship—not the movie I wanted to see with my mom. But it ended up being funny and sweet, and I found myself thinking I could learn something when the male lead told the female lead that she needed to stop pushing her mother away. Life was too short and other such deep thoughts.

After the movie my mom and I drove home to meet up with my dad, who had promised to be home before dinner. He was waiting when we got back, slightly miffed we didn't come home earlier. My mother asked him what did he expect when, after all, he'd gone into work the one day I was home? Then they looked at me and forced smiles as if they weren't really fighting. As if they still loved each other.

We made dinner and ate together as the dysfunctional family we were—distant daughter, husband and wife who wouldn't look each other in the eye, dead son's ghost lurking in the shadows. My mother didn't often mention Chris in my father's presence, and I hadn't heard my dad mention him once since he died. But my brother was present in the things we didn't say.

After dinner my mother made coffee and we sat around the

dining room table talking. They wanted to know every detail of my life in Seattle, or at least my mom did. My dad would probably have been content to talk about the stock market, frequent-flier miles, the cost of living in Seattle versus Chicago. He actually told my mom to get off my back a couple of times when I dodged her questions. I frowned at him. Admittedly she was too nosy, but I could take care of myself. And at least she cared enough to push. The only things he cared enough to dig into were his case files.

But I didn't say this and my mother didn't tell him off to his face like she had been threatening to do the last few days. And after twenty-four hours of hanging out with them and biting my tongue, knowing that they were both biting their tongues in their respective ways, I had to get out of the house.

I pushed away from the table and said, "Can I borrow a car? I feel like a drive."

"You do?" my mother said. "I thought maybe we could go for a walk."

"She just said she wants to go for a drive, Joyce," my father said. He fished in his pants pocket and tossed me his keys. "There you go, Sam."

"Thanks." How could he be so shitty to her and so buddy-buddy with me? "Can we go for a walk in the morning, Mom? I'd like that."

She nodded and I could tell I had managed to hurt her. She was always hurting about something. I hugged each of them (even though I wanted to strangle them both) and left the house, relieved to be on my own for the first time all day. I started my father's car and backed down the driveway. They were like children. Was this how they had felt about Chris and me when we were little? Could they not wait to get away from us either?

I headed down the street away from my childhood house, turned on the radio and searched for the station I used to listen to in high school. It had been replaced by static and fuzz and the echo of a Christian talk show. I drove without musical accompaniment through the quiet neighborhood near the university where Emily's family and mine both lived, easing up to the roomy brick house where Emily and Beth had grown up. I slowed the car under the tall old trees that shaded the front yard. The downstairs was lit up, and through the front window I could see Emily's parents in the living room sitting at opposite ends of a couch with their feet stretched out toward each other, reading. My window was open and so was theirs. Strands of classical music drifted from the house.

In that moment, spying on their solitude, my hope for the future crystallized. I didn't want to be alone any more. If you loved, you risked the possibility of feeling like shit. But if you locked yourself away from everyone and everything, what did you gain? I wanted what Emily's parents had. I wanted a house with a shady yard and someone to share the night with. Someone—but I knew who.

I drove up Elm Street, where my old elementary school hulked dark and empty for the summer, and turned left onto Main Street. Past Van's, the liquor store where my junior high friends and I used to lurk around hoping that someone legal might buy for us. Heading west through town, I continued past the new bike store that used to be a taco joint and before that a bank. Everything went in cycles, my mother liked to say.

Without planning to, I wound west toward the high school. I used to drive seventy down this residential street on mornings I was late. Or on mornings when I was just feeling trapped. I could never have run away, though. Chris had already done it. This route was also the way to the cemetery where Chris was buried. Strange to think I had passed it every day for four years. My brother had passed it on his way to the high school too, never knowing he would end up there well before his thirtieth birthday. But I couldn't say that for sure. He might have suspected.

I parked the car and walked down a row at the northern edge, hoping I was in the right spot. It had been a year since I'd packed up my truck, said goodbye to my parents and stopped here on my way out of town. I had wanted to visit at Christmas, but too much snow and not enough time killed those plans. I never mentioned it to my parents. They were depressed enough at the holidays, the first Christmas without Chris since he'd come back into our lives.

I stopped at his headstone, simple gray granite with his name, dates of birth and death and an inscription taken from his favorite Wizard of Oz song, "Somewhere Over the Rainbow"—fittingly, a line about troubles melting away and the singer being found up above the chimney tops. Chris wasn't wild about being buried. He would have preferred to be cremated he had told me once, but the idea upset our mother so much that he didn't push it. After all, he'd said, it wouldn't make any real difference to him at that point.

Joyce got her way and here he was, buried in a shiny black coffin in the cemetery next to our high school. From his plot, I could see the soccer fields where the team used to practice, the stadium where we played home games.

"Hey, bro," I said, looking down at the headstone. I waited for some feeling of him, some sign of his spirit, but all I heard was the breeze rustling lightly through the same trees that rained red and gold leaves onto our practice field each autumn. I waited a little while longer to see if the hair on the back of my neck would rise or a cold breath of air envelop me, but the summer night remained peaceful. Chris wasn't here.

"Happy travels," I said, and turned away.

* * *

The clock on the dash read midnight when I pulled into the garage. In the house, I set my father's keys on the kitchen counter and stepped out of my shoes, leaving them near the back door. I had already started up the carpeted stairs at the end of the hallway when I heard a sound from the den. Probably my dad watching SportsCenter and waiting up for me. I hesitated on the stairs. Then I went back down the hall.

In the den, the TV was tuned to *Saturday Night Live*, not ESPN. My mom was watching from the La-Z-Boy. She looked up when I stopped in the doorway.

"It's you," she said. "This show used to be better. I don't understand it anymore."

Her voice was bright and cheerful—her hostess voice, I called it, the one she put on at parties or fundraisers or the theater, the same one she'd used when we ran into the Sipsmas at the train station. Why was she using it on me? Then I saw the nearly empty vodka bottle next to the chair.

"Did you wreck your father's car?" she asked. "I hope not. He couldn't bear it if anything happened to his car. Now me, on the other hand, you could wreck me and I don't think he'd mind. Ask him. He'll tell you. He loves his car. It's still new. I'm not new anymore."

"Mom, don't you think you should go to bed? It's late."

"It's not late. I never go to bed until later than this, Sammy. Duh." She giggled. "Isn't that what you kids used to always say? 'Duh, Mom, you're like such a dork.'"

I walked over to the armchair, touched her shoulder. "Come on, I'll walk you upstairs."

"I don't want to go upstairs." She grabbed my arm. "I'm not new, Samantha. I'm old. I'm the old."

Her fingers on my arm were tight, painfully so. I pried them loose. "You're not old."

"I am. Old and useless. I'm not even a good mother. Out with the old, in with the new. Just like in that movie today. Ask him. Just ask your father."

Was she implying that my father was having an affair? I shook my head, trying to dismiss the idea as vodka-induced paranoia. But then I thought about how my mom had kept wiping her eyes during the scene in the movie today when one of the characters found out her husband was having an affair. I thought about the incessant fighting, my mother's inability to stand up for herself, my father's impatience. Maybe she couldn't do anything right in his eyes because she wasn't the one he wanted to be with.

It couldn't be that, I told myself. Not my dad. "Come on, Mom," I said. "Let's get you to bed."

"I am not going to bed, young lady," she said, glaring up at me. Then her face crumpled. "Oh, God, what am I going to do? What will I do without him?"

Was she talking about Chris? Or Dad? "You'll be fine," I said, and helped her to her feet.

"No, I won't." She leaned on me as I led her across the room. "I don't have any of you. You all hate me. You're all gone to me."

"I don't hate you."

But she wasn't listening. She was too wrapped up in her narrowed universe to hear. She passed out at the bottom of the stairs, leaning heavily against me, her eyelids fluttering. I lowered her slowly to the carpeting. I wasn't strong enough to carry her up on my own. I hesitated, then left her propped against the wall and ran upstairs to knock on my parents' bedroom door.

"Dad. Dad, wake up."

But he didn't come out of the bedroom. He emerged from the office down the hall, his bathrobe loosely tied, his salt-and-pepper hair tousled. "What is it?" he asked. "Is the car okay?"

Suddenly I hated him. "The car's fine. It's Mom. I can't get her upstairs by myself."

"Jesus." He didn't seem surprised as he followed me down the hallway to the stairs. "I'm sorry you had to see her like this, Sam. She just hasn't gotten over your brother yet."

"She might not ever get over him," I said, pausing at the top of the stairs. "You know, Dad, maybe none of us will ever get over losing him. Maybe it'll just always hurt."

"I don't believe that," he said. "It has to end. You can't go on hurting your whole life."

"Why not?"

"You just can't. It's not physically possible."

I wasn't convinced, but I let it drop as we reached my mother, still leaning against the wall at the foot of the stairs. We half-carried her up to the bedroom, one of us on either side, and set her on the still-made bed.

"I'll take it from here," my father said. "Don't worry. You get some sleep." He untied her shoes gently, and as he did, I noticed the dark smudges beneath his eyes, the slight slope of his shoulders. He looked exhausted.

In my room I stripped out of my clothes and went straight to bed. This trip had been more than I knew how to handle. And it wasn't over yet. I still had another day to get through in Logan. I closed my eyes and pressed my face against the cool cotton of the pillowcase. One more day until I could see Emily. Assuming she would want to see me.

* * *

The next morning, I carried my suitcase downstairs and rifled through the kitchen cupboards for breakfast. Only a few more hours with my parents. I'd have to catch the noon train to Chicago to be in time for my flight out of O'Hare. After the previous night's revelations, I couldn't wait to go home.

My father came in from the garage while I was pouring myself a bowl of Cheerios. "I see you found the cereal," he said, leaning against the counter. His outfit, mesh shorts and a T-shirt, told me he wasn't planning on working this morning.

Remembering what my mother had said about him the night before, I nodded without looking up.

"Your mother bought that especially for you. It's your favorite, isn't it?"

I shrugged. Actually, I ate granola and yogurt most mornings. But I wasn't about to give him more ammo to use against her in their undeclared war.

"So, what, you're not talking to me now?"

"I don't think you'd like what I have to say."

He frowned. "Remember, Samantha, there are two sides to every story."

"Sounds like you're trying to justify something, Dad." I set my spoon down on the counter. "All right, then, let's hear your side. Are you having an affair?"

His jaw tightened. "Is that what your mother told you?"

"That's not an answer."

"Well, I'm not. Not that it's any of your business. What's between your mother and me is our concern."

"Bullshit," I said, and felt my pulse pick up. I had never spoken to him like this before. "It became my business when you allowed what you felt to destroy this family. And Chris—" I stopped.

My father stared at me for a moment, then shook his head. "So that's it. We couldn't figure out why you moved away, but it's obvious. You blame us for your brother's death, don't you?"

"Don't you?" The moment the words were out I wanted to haul them back in. "Wait, I didn't mean that."

"I think you did. In fact, Sam, I think that's exactly what you meant." He turned away. "I was going to see if you wanted to shoot baskets, but I think I'll go for a bike ride instead." And he walked out the door.

"Fuck," I said, standing at the kitchen counter, my cereal growing soggy. "Fuck, fuck, fuck."

My mother came downstairs a little while later. She opened the window over the kitchen sink and set the kettle on the stove to heat. "Good morning," she said, no trace of the previous night's drama in her demeanor. I knew now where I had inherited my alcohol tolerance.

"Morning," I forced myself to grate out.

"Where's your father? He didn't go to the office, did he?"

"No, he went for a bike ride."

"On your last morning here?"

I dropped the newspaper I'd been pretending to read. "He left because we argued."

"Oh." Her movements stilled.

"About what you told me last night," I added. Apparently I was determined to alienate both of my parents before I got on the train and vanished for another six months.

"What exactly is that?"

"You don't remember? Are you kidding?"

"You don't have to be so angry."

"You implied Dad was having an affair." I brushed past her and dropped my bowl in the sink, flinching as the pottery clattered against the metal surface. "He left in a bit of a huff when I asked him if he was cheating on you."

"Oh, God." She rubbed her face. "I'm sorry. I don't remember. Your father's only affair is with his work. It always has been."

I shook my head. "What is wrong with you?"

"I don't know." She looked out the window over the sink. Across the street one of the neighbors was outside watering his garden. She lowered her voice. "Your father is never home. I'm alone all the time. And you live so far away. I don't have anyone to talk to."

"What about your friends? The women you golf with?"

"They wouldn't understand. They like their lives. And why shouldn't they? None of them have buried a child. Their husbands actually come home at night."

I stared at her. "You have a college degree. You could do something with that."

"True." She hesitated. "Do you want to know why I asked to meet you in Chicago? What I was doing while you were at the convention?"

I wasn't sure I did. But not knowing wouldn't change the truth of what was happening to my parents' marriage. "All right."

"I'm thinking of taking photography classes at the Art Institute. I had an interview with an instructor there. He looked through my old portfolio and said I should apply to the program. What do you think?"

I thought that Chicago was a long way from Logan. "It sounds like a great opportunity. But what about Dad?"

248

The kettle whistled. She poured herself a cup of tea before facing me again—Lipton's black, the same tea she had made every morning since I could remember. "That's something your father and I wanted to talk to you about this morning."

The cereal rumbled uneasily in my stomach, even though I'd been anticipating this conversation ever since Jim had announced he was sending me to Chicago. Actually, ever since Christmas. "You and Dad are getting a divorce, aren't you?"

"Not exactly," she said. "We're going to try a period of separation. We're practically strangers, Samantha. Your father has this compulsion to work all the time so that he won't have to deal with anything else."

"I had noticed."

"And I," she continued, calmer somehow than I'd seen her at any point in the past few days, "well, I have some issues too. Your father and I started marriage counseling a few months ago, and this is the decision our counselor has helped us reach. We need to step away and work on ourselves, separately, before we can bring anything worthwhile to our marriage. Maybe we'll decide we're happier apart, but we might also figure out how we can be better together."

"Right." I turned away. Bottom line, they were giving up on their marriage, just like they'd given up on Chris all those years ago when they realized he wasn't the son they wanted him to be.

"Don't shut me out," she said. "What's done is done. Your father and I have to do what's best for us now."

I could have walked away, could have gone out into the humid morning like my father and left the house—and my mother—behind. But instead I looked her in the eye and said what I never had before: "Everything is always about you guys. Even Chris dying was about you—the kind of parents you were and what you did wrong and what you wanted for him. You didn't even know who you wanted to be but you knew what you wanted for us."

"All I wanted was for my children to be happy."

"That is such a crock of shit. You wanted us to be these

249

perfect little robots you could show off to everyone because you weren't happy with your own life."

"That's not fair, Samantha."

"Was it fair that Chris had to run away to be himself? Anyway, who ever said life was fair?"

"Cynicism doesn't become you," she said.

"And vodka doesn't become you," I shot back. Now that I had started giving voice to my thoughts, I didn't seem able to stop.

"Well." She set her cup of tea on the counter. "I didn't know you felt that way about me. All this time I only wanted to be your friend. I had no idea you thought I was a terrible person."

And there she went, making everything about her again. "You just don't get it, Mom, do you?"

"No, Samantha, I don't. I was never friends with my mother. I could never talk to her. I knew that when I had children of my own, I would do everything I could to be a friend to them. But you've never wanted that. I'm sorry I wasn't a good mother to you. Obviously I've failed you."

"You haven't failed me." I couldn't tell her that I had always believed she didn't like me. I knew she loved me, but she never seemed to want me around. She'd chosen Chris every time.

"You were so hard to read," she said. "You weren't like your brother. I always knew what he felt. But you, I had to drag things out of you. I could never seem to reach you. Did you think I didn't try? Do you think I'm not trying now? You live on the opposite side of this country and I'm still trying to reach you."

I wanted to turn away from the need in her eyes, to drive away from this house, this town. But I clamped down on the urge, took a breath and said, "Do you really want to know me? Even if I'm not who or what you want me to be?"

She didn't hesitate. "I do."

This would change everything. But everything had changed already. My parents just didn't know it yet. "You were right before when you said I was different. It's not just soccer. I have met someone."

"Oh, honey, that's wonderful. I knew it." She took a step toward me across the kitchen.

I held up a hand. "Wait. It's someone you know, someone you probably wouldn't expect."

"Oh." She folded her arms across her chest and looked directly at me. "Who is it, Samantha?"

I took a deep breath and pictured Emily sitting on my couch, her head close to mine, her blue eyes smiling at me. "Emily Mackenzie."

"I see." My mother sighed and rubbed her eyes. "Christ. So you're gay, too?"

I could see the wheels spinning in her head—what would they think at the country club? What would her friends say? And how would she ever face Phyllis Sipsma again?

"I didn't say that," I told her. "I'm not sure what I am. I just know I'm in love with Emily." It was the first time I had said it aloud. The words felt right, at least to me.

"What about David? You were in love with him."

"Not like this."

We were both quiet for a minute. Then the back door opened and my father, with brilliant timing, walked in. He stopped when he saw the two of us facing off, went to the sink and poured himself a glass of water.

"She knows, Steven," my mother said.

He slammed the glass down on the counter so hard I was surprised it didn't shatter. "Damn it, Joyce, I thought we agreed we'd both be present for that conversation?"

"It's okay, Dad," I said. "I kind of guessed. Mom didn't bring it up." My eyes met hers across the kitchen. *Keep my secret and I'll keep yours.*

"Oh," he said, and ran a hand over his hair, windblown from his bike ride. "Well, you understand that nothing is irrevocable here, Sam. We're not getting divorced. It's just that losing your brother has been exceedingly difficult for both of us. We need to take a step back and get a better perspective on the situation. And since your mother wants to pursue her interest in photography, this seems like the appropriate time to do so."

He was polished, formal, as if he were presenting closing arguments to a jury. What would he have said if I had told him I was in love with a lesbian? What words would he have selected then? But that would have to wait for another day. I had already said enough.

"I understand," I told him. "I hope everything works out for you guys."

"We appreciate that," he said, and downed the rest of the water. "Right now, though, I need a shower."

As soon as he headed upstairs, my mother crossed the kitchen, stopped in front of me and set her hands on my shoulders. "I love you, Sam," she said. "I love you for who you are, not who I want you to be. Do you understand?"

Tears filled my eyes, but I blinked them away. I didn't want to cry in front of her. "I understand."

"Emily Mackenzie, hmm," she added, slipping her arm around my shoulder and walking with me toward the living room.

"Don't tell Dad yet, okay? I want to tell him in my own time."

"By all means, that's a conversation you should have with him when you're ready. You know, I see the Mackenzies around town quite a bit. I always thought Emily was a cute girl."

"You did?" I didn't bother hiding my shock.

"I did." My mother shook her head. "To be perfectly honest, I'm not thrilled by the news. But I knew you were hiding something. And you forget, I've been through this once already. I would hope I had learned something the first time around."

Chris used to always complain that he had to break our parents in with all of the stages—parties, driving, curfews, grades. I didn't think he ever would have predicted this one, though.

I slipped my arm around my mother's waist. I'd been taller than her since I turned twelve. I used to feel like I might break her if I wasn't careful. "Thanks, Mom."

"Thank you," she said. "It couldn't have been easy for you to tell me, not after your brother—well, you know."

We stopped at the window and looked out over the backyard. Summer flowers were blooming in the garden. I wondered how my mom would feel about leaving the house where she'd raised her kids, where Chris had come home to die. I wondered if she would feel freer without our family ghosts haunting her.

"We never went for that walk," I said. "Want to go now?"

"Yes, but let's wait for your father. I'm sure he'd want to join us."

We sat down on the couch and talked about gardening while we waited. Someday, I told her, I hoped to have a place where I could have a garden of my own. But that was still probably a ways off.

"There's no rush," my mom said, and covered my hand with her own. "You have plenty of time for all of that."

* * *

Three hours later I was on the train to Chicago, watching the Michigan landscape flash past. Through this same Amtrak window, or one very like it, I had observed snowbanks, freshly plowed fields and swaths of cut hay at different times of the year. The view beyond the train window, though, was about the only thing from my old life that had remained constant. When you went home after a long absence, I was beginning to realize, you had to accept that the people you'd left behind weren't going to be the same anymore, even as they struggled to adapt to the changes in you.

As I left my hometown behind, I hummed along to Shawn Colvin on my iPod and gazed down at the blank first page of a journal decorated with Vincent Van Gogh's "Starry, Starry Night." My mother had pressed the small book on me just before I boarded the train.

"I saw you pick it up at the bookstore yesterday," she'd said. "If an old lady like me can get back on the horse, you can too."

"You're not old," I said, and hugged her. Then I hugged my father. "I'm sorry about this morning. I didn't mean to be so harsh."

"It's okay," he said. "Just take care of yourself, sweetheart."

I boarded the train and found a seat, and when I looked out the window, my parents were still standing on the platform together. I wondered if it would be the last time I ever said goodbye to them as a couple. I waved and they waved back. My mother had even given a thumbs-up. Such a sporty gesture for her.

Now I touched my pen to the blank page and began to write as the train rolled and rattled toward Chicago:

Dear Chris,

You wouldn't believe the weekend I just spent at home. I came out to Mom, and she told me she and Dad are separating. I wish you were here. You're the only one who could appreciate the surreal quality of all of this.

I visited your grave, too. Don't know if you keep track of things like that. I got the feeling you were far away, soaring through the atmosphere maybe. That's how I like to think of you—free of your body, free of everything. I'm starting to feel that way too. Telling Mom about Emily was awesome. Now I just have to tell Emily about Emily.

Wish me luck. I miss you. Happy flying.

Love,
Your Sis

I closed the journal and sat back to watch forest-lined farm fields pass. Shawn Colvin was singing now about riding shotgun down an avalanche. I thought I knew what she meant.

* * *

At O'Hare I had a couple of hours to kill. A row of phones beckoned from one side of the gate, so I wandered over and used my calling card to check voice mail, thinking as I did so that it might finally be time to give in to peer pressure (i.e., Tina's haranguing) and buy a cell phone. I had three new messages. I listened hopefully—one was Tina who said I should call her when I got home; one was Jim telling me to take my time getting back to work in the morning; and the last was Sarah, who knew she acted like a jerk at the barbecue and would like to meet me for coffee sometime soon. I hung up, then punched in Emily's number, quickly, before I could think about it.

Voice mail. I cleared my throat and, at the beep, spewed out a completely unrehearsed message: "Hey, Emily. I was really hoping you'd pick up. Anyway, this is Sam. I'm in Chicago about to get on a plane. I've been doing a lot of thinking and I wanted to apologize for Sunday." I paused. "I guess you could leave me a message on my voice mail, if you wanted. I'll check it when I get home. Maybe we could meet for coffee or something and talk? Or whatever. Hope you had a good week."

I set the phone down and returned to the waiting area, trying to silence the little voice inside telling me I had just made an utter fool of myself. What if she got my message and let her new girlfriend listen to it? Saying, "This is the woman I was telling you about?"

The next two hours crept past. When my flight finally started to board, I checked my messages again, just in case, but to no avail. I boarded the plane and watched out the window as we lifted off and flew away from Chicago, away from the Midwest, away from my parents. I hoped they would be okay. They had survived the death of their child. I'd heard that everything else was supposed to seem easier in comparison.

The flight was smooth as we headed west, chasing the summer sun. I peered through the window at the earth thirty-five

255

thousand feet below. The flight was sunny, and I gazed upon the wispy tops of clouds, noticing the shadows they cast far below. The summer I turned eleven, Chris and I had taken our bikes to nearby Jones Park almost daily. We would lie on the ground, chew grass and tell each other stories about the clouds. They were mythological creatures, and warrior heroes and animals with magical abilities. And us, sometimes, flying higher than ordinary mortals ever could.

* * *

When we landed, I filed off the plane with the rest of the passengers, accompanied by the salient odor of jet fuel. At baggage claim I looked around, but saw only strangers embracing their loved ones. I had forgotten to set up a ride after Emily and I stopped talking. Looked like I would be catching a cab home.

The baggage carousel silent and unmoving still, I checked my voice mail on a nearby pay phone. Still no new messages. It had been six hours since I'd called her. Either she was totally wrapped up in somebody else and hadn't received my message, or she didn't want to talk to me. Or both.

The baggage carousel groaned to life. And all at once, I couldn't wait to get home to my apartment with its view of the Rose Garden and the zoo gates, to Chloe's low purrs and trills of affection. I hoped Tina had kept her company like she'd promised.

I had just spotted my suitcase tumbling down the chute when a hand pressed my shoulder.

"Sam."

I knew that voice. I turned quickly.

"Your flight was early," she said, her eyes crinkling with her smile. "I'm glad I didn't miss you."

"Emily," was all I could say as I stared at her. She looked tanned and fit in a tank top and low-slung jeans, her cheeks rosy, her hair damp. I couldn't believe she was standing in front of me.

Then her words sank in. I took her hand, pulling her away from the crowd jockeying for position around the carousel. "You got my message?"

"Even if I hadn't, I said I would pick you up, remember?" She touched my face, the palm of her hand gentle against my cheek.

"I know, but that was before…" I trailed off, still holding onto her.

"I couldn't just let it go," she said, uncharacteristically serious, her eyes on mine. "I couldn't just let you go."

"I don't want you to." I leaned forward and kissed her there at the edge of baggage claim. She kissed me back, and then we were both laughing, and she was asking me about the trip, one arm around my waist, and I was starting to tell her about the craziness of my time at home. Then I remembered I'd seen my suitcase just before she reached me.

"I'll get it," she said.

A minute later we walked out to the parking lot where we wandered the rows of shiny, rust-free cars. Back to the Pacific Northwest—land of mountains, evergreens and salt-free winters. And, best of all, Emily.

"I couldn't believe you called," she said, my hand clasped in hers.

"I didn't want to leave things the way they were."

"Neither did I. The last week was awful."

"Tell me about it."

She stopped beside the Miata, angled away from the other cars, top down.

"Nice wheels," I said.

"Jessie insisted. It might make talking a little difficult, though."

"That's okay. We've got time," I said, relaxing a little as I realized it was true. There was nothing to keep us apart. I hoped.

She smiled at me again and ushered me into the convertible. When she slid in next to me, I leaned over and kissed her again, really kissed her. I couldn't help it—she looked too cute and pleased with herself. I didn't even care who saw us.

After we'd greeted one another sufficiently, Em started the car and drove us away from the airport, taking the back way into the city. Highway 509 joined 99 just south of downtown, and we cruised along the waterfront where the sun hovered above the Olympic Mountains and reflected unevenly across Puget Sound. I looked out over Elliott Bay, tracing the Olympics, jagged against the western sky, the skyscrapers towering over the Viaduct to the east. The Washington Mutual Tower, with its granite frame and emerald green windows, arched above us.

"Welcome home," Emily said over the sound of air rushing past.

I pressed my lips against the soft inside of her wrist as we rode on across the Viaduct into Seattle, passing now-familiar landmarks—the Space Needle, the Pink Elephant, the Pepsi sign—bridges and bodies of water simultaneously receding and approaching.

"It's good to be home," I said, and smiled out at the city, her hand in mine.

Publications from
Bella Books, Inc.
The best in contemporary lesbian fiction

P.O. Box 10543, Tallahassee, FL 32302
Phone: 800-729-4992
www.bellabooks.com

TWO WEEKS IN AUGUST by Nat Burns. Her return to Chincoteague Island is a delight to Nina Christie until she gets her dose of Hazy Duncan's renown ill-humor. She's not going to let it bother her, though…
978-1-59493-173-4 $14.95

MILES TO GO by Amy Dawson Robertson. Rennie Vogel has finally earned a spot at CT3. All too soon she finds herself abandoned behind enemy lines, miles from safety and forced to do the one thing she never has before: trust another woman.
978-1-59493-174-1 $14.95

PHOTOGRAPHS OF CLAUDIA by KG MacGregor. To photographer Leo Westcott models are light and shadow realized on film. Until Claudia.
978-1-59493-168-0 $14.95

SONGS WITHOUT WORDS by Robbi McCoy. Harper Sheridan's runaway niece turns up in the one place least expected and Harper confronts the woman from the summer that has shaped her entire life since.
978-1-59493-166-6 $14.95

YOURS FOR THE ASKING by Kenna White. Lauren Roberts is tired of being the steady, reliable one. When Gaylin Hart blows into her life, she decides to act, only to find once again that her younger sister wants the same woman.
978-1-59493-163-5 $14.95

THE SCORPION by Gerri Hill. Cold cases are what make reporter Marty Edwards tick. When her latest proves to be far from cold, she still doesn't want Detective Kristen Bailey babysitting her, not even when she has to run for her life.
978-1-59493-162-8 $14.95

STEPPING STONE by Karin Kallmaker. Selena Ryan's heart was shredded by an actress, and she swears she will never, ever be involved with one again.
978-1-59493-160-4 $14.95

FAINT PRAISE by Ellen Hart. When a famous TV personality leaps to his death, Jane Lawless agrees to help a friend with inquiries, drawing the attention of a ruthless killer. No.6 in this award-winning series.
978-1-59493-164-2 $14.95

A SMALL SACRIFICE by Ellen Hart. A harmless reunion of friends is anything but, and Cordelia Thorn calls friend Jane Lawless with a desperate plea for help. Lammy winner for Best Mystery. No.5 in this award-winning series.
978-1-59493-165-9 $14.95